The
QUEEN'S
LADY

Also by Eve Edwards

The Lacey Chronicles I: *The Other Countess*

The QUEEN'S LADY

EVE EDWARDS

DELACORTE PRESS

Text copyright © 2011 by Eve Edwards
Jacket photograph copyright © 2012 by Lara Jade

All rights reserved. Published in the United States by Delacorte Press, an imprint of Random House Children's Books, a division of Random House, Inc., New York. Originally published in paperback in Great Britain by Razorbill, an imprint of the Penguin Group, UK, in 2011.

Delacorte Press is a registered trademark and the colophon is a trademark of Random House, Inc.

Visit us on the Web! randomhouse.com/teens

Educators and librarians, for a variety of teaching tools, visit us at
randomhouse.com/teachers

Library of Congress Cataloging-in-Publication Data
Edwards, Eve.
The queen's lady / Eve Edwards. — 1st U.S. ed.
p.   cm. — (The Lacey chronicles ; #2)
ISBN 978-0-385-74091-3 (hc) — ISBN 978-0-375-98338-2 (ebook) —
ISBN 978-0-375-98975-9 (glb)
[1. Kings, queens, rulers, etc.—Fiction. 2. Courts and courtiers—Fiction. 3. Love—Fiction.
4. Great Britain—History—Elizabeth, 1558–1603—Fiction.] I. Title.
PZ7.E25252Qu 2012
[Fic]—dc23
2011026177

Printed in the United States of America

10 9 8 7 6 5 4 3 2 1

First U.S. Edition

For Lucy Drake

PROLOGUE

1583

Rievaulx House, Yorkshire

IT WAS A SAD FATE TO HAVE ONLY three people in the world who really cared about her. Resting a palm against the cold pane, Jane gazed out at the redbrick gatehouse and the rutted road leading onto the moor as she counted those people off in her mind. Worse was the fact that the first was denied her after marrying a man Jane had so abruptly jilted; the second was far away, finishing her a suit of mourning clothes; and the third lay dying in the chamber next door.

"Jane?" Jonas's voice had grown weaker this past hour.

Gripping the stone windowsill, Jane struggled for the composure she sorely needed. She couldn't bear it if he left her, but they both recognized he now had no choice.

"I'm here, Jonas." Jane turned from the view of barren hills to hurry into his chamber, her heavy pink satin petticoats rustling in the hush of the sickroom. Drapes were drawn across the windows, leaving the bedroom in perpetual twilight. The feeling of gloom was deepened by the somber arras covering the walls and the deep red bed hangings embroidered with gold thread—so old-fashioned, but she had not had time to change them for something more cheerful. The air, sweetened with lavender and dried rose petals, still bore the unmistakable undertone of sour sweat.

Jonas reached out a frail hand, the back a knot of blue veins, knuckles prominent like limpet shells sticking to a sea-washed rock. "You've been a good girl, Jane."

That was not how she saw herself, but then he had always believed the best of her, ever since he had come to her rescue six months ago. Jane blinked away tears, determined not to burden him with her sorrow.

"Jonas, try not to speak—don't waste your breath on me."

Gray hair curling from under his nightcap, face frozen on one side, Jonas Paton, Marquess of Rievaulx, had been felled by a stroke two weeks before. Already in frail health as he was, his slide towards the grave was now inevitable. At seventy, the marquess was content, believing he had had more than his fair share of life. He regretted only one thing, and that was the plight in which he would leave his young bride.

"My sons—they gather below—crows coming to feast on my corpse." Jonas fretted at the velvet counterpane. His words came out thick as his mouth refused to cooperate with his quick brain.

"Hush now." Jane knelt by his side, stroking the back of his hand.

"'Tis true, and you know it, Jane. They showed little love to me while I lived; they'll show you no mercy once I'm gone."

Jane shook her head, denying this, but she knew he only spoke the truth. Her stepsons hated the seventeen-year-old girl their father had wed in what they considered an outbreak of senility. They did not understand that the marquess had wed Lady Jane Perceval not for a wife but as a rescue. Punished harshly for breaking a match with an earl, Jane had been sent in disgrace to the Perceval family seat at Stafford Grange, North Yorkshire, and left there "to rot on the moors," as her father, the Earl of Wetherby, had so bluntly put it. He had imposed a regimen of prayer and fasting, combined with corporal punishment to bend her rebellious flesh to his will, treating her as if she were a child. Jane's confidence, once so high as she charmed lords at Elizabeth's court, had been destroyed, her belief in her own worth undermined. Written off by her father as an expensive failure, she had truly begun to think herself one. While her brother, Henry, flourished at court, and her onetime lover, Walter Raleigh, reigned as the Queen's favorite, she languished in her rustic prison.

That was until Jonas Paton came to visit Stafford Grange for the hunting. Expecting to kill a few deer, he came away with quite another quarry. A clever man of quiet Catholic persuasions, the marquess recognized Jane's persecution for what it was—a sentence without fair trial or hope of paternal forgiveness. He took pity on the girl and saved her by offering marriage, the only key that would open her prison door. The arrangement had proved a happy one for both parties: he got a youthful friend to brighten his final days, and she a wise companion. In the last six months, Jonas had been more of a father to Jane than her own had ever been. There had been no question of him taking her to his bed—he had no desire for more children, with a clutch of legitimate sons to inherit—but he had certainly made her feel cherished with his tender consideration.

"Ah, Jane, there'll be little money in the settlement—my sons will fight even your dower rights, as they know our union was not consummated," Jonas said softly. "But I've made sure you keep your dowry—you'll need it again."

"I don't want money." Jane curled her lip as she remembered with disgust her own selfish thoughts of but a year ago, when she had considered marriage to an ailing nobleman who would leave her a rich widow the summit of her desires. Now that she had gotten her wish, she cursed herself for ever tempting fate to punish her by giving her what she had wanted.

"But you will need it, little bird. And this time it will be under your control, not your father's. I got that promise on our wedding day. There's a trust—my lawyers, Baines and Rochester, are your official guardians until you are twenty-five, but they understand you are competent to manage your affairs yourself."

"Jonas—"

"No, Jane, we have to talk of these matters. When I die, you must get away from here. You won't be safe from my sons. Richard will be after your money to sustain the Rievaulx estate, and Otho and Lucres have always followed his lead, more's the pity. But with my title and your beauty, you are sure of a welcome at court. I've asked an old friend—Blanche Parry—remember me mentioning her? She'll see you to a good position in the Queen's household after your mourning is over."

Jane bent forward and rested her forehead on his hand, trying to smother her sobs.

"There, now, we got you free, did we not?" Jonas fingered a lock of her heavy honey-blond hair as it escaped from her headdress, twining it round his thumb, then letting it go. "Time for you to soar. It pleases me to think of you like that—happy."

She kissed his fingers. "Jonas, you are the best man I've ever known."

"I think, my dear," he whispered, voice sinking a notch lower, "you should send for the priest . . . and my sons. I wish to bid them farewell while I still can. I'll make them promise to look after you . . . but I have little hope they will hold to their word."

She sat up, recalling the many duties that fell to her as mistress of a marquess's household. "I'll fetch them. And . . . and if they vex you, I'll box their ears, see if I don't!"

Her defense of his peace made Jonas smile, as she had hoped. "Don't mourn me long, Jane. I'm not worth so many tears. Had to do things in my life I regret—so many terrible choices . . . to survive. Pray for my soul. Fetch Father Newton now."

"Yes, at once." Jane brushed a final kiss on his brow and went to summon the family.

The Spanish Low Countries, near Dunkirk

A bitter wind blew off the Channel, wiping away the smoke still rising from the burnt-out village like a damp cloth over a schoolboy's slate. The black silhouettes of inn, houses and barns stood out starkly in the gloom against the frost-hardened lake where once the children would have skated in winter sports. James Lacey knelt by the body of one of them, covering the girl's face with her little apron. His hands shook as he saw the message embroidered on the pocket—a mother's blessing on her child. A lot of good that had done her. Philip of Spain's troops under the Duke of Palma had carelessly destroyed this nameless village in some senseless reprisal for an attack by the Duke of Anjou's Dutch fighters. Spanish Fury, the locals called it. James called it a massacre of the innocent.

It wasn't the first outrage he had witnessed, nor would it be the last in this ugly war, but this particular one had finally killed something inside him—the last glimmer of faith that a military campaign could be honorable.

"My lord?" His blackamoor manservant approached, leading two horses. They were hard to make out in the darkness, as the metalwork on the harness had been dulled, hooves muffled by sackcloth. "We must go, sir—they may come back at any moment."

"God's mercy, Diego, can't we even bury the children?" James's question was not one he expected his servant to answer; they both knew they had little time to complete this surveillance mission behind enemy lines. James was carrying information that had to reach Anjou and his English military advisers.

Diego bowed his head.

"Aye, I know it. But why?" James addressed the last to the blank skies. The only answer he received was a flake of snow that caught on his eyelashes like a frozen tear. God had hardened his heart against his people, leaving them to suffer the two plagues of rampaging troops and cruel Inquisition from their merciless overlord, King Philip of Spain. With the Protestant Dutch hard-pressed in the Low Countries and the Spanish in possession of Dunkirk and Nieupoort, a bridgehead to England, should they wish to invade, it seemed to James that God had turned Catholic and was intent on bringing Elizabeth's nation to its knees.

"Come, my lord." Diego held out a hand.

James took the blackamoor's strong palm in his and got to his feet. Diego was only a year younger than he but appeared to be coping with the traumatic sights far better than his master. James swayed, the corpse dragging on his spirits like a sea anchor.

He took a deep breath, swallowing against a surge of nausea. "You have the reports?"

Diego tapped the leather pouch slung across his chest. "Secure, my lord."

"Then we ride on." James mounted his black gelding and urged the horse off the exposed road. Taking to the countryside to avoid Spanish patrols, Her Majesty's spies disappeared into the woods.

CHAPTER 1

1584

Richmond Palace, Surrey

"Now, when the Queen wakes, she is never in the best of spirits," advised Blanche Parry, leading Her Majesty's newest Lady of the Privy Chamber into the Queen's private apartments. Elizabeth was out hunting in the park of Richmond Palace, leaving the way clear for the induction into a lady's duties. The court had followed the sovereign like the train dangling from the back of her petticoats, sweeping across the snow in a glorious swatch of rich velvets and plumed hats, all mounted on first-rate horses—quite a pageant to entertain the commoners lucky enough to witness their passage.

"Your ladyship may be asked to sleep nearby to be on hand for messages. I, or one of the other Ladies of the Bedchamber, sleep within." Blanche gestured to the canopied bed in the room beyond. The apple-red hangings were exquisitely embroidered with flowers—pansies, roses and love-lies-bleeding.

The Dowager Marchioness of Rievaulx, as Jane was now known, smiled down at the stooped elderly attendant who was her guide in her first days as one of the Queen's ladies. Mistress Parry had served

Elizabeth since before her coronation; now, at seventy-six, she surely had earned a better bed to sleep in than the one at the Queen's feet. Then again, perhaps the faithful retainer did consider it the best place in the kingdom. "I will await your commands, mistress," Jane said with a smile.

Blanche returned the smile and wagged her finger at the young widow. "I know what you are thinking, my lady."

"Oh?"

"That someone as aged and half-blind as me should have been pensioned off some years since."

"No, mistress, not at all." But she had been thinking something a little similar, truth be told.

"All you young girls do. You try to sit me in the chair nearest the fire, make possets and other such foolishness as if I'm already an invalid. But as I've told Her Majesty, this old warhorse has served her for over fifty years and intends to die in harness."

Jane thought that to have survived the reign of four Tudors so close to the center of power was something of a miracle and certainly not to be rewarded with the patronizing treatment of untried youth. Jane touched the lady's arm gently. "If I make you a posset, I give you permission to pour it over my head."

The Queen's chief gentlewoman bubbled with laughter and patted the back of Jane's hand where it rested on her elbow. "That I will, my lady. Come, I'll take you to the steward so he can find you a room. You may have to share with one or two others, depending on how many are at court. I tell all my noble ladies that they would have been much more comfortable had they stayed with their families, but still you all beg for the honor of serving our sovereign—it speaks well of you."

"Thank you, but your praise is undeserved. I am proud to serve the Queen, but I have to admit that I came in the main because the late marquess my husband asked me to do so."

"Ah yes, dear Jonas." The lady's eyes flicked over the pretty widow shrewdly, taking in the mourning weeds still worn long after the month's mind had passed. "You grieve him truly, I see."

Jane twisted the heavy wedding ring of the Rievaulx on her finger. Before Jonas was cold in his grave, his eldest son, Richard Paton, had demanded it back for his own wife, and Jane had taken great pleasure in refusing to part with it. The sons had been predictably cruel from the moment Jonas had been laid in the family vault, spreading foul rumors about the young widow. She knew many—if not most—people at court would think she had married Jonas for mercenary reasons; Blanche's insight came as a surprise and a blessing.

"Yes, I miss him. He was a kind and wise husband. I had him for too brief a time."

"It gives me great pleasure to find a place here for his widow, though that is scant payment for the generosity he always showed me. Which reminds me: when you receive gifts from those trying to gain an audience with the Queen, it is appropriate to declare them to me or one of the other senior ladies. There is a fine line between a gift and a bribe, but we can help you discern the difference."

And so the instruction continued until Jane felt quite dizzy with information. Having spent her time since Jonas's death four months earlier on her own in Yorkshire, she found herself shocked by the sudden flood of people, noise and movement that made up the continual parade of court life. Jonas had passed peacefully, and his sons had let her remain in her home until the details of his will were settled. It was only when the lawyers had locked horns over her widow's rights that the new marquess had ousted her from Rievaulx House and refused to move the tenants from the dower property that by right should have been hers for the remainder of her life. Having no desire to put herself back in her father's care, Jane had been thankful for the foresight that had caused Jonas to arrange a place at court for her.

Blanche led Jane at a slow pace to the steward's apartment not far from the Queen's suite.

"What else can I tell you? Ah, yes. Naturally, you are entitled to the bouge of court, meaning lodging, food, lights and fuel for your fire if your room has a grate. Two suits of livery are also yours—I'll give you the cloth; you'd best see a tailor as soon as possible, as the Queen likes her attendants to be appropriately attired, the better to emphasize her appearance. We are the setting; she is the jewel—do not forget this."

"No, mistress. Then may I beg leave to go to my needlewoman this afternoon?"

"You have your own? Will not one of our court servants do?" Blanche did not sound too impressed by the fastidious habits of the rich ladies who thought themselves above a service that served others well.

"I am patron to a deserving woman, mistress—an old friend before her father's fortunes were overset. She depends on my custom for her finishing business. I would not want to wreck her prospects by withholding my custom."

"As kind as you are beautiful," chuckled Blanche, her opinion of the young marchioness restored. "I am sure you can be excused. You are not due to be sworn into the chamber until the morrow, so the Queen will not look for you this day."

Jane took a boat downstream from Richmond to London, accompanied by her maid and two footmen. The Thames, a chilly slate color, flowed at a rapid clip as the tide raced out, leaving the banks muddy wastes. As a marchioness, she could, of course, have summoned Milly Porter to come to her, but Jane craved the privacy and informality of her needlewoman's workshop. There she would be guaranteed a warm welcome, and a chance for a lively gossip without fear of interruption.

As they neared Westminster, Jane noticed that the two men at the oars were staring at her boldly. She flicked a glance at the elder of her footmen and he immediately had a sharp word with them, demanding more respect for his mistress. They dutifully lowered their eyes.

One had to keep the lower orders in their place, of course, but there were limits. Jane had never felt quite right ordering around her old friend even though she had turned seamstress. Before Milly's father had gotten mixed up in a plot against the Queen five years before, he had served Robert Dudley, the Earl of Leicester, as his chief sergeant-at-arms, and his only daughter had been treated as a gentlewoman. As the families lived close to each other and the children were of the same age, Jane and young Milly Porter had shared a tutor. Then the Porters had hit their rock. Imprisoned for informing Her Majesty's Catholic enemies of the doings in the Leicester household, Silas Porter had been stripped of rank and wealth and sent to the Tower; Milly had been made destitute, no longer welcome in Leicesters' household. Loyal to her blameless friend, Jane had kept abreast of Milly's plight as she was passed from house to house of her distant family. When Jane had assumed control of her own fortune on marriage, it had given her great pleasure to help Milly set up her fine finishing and embroidering workshop, freeing her from the humiliation of living as a disgraced poor relation. Not accepted as a tailor—the guild system was too strict to allow a woman entrance to that profession—Milly had found her niche as a finisher of their work in the feminine skills of embroidery and lacemaking.

At the landing place, a network of planks led Jane safely over the muddy banks exposed by the low tide. Taking a horse-drawn litter to the workshop, she was spared walking in the filthy streets of the capital. Her maid and footmen were not so fortunate, having to avoid as best they could the horse manure and rubbish dumped in the gutter. As the litter jogged along the streets, Jane lifted her gaze to the tower of St. Paul's; it dominated the London skyline, rearing over the rooftops like a giant's castle from one of the tales she had heard in the schoolroom. She had spent many happy days with Milly, acting out the stories. Jane remembered with some chagrin that she had always demanded to be the princess. Milly had had to make do playing a variety of heroes and villains, but she hadn't seemed to mind; that was until life had forced them on to their different paths, Jane's upwards and Milly's down.

The litter stopped outside the little workshop in Silver Street, just north of Cheapside. Not having yet had the opportunity to visit, Jane was pleased to see that it was a handsome property with a bow window and an overhanging upper room almost meeting the house opposite. The window was draped with tempting samples of Milly's needlework—best-quality linen worked with intricate red detail, flower-bejeweled silks and night-black velvet sprinkled with gold embroidery. A beautiful lawn ruff edged with lace, almost as elaborate as the Queen's own, sat in pride of place on a red satin cushion, indicating that this particular establishment supplied only the most elegant customers, either those who frequented court or the rich city wives who followed the same fashions.

"Well done, Milly," Jane murmured, pleased to see the use her friend had made of her prime location. Jane accepted a hand from her footman as she descended from the litter. Her other attendant was already opening the door, ushering her into the haven of the shop, past the watchman guarding the entrance and out of the dangerous chaos of the streets.

A young servant waited within and bobbed a deep curtsy. "My lady, how may we serve you?"

Jane was still looking around the room, enjoying the signs of a flourishing business: orders ready wrapped on a table, a customer examining buttons in a layered jewelery box.

"Tell your mistress that the Marchioness of Rievaulx is here," her footman replied on her behalf.

Soon after the servant had disappeared upstairs, a shriek of delight greeted this message. Jane would have laughed if she were not so mindful of her dignity before strangers. Her presence had already attracted the attention of a couple of passing housewives who stood on the pavement outside; they were eyeing her fine bronze satin doublet and skirt striped by panes of black ribbon, pricing every yard from gold thread to amber beading. Pretending to be ignorant of their interest, Jane turned slowly to display the outfit in full, hoping they would be encouraged to return later and place their orders for fancy work here in the future.

Her attention sprang back to the stairs as a bright-eyed Milly clattered down the narrow flight and rushed into the room, hands outstretched, as she would have once greeted Jane after a long holiday apart. Milly checked herself just before she collided with her friend and sank into a curtsy.

"My lady," she said breathlessly. Several inches under five feet, Milly was a great deal shorter than her friend and slight with it. She always jested that she used half the material in her own dresses than the tailor did for Jane's fuller figure, claiming it a useful economy for someone of her scanty means.

Aware that they needed to keep up appearances before others, Jane gave her friend a regal dip of her head. "Mistress Porter. I wish to bespeak two suits of livery from your tailor, finished by you, of course."

"For your servants?" Milly asked, darting a look at the brawny footmen.

Oh yes, her friend would like to get her hands on those two fine specimens for their inside leg measurements, thought Jane with a smile. "No, for myself. I have taken service—with the Queen."

Milly shrieked again—then clapped her hand over her mouth. Jane nearly lost her composure—she'd forgotten how Milly always squawked and squealed at the most inappropriate moments, habitually getting them both into trouble. "You are fortunate, my lady. To be at court—with the Queen—and all those fine gentlemen!"

"Quite." Jane bit her cheek to stop her amusement from bubbling over. "I have the cloth with me." She gestured to her maid to hand over the bolt of white satin wrapped in a protective sheath of canvas.

"May I take your measurements, my lady?" Milly gestured to her stairs.

"Of course." Jane swept ahead to the private chamber above. "Wait below," she ordered her attendants.

Once safe upstairs, Jane dropped her starchy marchioness's manner and sank into a chair by the window to give in to her laughter. Milly joined her, leaning against the sill.

"Oh, it is so good, my lady, to see you again!" Milly exclaimed, her face flushed with excitement.

"You have 'my lady-ed' me enough, Milly. To you, when we are alone, I insist on being Jane."

"Not Jane the Vain?" teased Milly, recalling her friend's old nickname in the schoolroom.

"Only if you want me to call you Silly Milly." Jane linked her hands across her stomacher, relaxing into the chair as much as her boned garments would allow.

"I think I will pass on that honor." Milly perched on a footstool. "So, Jane, any change to your measurements since the mourning weeds? Master Rich still has the old patterns he used for them."

"None."

"Excellent, so we have plenty of time for our gossip. Tell me everything." She twirled her hands encouragingly.

Jane's smile dimmed. "You know most of it already."

Milly sobered and hugged her knees. "You must miss him."

"More than I thought possible." Jane sighed. "He helped me mend after the Earl of Dorset disaster."

"Not to mention that you jilted the earl in part because you were madly in love with his younger brother," Milly said sagely.

Jane pulled a wry face: this was the problem of having so good a friend—they did not forget your confidences even when you wished they would. She'd poured out her miserable heart to Milly letter by letter when imprisoned in her family home, every last humiliating detail of her failed betrothal. The charming, teasing James, brother of the earl, represented all that she had loved and lost, and she had spent rather too many letters recounting her fascination with him. "Well, James Lacey was never going to be for me, was he? I threw over his brother in a very cruel way—or so it would seem to the family."

"Even though you did it for Lady Ellie's sake?"

"Neither James nor the earl knows that. I hoped that his countess might guess, but we've not seen each other since she married him."

Milly brushed some mud from the hem of her friend's petticoats absentmindedly. "So Lady Ellie does not understand what you did for her? I've not met her, but she sounds from your account a very kind person. Why not write to her?"

Jane shrugged. "At first it was too awkward—then too much time passed."

"You'll meet them now that you are at court, surely? Have a chance to restore your friendship?"

"Maybe, but the Dorsets aren't rich—they won't be able to afford to attend frequently. Our paths may not cross for some years." Jane mourned her fractured friendship with Ellie almost as much as she missed seeing James. "Oh, but that's too gloomy for this day. Let's not talk about me—I'm sure I've written it all—the horrid sons, the grim few months I spent after Jonas's death—all very predictable and ugly. Tell me about yourself. How fares your business?"

Milly gave her a smug look. "Well now, as you are my main investor, I should report that I'm turning a decent profit, thanks to your patronage and the ladies you have sent my way. I have two girls in my workroom and Henny to mind the shop, so I am quite the woman of business. And I have Old Uriah to defend my doors, on your late husband's insistence." Milly grinned at her friend, seeming very young to have such responsibilities. She was sweet-looking rather than classically beautiful, with lively hazel eyes and silky auburn hair, though that was currently hidden by her modest coif. Jane did not doubt that she would attract more than her share of admirers among her neighbors and would be regarded as a good marriage prospect.

"And the tailors you work for take you seriously? Jonas was worried that you would struggle to get good terms, being so new . . ."

"And so female," finished Milly. "Aye, I've had my share of problems. Most of them do not know if they should flirt with me or dismiss me as witless cotton-fluff."

"The fiends!" laughed Jane.

"Fortunately, one of my workers is the daughter of a merchant-draper. He helps me when I need a man to intervene or run into difficulties with the Company of Tailors. Most of my work is with my neighbor, Master Rich, and he says he is happy with our collaboration."

"Not to mention that he is a man without any urge to flirt—not with our sex, at least."

"Shhh! I know the court has lax ideas about such things, but round here you must not mention it. He's a dear and I don't want to get him into trouble. Where was I? Oh yes: the marquess's man of business—he holds the lease on my behalf, so really I have little to worry about on that score. I'd say that most of the tailors in Cheapside now welcome my finishing services, as I am known to refer new customers on to them."

Jane was relieved to hear this news. It was almost impossible for a woman to set up in business; only the protection of a marquess had made it a reality for Milly, and Jane had worried that Jonas's death would be felt badly by her protégée. But they were not out of the woods yet.

"I hope Master Rochester continues to follow Jonas's instructions. My stepson, the new marquess, may not notice this little detail in the Rievaulx holdings, but if he knew you were my friend he would make trouble just to spite me."

Milly waved the matter away. "I count my blessings each day and try not to worry about the morrow."

"And your father?"

Milly huffed a sigh. "Some improvement there, praise the Lord. He has been released on condition he serve in the Low Countries campaign as adviser to the Duke of Anjou. If he proves himself loyal, he may be allowed back from exile."

"Did you see him before he left?"

Milly shook her head. "Nay, it chanced that I was away from town on a commission for Lady Norton when he was sent out. They decided they needed him after the fall of Dunkirk. That disaster proved a blessing, as even military gentlemen under a cloud are in demand. They say the war has reached a crisis and the poor Dutch are being crushed."

Jane had always rather liked Milly's bluff soldier father, despite the fact that he had been a fool for being talked into his treachery and was lucky still to have his head. "I wish I could exile my father and bring yours back."

"Has your father bothered you since your husband's death?"

Jane fingered the amber beads on her doublet, a nervous habit she wished she could conquer. "No, but it's only a matter of time. He will seek me out either to make use of me or remind me of my failings—he can't resist the chance to bully someone."

Milly picked up a piece of bone-work trimming from her work-basket and threaded a needle. Jane liked the sign that Milly had forgotten her guest's new, exalted rank and was behaving again as she once would have done on any previous cozy visit.

"I think, my dear Jane, you need to marry again. Find yourself a strong gentleman to protect you from your family—not a fatherly old lord this time, but a lusty young lover."

Jane tried in vain to dismiss the image of James as she had last seen him—an imposing figure in his favorite blue doublet and hose, dark eyes and brown hair, effortlessly charming and capable. But then, she reminded herself, she had also been attracted to Raleigh's handsome appearance at first, and look where that had led her.

"I'm not sure my judgment is all that it should be in matters of love," she admitted. "The one lover I've known turned out to be a great disappointment."

Milly pricked the cloth, a frown wrinkling her forehead. "Well, Master Walter Raleigh may look very fine, but he has no heart. You deserve much, much better—and, they say, once bitten, twice shy."

"Meaning I've learnt from my mistake?"

"Mmm-hmm." Milly held pins in her mouth as she fixed the bone work to the neck of a gown.

"And what about you?" probed Jane, leaning forward. "Any suitors after the pretty new seamstress?"

Milly smiled and stuck the last pin in place. "Maybe."

"Oh, don't be coy—tell me!"

"There's the butcher, the baker, the candlestick maker . . ."

Jane threw herself back in the chair and laughed. "Oh, you tease! I thought you were being serious!"

Milly grimaced. "Maybe I am, for sadly, none of them makes my heart go pit-a-pat."

Jane glanced out the window. In February, night came early, and she had to go if she was to return to her lodgings at a decent hour. "And thus far none of the fine gentlemen at court have made my pulse race. We are a sorry pair, are we not?"

"I blame the men: either they are all show and no substance, or all substance and no show." Milly waggled the trimming, suggestive of a disappointing encounter.

Jane snorted with laughter. "My dear friend, you are quite vulgar."

"My dear Marchioness, you are quite right."

Standing at the upper casement, Milly watched Jane depart in her litter until it turned the corner and went out of sight. With a sigh, she returned to her chair, playing with the bead bracelet she always wore, finding it an aid to thought and a holder of memories. She was so pleased for Jane—she deserved her chance of happiness at court, free of her wolfish family. If the truth be told, Milly liked Jane even more now than when they had shared a schoolroom. At ten, Jane had a streak of her father's hardness and not a small dose of vanity about her beauty; the events of the past few years—being thrown over by Raleigh and suffering disgrace for her choices—had softened that brittle shell and added an attractive dash of humility. Milly was touched that Jane, now an exalted marchioness and lady-in-waiting to the Queen, still wanted her friendship; indeed, she seemed more anxious to maintain it than ever before. Perhaps that was a result of losing Jonas and realizing how alone in the world she could be without friends around her.

"Hey-ho, Milly-o!" A voice from the street broke in upon her reverie.

"Master Turner!" Milly saw the player approaching from the direction of the theater north of the city walls, his scarlet cloak as loud as a trumpet blast.

"How is my fairest flower of the Cheap?" Christopher Turner stopped below her window and swept off his hat in a flourishing bow.

Milly laughed. "I am well, sir. Have you come for the king's robe?"

Christopher clapped his hand to his chest. "You wound me, lady. I came to gaze upon the picture of fair Persephone framed by her casement, the maiden of the needle, who brings spring early to our sad city."

"Come on in, you rogue. I know you are only here to carry the costumes for your master."

With a theatrical groan as if mortally struck in the heart, Christopher staggered through the door to repeat his performance for Henny. Milly took her time going down the stairs to allow Henny her fun, not in the least offended that to the young player every girl was a Penelope, a Helen of Troy or a Venus. He could no more keep hold of his poetic utterances in the presence of a maiden than the tide could be stopped from turning.

"So, my turtledove, my honeybee, have you retrimmed the cloak as required?" Christopher asked as she descended to the shop. A vital presence, nearly six feet and blessed with curly black hair, he filled the room, making it his stage. Poor Henny and the doorman were quite cast in his shade. But while Milly had a very soft spot for Christopher, she knew better than to cast her affections away on him, as that was the path too many girls had trodden to heartbreak.

She returned his compliments in the same coin. "But of course, my crowing cockerel, my glowworm, I've done my very best." Milly plucked a package from the shelf and shook it out to show him the new gold fringe and fur collar. "I have refurbished the fastenings so that they are almost as fine as when its first owner wore it at court."

"Oh, lackaday, who can sing the sad tale of the cloak that once sat on my Lord Leicester's shoulders, attracting the sovereign's favor, now to bear the hoots and scorn of the groundlings on a player's back?" Christopher struck a tragic pose, cradling the cloak in his arms like a dying heroine.

"If someone's to tell the tale, I would've thought it should be you."

He handed the garment back to her. "Aye, I know all about being a noble castoff."

Milly kicked herself for her misstep—she had not meant to offend, but he had taken her comment as a reflection on his birth. It was an open secret among Christopher's friends that he was the illegitimate offspring of the last Earl of Dorset and his mistress, Judith Turner; the bastard son had been haphazardly supported during the earl's life and cut off from the family since his negligent father's demise. That made him half brother to the James whom Jane loved—not something Milly had thought wise to reveal to either friend, as they were worlds apart.

Having no wish to dwell on a painful subject, Milly turned the direction of the conversation as deftly as she turned a seam. "Master Turner, I beg of you to tell your master to die with more discretion—less rolling about on the boards, please. I can only patch, not produce miracles."

Dark thoughts passing swiftly, Christopher waggled his coal-black eyebrows at her as he leapt at the new opening for a well-fashioned compliment. "Ah, but every breath you take is a miracle, dear one, sweetening the very air with the perfumes of Arabia."

Milly swatted his arm. "Too much, Kit."

He stood back and scratched his chin. "You think so? All right—I will strike that out of my sonnet."

"You're writing sonnets?"

He nodded. "Fourteen lines for seven shillings. Twenty-eight lines for ten—quite a bargain if you are a prosaic baron courting some pretty noblewoman."

"Oh, in that case, perhaps it will pass—Arabian perfumes are fine enough for a knight."

He took out his notebook and snatched a quill from the table. "No, no, I will be guided by the lady's taste. I get a bonus if these sonnets secure her hand in marriage." He crossed out the offending words.

Milly peered over his shoulder at the correction. "Poor thing, she will be mightily disenchanted after the wedding to find her romantic songbird a plain old duck."

Turner caught her hand and kissed her fingers. "But that is marriage, my love, mutual disillusionment."

She pulled her hand free. "Go to, you devil. I'll listen to none of your cynical speeches today. I still hope for a husband and happiness."

He laughed. "Settle for one or the other, sweet—that way you will not be disappointed."

CHAPTER 2

Lacey Hall, Berkshire

THE EARL OF DORSET HAD AN HEIR—an heir who at a week old was bawling red-faced as the priest doused him with tepid water at the font in Stoke-by-Lacey church. James pitied his little nephew, fretting in his baptismal whites, eyes screwed shut against a cruel world that had taken him from his cradle to this cold stony place and then had the nerve to get him soaked. James also pitied him because, in addition to his sister Catherine, and her husband, Sir Gilbert Huntsford, the poor scrap had got James as a godfather. A raw deal when this particular sponsor barely knew if God existed anymore.

James had tried to put his older brother off the idea of asking him to stand for the boy, but Will had been insistent.

"You wouldn't want him to have to rely on Tobias, now, would you?" Will jested, having just finished telling James how he had had to placate their youngest brother's Cambridge tutor, who was threatening to send the boy down for numerous infractions.

James privately thought the baby would do better with sunny-natured Tobias as a godfather, but dared not add to his manifold shortcomings by hurting Will and Ellie with a refusal.

"Just so as you understand what you're getting, Will," he had warned.

"I know exactly what he's getting," Will replied warmly, throwing an arm round his brother's shoulders. "A good man for a godfather."

James knew he was no longer a good man—if he ever had been—but had agreed so as not to cast a shadow over what should be a perfect day. Will's joy was a pleasure to see—he deserved it. The earl had a wife he loved more than life itself, and now a child to pass on his title. James did not mind being knocked off his perch as his brother's heir—indeed had expected it ever since Will married Ellie—but it did rub in the fact that he was no longer needed at Lacey Hall. With her usual foresight, their mother had already realized this and moved out to the dower house, taking their little sister, Sarah, with her, despite Will and Ellie's earnest protests that they should both stay. The earl and his countess did not intend to make other members of the family feel unwelcome, but they were so in love with each other it made bachelors like James feel surplus to requirements. He now wished he had arranged some employment before returning home, something to take him away and give him a purpose in life. As long as he did not have to return to the war in the Low Countries—he did not think his sanity could bear another taste of Spain's war on its Dutch subjects.

The family walked the short distance back to Lacey Hall. The proud mother had not attended, still confined to bed for her month's lying-in. The dowager countess whisked the child from the earl's arms and led the retreat of the married ladies as they trooped upstairs to join Ellie for the celebration in her bedchamber. This left James in charge of Sarah.

"Why can't I go upstairs, Jamie?" Sarah begged for what felt like the hundredth time, swinging on his arm as he towed her into the family parlor.

James, never the world's most patient brother, was feeling itchy in his skin, as if his shirt had been impregnated with some vile poison. The Stoke-by-Lacey children had been skating on the pond when the baptism party had passed through the village, their screams so like the cries of the victims of the massacre he'd witnessed from the edge of the woods that he had had trouble remembering where he was. *He'd had to stand and watch them fall, powerless to save even a single life.*

James shook himself, bringing his attention back to the present with difficulty. "You know why you can't, midget. The ladies talk about things not suited to a maiden's ears."

"Exactly! They get to hear all the exciting gossip and I'm left with my boring old brothers. I don't even get to watch Ellie feed Wilkins. Please, I'm almost grown up now; can I go upstairs?"

"No, now, hush!" *Those cries, cut off so suddenly. God in heaven, what a waste.*

"It's not fair!"

"Be quiet!"

"But, Jamie—"

Desperate to escape, James swung round, raising his hand. "I said no! Dammit, Sarah, can't you take no for an answer!" He glared at her, only to find her looking in openmouthed horror at his bunched fist. The room had fallen silent as all the men gathered there, from his older brother to Vicar Bagley, broke off their conversations to see what passed at the entrance.

"Jamie?" whispered Sarah, her bottom lip trembling.

With a struggle, James unclenched his fist, disgusted with

himself. He had never raised a hand against his sister in a temper, and he had no idea from where the sudden gust of violence had sprung.

"I said no," he repeated, moving back from her. He wished he could step away so easily from himself. "Pray excuse me." He gave the watching company a cursory bow, then quit the celebration. He couldn't stomach making polite conversation when his brain felt like a keg of gunpowder on the point of combustion.

Striding from the house, he made for the stable, where Diego intercepted him.

"Your horse, my lord?"

"Why else would I be here?" James kicked the trough while his servant saddled Tartarus.

"I come with you?" asked Diego as he led the gelding out.

"No. Stay. I'm not fit company for anyone." James swung into the saddle and kicked the horse into a gallop, attempting to outrun himself as he fled across the meadows.

A frown knotting his brow, Diego watched his master streak off until he was lost in the mist rising from the river, cloak flapping behind him like wings. James had not been himself since their mission near Dunkirk; the ugly scenes they had seen in that devastated village had snapped something inside him. He was not sleeping—or when he did finally manage to drop off, his sleep was plagued by nightmares. More than once James had actually stabbed the mattress with the dagger he kept under his pillow. Diego hid it when he could, fearing James would do himself an injury one night, but his master always demanded its return, saying he did not feel safe without it close by.

Diego straightened a tattered saddle blanket claimed by the stable yard dog as a bed. James had kicked it over in passing, but Diego doubted he had noticed; so sunk in his gloom, James had stopped caring about his effect on others—a notable change for one who had been loved for his good humor and interest in the world around him.

The mongrel whined his thanks, licking Diego's hand.

"Hey, boy, he is gone; no need to be afraid."

For all his soothing words to the dog, Diego had to admit he was scared. He feared that his lord was troubled by a haunt, an uncanny creature like those the elders of his village in Africa used to speak of in hushed tones, as even to utter their names was to invite their attention. James must have picked up the spirit of one of the people in that massacre who had not been laid to rest as was seemly; he would not heal until he was freed of it. Diego credited his own escape to the bead talisman he wore round his neck—he wished he'd thought to protect his master with one. Perhaps it still was not too late?

Diego took up his pitchfork and returned to mucking out Tartarus's stall, talking in his own tongue to Barbary, the earl's favorite mount, housed in the neighboring enclosure. He confided more to the horses than he did to any person. He told the stallion about the horrific mission in the Low Countries. He went on to his own nightmares of his early years—being taken from his homeland and passed from hand to hand as a servant, from Turk to Venetian, from Venetian to Spaniard and lastly to an Englishman. That gentleman, one Silas Porter, had been thrown into the Tower for treason, and Diego had ended up with the Laceys. Diego admitted to Barbary that, fond though he was of his current family, he had never truly been touched by the suffering of these strange people in the north—their ways were alien to him, their cruelties so flagrant. He pitied the Dutch children, though. No child of any nation should be cut to pieces on the whim of some distant overlord.

Barbary agreed with a snort.

"Diego?" The earl had come in search of his brother. The two oldest Laceys were a contrast of light and dark—the earl blond to his brother's chestnut coloring—but they were clearly devoted to each other.

"My lord?" Diego propped his fork against the wall and ducked out of the stall.

"My brother's gone?"

"Indeed he has, O most worshipful lord." Diego wasn't really feeling up to his usual jesting overuse of titles for the earl, but he felt he should make the attempt on his lordship's special day.

"Was he . . . was he quite himself?"

No, he was not. That was as plain as the nose on Dame Holton's face, which was the largest in the village. "He required some time apart, my lord."

The earl pulled off his velvet hat and ran his fingers through his hair. "What happened to him, Diego?"

"My lord?"

"In the Low Countries. He's been different since he came back. Before he left, he was all fire and brimstone, eager for the adventure, for the military life; now he is . . . he's sad, is he not?"

"Aye, my lord."

"So what happened?"

Diego found himself in an awkward position. If James had not confided in his brother, was it his servant's place to do it for him?

"Please, Diego, I only ask because I care for his welfare." The dog nudged his master's hand and the earl scratched him behind the ears. The casual affectionate gesture swung Diego in Will's favor.

"It was not what happened to us, my lord, but what we witnessed that troubles Master James," Diego finally admitted. "Your brother suffers because he could not stop the slaughter. It haunts him."

"And so it would. He was ever one to rush to the defense of another." The earl tapped his fingers restlessly on the stall only to have his stallion, Barbary, lip his knuckles. He stroked the horse's nose, finding it easier to have this conversation when not meeting Diego's eyes. "Do you have any idea what would cure him of his melancholy?"

Diego frowned. He did not understand this talk of humors and melancholy so beloved by the learned men of this country; he believed James's problem belonged to the spirit world. But perhaps the cure was the same?

"You should give him something to do, sir. He needs a task to take him beyond the reach of his haunt. Wise men claim that passage over water is said to lose them. The English Channel did not prove far enough."

The earl had grown accustomed to his groom's way of seeing the world and sorted through the talk of haunts to the essential advice. "A long voyage?"

"Aye, my lord. To a land where the haunt would not dare travel."

The earl stood up straighter, his burden of worry lightened. "How strange you should mention that; I have an interest in such an enterprise." He closed his eyes, consulting his god, then smiled. "Yes, I think perhaps this is the Lord's will. Pack your bags, Diego, I believe you are headed to the New World."

Diego's jaw dropped: he had not intended to leave Lacey Hall again so soon. There was a village girl or two he had been courting. "Me, sir?"

"Naturally. How else will James lose his haunt if you do not go with him to chase it away?"

Diego wanted to protest that he hated sea travel, having had his fill by his twelfth year, when he arrived in England, but what was the use? His role in life, it appeared, was to obey. "Aye, my lord. I will ready myself for the voyage."

But not without making a few prayers to his own gods.

"Raleigh's planning what?"

On his return from his punishing ride, James had been cornered in the study by his brother and their sister's husband, Sir Gilbert Huntsford. Will had blocked his attempt to raid the wine while Gil had wrestled him into a chair. Now he was forced to listen to them both with a clear head.

A long-standing friend of the earl, Gil was a dependable man in his early twenties. With his no-nonsense brown hair cut short, neat mustache and kind eyes, he suited their practical sister Catherine to the ground, and James suspected the arranged marriage had rapidly become a love match, despite the sadness that so far they were yet to have a child survive infancy. Gil was the last person one would expect to be interested in Raleigh's dream of settling a strange land on the merest thread of hope that they might strike gold.

"Raleigh's idea is not so wild as it may sound," Gil explained patiently, his voice a rich bass to go with his broad-chested frame.

"If I'm going to listen to this, at least give me a drink," James groaned.

Will showed mercy and thrust a glass of white wine into his brother's hand, then poured two more, for Gil and himself.

Gil seated himself in a chair opposite. "Raleigh plans to establish a colony on the coast of America where the land has not yet been claimed by a Christian prince."

James sipped, barely noticing the taste. "I thought that had been tried. Did not his half brother die in the attempt to find riches there but last year?"

"Aye, 'tis true that many have wrecked their fortunes that way, but I am convinced that soon, one day, we will succeed."

"The accounts of that land are marvelous," Will added. "And look how Spain fills her coffers each year with gold and silver from Peru."

"That is so," agreed Gil. "If God lets the devil Philip have such an empire, why not our Queen?"

James couldn't stir himself to feel excited by the venture. To be sure, a few years back, like the rest of the nation, he had lapped up the tales of Sir Francis Drake's momentous circumnavigation of the world and the riches he had plundered in the Americas. For a time, it had been every boy's dream to go pirating for Her Majesty across the Atlantic, and Drake was venerated as their patron saint. But now James had no spirit left to pretend to care.

"I really believe this plan by Raleigh has a chance, Jamie," Will continued. "You know he and I do not like each other much—"

James snorted. That was an understatement: every time the pair met on the jousting field, they tried to beat the stuffing out of each other.

"Even so, I have been impressed by his careful preparations and am of a mind to invest in the scheme."

James put his glass down with a rap on the little oak table. "You are thinking of handing over some of your money to him? You must either be sickening for something or be serious about this."

"The latter, I think. Gil's putting up fifty pounds as well."

Gil winked at James, tapping the empty pocket in his doublet. "You have to spend some to make some."

"Indeed." James scrubbed his hand over his face. There was some undercurrent here that he hadn't quite grasped. "Well, this is all very interesting, but as I barely have two shillings to rub together, my name is unlikely to appear on the list of sponsors."

Will pushed up from the desk where he had perched. "It's not money I'm thinking about. I admire Raleigh's vision, but I still find I doubt the man."

"Hardly surprising, seeing how he's an ill-natured upstart only where he is now because he's got a pretty face and an overstuffed codpiece."

Will smiled. "Jamie, please, don't feel you have to hold back on my account."

"Yes, well, you know what I think about him."

"Same as I do. But, leaving that aside, he's clever, and indisputably a man of action. One day, unless he's very unlucky, one of his ideas should bear fruit."

"And you think this might be it?"

Will shrugged and unfastened the hooks of his doublet, letting himself relax after a day on duty before the gaze of his tenants and guests. "It's worth looking into—North America might have a future. But we need a man on the inside to protect our investment. I wouldn't put it past Raleigh to hide half the gains he makes."

James began to guess what was coming. "And this means?"

"You. Volunteer yourself for the voyage."

James picked his drink up again and swirled it in the firelight, hints of gold flashing against the glass. "So now that you have Wilkins, I really am expendable."

Will folded his arms. "That's a low blow, Jamie."

James knew it was, but he would be damned before he apologized. He gave a bitter laugh. "I fear my thirst for roving has been quenched by the Low Countries."

"Not roving, Jamie, but exploring—building a settlement in a new land. A fresh start. I thought that would appeal to your sense of adventure. We used to play at sea captains, remember?"

Indeed, they had and fought many a battle of command over their tree-house ship. Poor old Tobias had always been the Spanish prisoner fed to the sharks. "I'm wiser now, Will. It would very likely kill me—you know how few return from the sea."

"But aren't you dying by inches staying here, Jamie?" Will asked softly.

Ever tactful, Gil got up and moved farther off to allow the brothers some privacy.

Jamie felt a strange sensation in the back of his throat. He wasn't going to cry, dammit.

"We can all see that you are on the rack, and I would give anything I own to get you off it. Even your servant thinks you are haunted—he was the one who suggested a voyage as a cure."

"Remind me to dock his wages."

"He meant to help."

James stared at the flames rather than meet his brother's eye. Was Will right? Was he killing himself slowly, languishing in a self-built hell? But how could he break free of it? He couldn't sleep, had no appetite, felt so alone even when among those he loved. Men were supposed to be stronger than this—not crack under the first trial of their character. Thousands had seen much worse, experienced harsher torments, yet he was the one plagued by nightmares and barely able to control his violent urges. If he hadn't caught himself, would he actually have struck his sister? The thought terrified him. Maybe it would be best for his family if he did take himself away. So much the better, perhaps, if he never came back.

"All right, Will, all right, you've persuaded me: I'll do this. What do you have in mind?"

His brother unfolded his arms and leant forward intently. "Go to court and present yourself to Raleigh. I'll write to him to explain our interest in his project. He's so eager for backers he won't scorn my money. Involve yourself in the preparations, and, if you think it a sensible scheme, maybe you should take part in the expedition. It's due to leave this April."

"You want me to go to America? What, permanently?" James felt the sting of hurt that his presence had become so insupportable to his brother.

Will shook his head adamantly. "No, you halfwit. We want you to come back and report. This voyage is merely to locate the most promising site for a colony—it should only last the summer. The risk is as low as it can be for any voyage of discovery. 'Swounds, the last thing I want is to lose you to some savage land!"

Feeling a little placated, James nodded his assent. He found the prospect of a voyage into the unknown neither exciting nor terrifying. What did it matter what happened to him?

Will frowned. "I was hoping for a little more enthusiasm from you."

James tossed back the last of the wine. "It's your plan, my lord, not mine."

"Still—"

Gil intervened before they could fall to arguing. "Good my lords, I'm for bed."

Will stood and stretched. "Excellent idea. Ellie will be wondering what's become of me. Jamie, are you retiring now?"

And lie sleepless staring at the ceiling? No thanks. "I'll sit here a while."

Will was reluctant to leave him. "Shall I stay? We could play chess if you like."

James had had enough of Will's well-meant concern. "Heaven's sake, Will, your wife is not yet safe from her lying-in. She needs you more than I do. Get thee gone."

Finally, he had the study to himself. He threw another log on the fire and watched the sparks fly up the chimney. Midnight. Never his best time—too many hours to dawn, no chance of fooling yourself that the night was almost over. He half rose to refill his glass, then sank back knowing that there was no comfort to be found in the bottom of a flagon. He didn't want to be around his family with drink-sodden wits.

"Jamie?" While he'd been brooding, a little mouse had crept in.

"Sarah." His guilt rushed back as he remembered how he had snapped at her earlier.

His little sister came closer, her bare feet peeking out from the bottom of her ankle-length smock. Her long red-gold hair hung in two braids from beneath her white bed cap.

"I'm sorry I pestered you," she whispered, looking at his toe caps.

Now, if that didn't make him feel a hundred times worse, knowing he'd spoiled his little sister's day.

"No, no, sweeting, don't apologize to your grumpy bear of a brother. I should never have lashed out at you like that."

She knotted her fingers in her skirt. James knew she had embroidered the loose long-sleeved bodice herself, covering it with stylized figures of knights-in-armor bearing the Lacey colors, one for each of her brothers. Now she would realize that one of her heroes had feet of clay.

"Oh, come here, Sarah." He beckoned her to squeeze in the chair beside him and put an arm round her shoulders, relieved when she did not hesitate. "Feet warmer now?"

She nodded, settling against him with a dig or two of her sharp elbows. A gangly thirteen, she seemed all thin limbs and bony angles. "I love you, Jamie."

"I love you too, grasshopper."

"Love you best."

"Love you most." He tweaked her nose. "Don't worry if you go to sleep—I'll carry you up."

She relaxed against his side, swinging her toes lazily. James let out a deep sigh, strangely comforted by her acceptance of him and his moods. After only a few minutes, she was asleep. Carefully, he lifted her into his arms and took her up to the chamber she was sharing with her maid. Tucking her into bed, he sought his own room and lay fully dressed on the cover, waiting for morning to arrive.

CHAPTER 3

Whitehall, Westminster

THE COURT HAD MOVED TO WHITEHALL, so Milly did not have far to go to deliver Jane's new clothes. She arrived just after the noon meal, riding pillion behind her watchman, Old Uriah, with an exciting collection of parcels in her basket panniers. Jane watched out her chamber window as her maid greeted the needlewoman and conducted her upstairs. Clothes had always been something of a weakness for Jane; she could barely wait to see what Milly had brought her.

"My lady." Milly dipped a curtsy in the doorway, her quick eyes taking in the plain room, evidently disappointed that it wasn't dripping with gilt and velvet. The palace at Whitehall, while finely painted on the exterior, was a ramshackle place within; many a lord lodged in chambers that a tavern would have been ashamed to offer for hire.

"Mistress Turner," Jane replied formally, waving her servant away after she had piled the parcels on the bed. The door closed.

"Oh, horrid!" Milly blurted out, wrinkling her nose at the cracked plaster and lack of fireplace.

"Isn't it—and this is one of the better rooms." Jane blew on her chilled fingertips. "So now you know, being the Queen's lady is no bed of roses. At least here I have my own chamber. We all dread the summer progress, where they say we are frequently lodged like soldiers in a military camp." She gave an impish grin. "That is why I need you to add some sparkle to my life. Show me, show me!" Expertly dodging Milly's restraining arms, she darted to the bed and began unwrapping the parcels.

"Uh-uh," Milly scolded, and tapped her chest. "You can't rush the work of genius. Let me open them for you."

Jane flopped back on the pillows. "Very well—but hurry."

Milly laughed and unfolded the first of the two suits of livery: a white gown that nipped in at the waist and fell to the floor in a simple skirt. "Master Rich and I have had a wonderful time creating these—he really is a marvel at cutting fabric. You wear this with a high-necked chemise." She held up the lawn garment with frills at the neck and cuffs embroidered with gold thread. "And your brocade petticoat."

"Oh, it's lovely—so unfussy."

"You'll need a farthingale and a French roll round your hips if you wish to give it more shape."

"I like it like this," Jane admitted, fingering the smooth satin.

"And we made this sable-edged sleeveless coat to wear over the top—good news, seeing how you've no fire." Milly displayed a black velvet garment with pearl buttons and a trim of fur cut to a similar line as the gown so Jane's figure would be well displayed.

"But I didn't ask you—" Jane began to protest.

Milly pushed it into her hands. "You don't need to—I'll take it out of your share of the profits from my workshop."

Jane danced round the room with the coat. "I love it! What else?"

The second outfit was a dream: a full skirt in cream split down the middle to reveal a pearl-encrusted forepart, a stomacher embroidered with spring flowers and a white bodice and sleeves.

"What happened to the rest of my white satin?" Jane asked, looking suspiciously at the much nicer cream damask Milly had used.

"The mice ate it?" tried Milly.

"No, really, you must tell me!"

"I interpreted my orders a little creatively. I told Master Rich it was too tedious for you to have two dresses in the same fabric, and the Queen won't mind as long as you are wearing a pale color to complement her, so there we are." She frowned, having second thoughts. "You won't get into trouble, will you?"

Jane chuckled and shook her head. "Oh no, there are rules here, but it is not quite as strict as that. I'm going to be the envy of all the ladies—and you and Master Rich will be rushed off your feet with new commissions when I tell them who made my clothes."

"That's the idea—see, I did it for purely business reasons."

"And not to cheer up an old friend?"

"Absolutely not."

Jane held the dress to her. "How does it look?"

"Beautiful—but I knew it would."

"I'll wear it to the masque tomorrow."

"What masque is that, pray, and why haven't you told me before?"

"I only found out about it yester eve. It's our last chance for some frivolity before Lent. I've been given the role of Diana. The Queen's been drilling us all day like a fearsome general."

"You in a masque?" Milly snorted. "Do they know you can't hold a tune to save your life?"

"It's a nonsinging part," Jane replied, biting her lip to keep from following Milly into a painful fit of the giggles.

When Milly had recovered, she helped Jane fold the clothes into her trunk and then sat with her in the window, sharing a blanket to keep out the chill. A light frost dusted the roofs opposite, the white slowly retreating as the sun reached the shaded tiles. The maid brought in two tankards of warm spiced ale, then left again. Milly cradled hers and breathed in the steam.

"Ah, heaven."

Jane just gave her a secretive smile.

"Correct me if I'm wrong, my dear friend, but you seem in extreme good spirits," Milly probed. "Even before I came into the room you were buzzing like a bee in springtime. What has brought this upon you? I can't believe it is just the prospect of participating in the masque."

Jane hugged her edge of the blanket tightly. "There's a newcomer at court."

"Oh, do tell. Who?"

"James Lacey."

Just in time, Jane covered her ears as Milly squealed. "No!"

"Yes!"

"Have you spoken to him yet? What did he say? Did he kiss you?"

Jane held up a hand. "Slow down, slow down! We've not met yet."

Milly thought for a moment. "But he'll be at the masque, won't he?"

"Oh yes, undoubtedly."

"So you'll have a chance to explain."

"I think so—I hope so."

"Oh, Jane, this is good news." Her eyes turned to the trunk. "Shall I lower the neckline—Master Rich made it widow-modest, not maidenly alluring."

Jane pulled Milly back down before she could chop up what Jane considered perfection. "Widow-modest is just right."

Milly thumped her forehead. "Of course, sorry. I was just getting carried away."

"As usual."

"As usual." She held her peace for two seconds. "But the chemise is semi-sheer, if it gets that far."

Jane found herself blushing. "Stop it, you hussy."

Milly sucked in her cheeks in a vain attempt to forestall a smirk. "Don't say you weren't thinking it too."

Durham House

On arrival in London, James had lost no time in presenting himself at court, then had traveled the short distance downstream to Raleigh's Thames-side home of Durham House, a recent gift from the Queen to her favorite. The residence had the appearance of a castle from the outside, with thick stone walls rising from the river. It was damp and gloomy as a dungeon; Raleigh had spent a fortune on hangings and furnishings to make it fit for his role as first gentleman in the realm. As Will had predicted, Raleigh was more than welcoming when he understood the Laceys were backing his venture. James had immediately been invited to lodge there as if no bad feelings stood between the Earl of Dorset and Raleigh.

"How is your brother?" Raleigh asked casually as James joined the gathering in the turret-room study overlooking the river. The chamber was lined with books and navigational instruments; water reflections danced on the ceiling, enticing the occupants to plot this voyage into the unknown. The other speculators in the American experiment turned out to be an eclectic mix of merchants and scholars, leavened by a few noblemen like James. They were all currently studying the best maps yet made of the coast they intended to explore. Even to James's untrained eye, there were far too many blanks to be filled in. The north, Newfoundland, was fairly well known to the cod fishermen; Florida and the Caribbean were familiar to the Spanish and French; but the middle stretch was truly a mystery.

James ran his finger over the spot that marked the Gulf of Mexico. "He is well, sir. Celebrating the arrival of a son."

"The lovely countess has given him an heir. I see." Raleigh's shrewd dark eyes narrowed. "And he's sent you on this voyage."

How like the Queen's favorite to turn the knife in what he thought was a wound. "It is an honor to serve my family's interests, Master Raleigh."

"Naturally." Raleigh seemed quite cheered by the hint of another's unhappiness. He caressed his black beard to a dagger point. "We are eager to welcome the bold on our venture. I won't be going myself this time, but my captains are both good men. You'll be in the best hands. What skills can you offer us?"

James had given this some thought on the journey to London. "Like yourself, sir, I've military experience. I can advise on the security needs of a future colony."

Raleigh removed the map from under James's hand. "I have not heard of any distinguished service in Her Majesty's armies on your part, sir."

James steeled himself not to take offense. "That is because I spent most of my time in enemy territory—my presence was not bruited abroad. I suggest you ask my lord Leicester if you want confirmation."

Raleigh's expression brightened, as he was quick to understand the hint. "Ah, you were a scout. Excellent. You will know then how to survive in a land held by hostile forces. We have need of trackers too. You can do this?"

"I have some talent for it, I think."

"Good. You may turn out to be a more valuable investment than your brother's stake in this affair."

"I'll endeavor to be of use," James said drily.

Raleigh stood up from the table and stretched as a nearby church bell struck the hour. "My lords, gentlemen, we must adjourn for this day. Those of you invited to the masque this night are welcome to travel in my barge if you so wish."

The city men tactfully excused themselves, leaving only the courtiers to discuss their evening plans.

"Lacey, are you going?" Raleigh asked.

James would have preferred to stay in his room but knew he would be expected to show his face, if only for an hour. "Aye, sir."

"Then we'll meet you at the landing stairs anon."

Raleigh swept out to consult his famous wardrobe for a suit to impress his mistress. James ambled off to his small chamber to unpack a clean shirt—the best he could do in his straitened circumstances.

Waiting in the cold passageway for her entrance, Jane shivered in her new dress. Despite the layers of chemise, farthingale, petticoats, kirtle, bodice, sleeves and stomacher, the February chill still managed to creep into her bones. Mary Radcliffe, another of the Queen's ladies, rubbed her arms.

"I swear I have goose pimples," Mary muttered, craning her neck to peek through the doorway. "When is it our turn?"

Jane listened for the musical cue. The courtier playing Jupiter was concluding his speech to the sovereign, and then it would be their chance to process across the stage, each wearing a mask and carrying a symbol of their divinity. Hers was a bow and arrow for the huntress; Mary Radcliffe bore a basket of apples, symbolizing love and temptation for Venus.

"If that windbag doesn't hurry up, I'm going to pelt him with my fruit," grumbled Mary.

"No need, I'll have shot him with my arrow before then," whispered Jane, frowning as she spotted her brother Henry seated not far from the Queen. Two rows down from him were Jane's least favorite courtiers, Richard Paton, the new Marquess of Rievaulx, accompanied by his usual shadows, Otho and Lucres. How had Jonas managed to produce such an unpleasant crop of sons? Stout-bodied Richard was arrogant beyond all bounds; lank-limbed Otho never happier than when tormenting someone weaker than him; and Lucres, sharper in features as well as in brain, the one who plotted the most fiendish mischief. She could only suppose that Jonas's long periods of absence from home while attending court had allowed his boys' characters to run to seed and it was too late to prune them into shape now.

Another party of gentlemen came into view, and Jane felt a delicious tingle of excitement: James Lacey had just entered with Raleigh and taken a seat near the Queen. James looked very serious in his black doublet and long venetians compared to the spangled finery of Raleigh in his gold velvet jerkin worn over a white pinked doublet and puffy satin trunk hose.

The musicians struck up their tune. Jane took a breath to steady her nerves, then entered in her place in the procession of gods and goddesses. The sequinned mask gave her the confidence to display herself before James after eighteen months apart. Would he recognize her? she wondered. She had never been entirely sure of his regard, but thought he had liked her when she had been a guest at Lacey Hall. She had certainly felt a spark between them, but had he?

The gods did a complete revolution of the room, bowing or curtsying on every count of twelve. Finally, they came together to hold a dramatic pose before the Queen, Jane in the front row holding aloft her bow and arrow as if to shoot the ceiling. She slid a look to the spectators and noticed with chagrin that James was studying his toe caps, seemingly indifferent to the performance.

The Queen led the applause. The actors dispersed to make way for the dancing to follow. Jane moved to one side, handing her bow and mask to a waiting page.

"La volta," demanded Elizabeth, signaling the musicians to play the strenuous dance that was one of her favorites. Though past fifty, she still reigned supreme as the foremost dancer at court. Raleigh immediately offered his services as her partner, lifting and turning

Elizabeth as the steps demanded, her crimson skirts swishing as she leapt with the energy of a much younger woman. After they had completed a circuit of the floor, other couples joined the dance. Jane hovered at the edge, hoping James would look up and notice her, but he was still sunk in a brooding inspection of the floor.

"You wish to dance, Marchioness?" Jane's brother, Sir Henry Perceval, appeared at her elbow. A large-built man with her fair coloring, he was not usually short of partners, despite not being the heir to their father's earldom—that honor rested with their staid eldest brother, David, who rarely ventured out of Yorkshire. Henry had served with Raleigh in Ireland and been knighted for his military prowess.

Jane gave up on waiting for James. "How kind, brother, thank you."

Henry seized her by the waist and threw her into the first leap, her skirts belling as she landed. La volta was too vigorous a dance to allow for discussion between the participants, and Jane concentrated on keeping time while wondering at her brother's motives for asking her to partner him. His renewed interest in her presence at court was likely herald to an attempt by her family to use her once more. At the close of the music, her suspicions were justified, as Henry immediately drew her aside.

"How are you faring as the Queen's lady, Janie?"

"Very well, thank you, Henry," she replied coolly, distrusting his use of his old nickname for her.

Henry signaled to a serving man to bring them wine. "I've been talking to your stepson." He said the last word with a sneer.

"Oh? How is dear Richard?" Her tone was acidic as she feigned calm but a frisson of fear shivered along her spine. The Paton sons' presence at court was unlikely to mean good news for her. She hoped they stayed far away from her on the other side of the dance floor.

"Spitting mad at you, sister. Something about a wedding ring and dower properties—I confess I stopped listening after the first hour of his rant. Remarkable talent you have for making enemies."

"One we both inherited, I think."

Henry leant back, considering her. "Father and I have been talking."

Here it came: the reason he was making such friendly overtures.

"We could help you against the Patons, gain your rights to your husband's estate."

"Could you indeed?" Jane sipped her wine, scanning the crowd for any sign of James. "And what would it cost me?"

"Nothing. We merely would like to explore with you the possibilities for another match. You surprised Father landing a marquess; he has revised his opinion of your potential."

"How pleasing for him."

"He thinks if a marquess before, why not a duke next time?"

"Why not indeed? But for the fact that there are no dukes to be had in England at present."

"Who said anything about England?"

"Oh, I see. Father is thinking outside his usual patriotic prejudices. I suppose he has his eye on some trading advantage he thinks I can bring him."

Henry did not contradict her guess.

"You can tell him that this particular daughter is tired of being a pawn in his interminable game of chess. I do not want to be traded for a more valuable piece."

Henry laughed. "I knew you'd say that, which is why we had to look for an incentive that would make you more inclined to carry out your duty."

Jane felt a pang of fear. "Incentive?"

"Ah, look. Here's that Lacey fellow. James, isn't it?" Henry deliberately ignored her inquiry and tapped James on the shoulder as he made his way to the door. "Lacey, good to see you at court once more! You remember my sister, of course?"

Still on edge from Henry's veiled threat, Jane felt her heart flutter in her chest. She could have done without her brother's presence, but at least he had brought James to her side. She dipped a curtsy. "Sir."

Disdainful brown eyes swept over her. "My lady, Perceval," James said curtly, giving them both a shallow bow, intent on escaping the chamber.

Henry refused to let him slip away so easily. "I don't know if you've heard, my lord, but my sister is a widow now—a marchioness, no less."

Henry had always been crass, but his bluntness made Jane cringe.

"My condolences, madam," James murmured, his eyes skipping to the exit.

The musicians began another dance, a stately allemande.

"Happily, her mourning is past and she is quite able to participate in our revels," Henry continued, enjoying his sister's discomfort at the reluctance of the young nobleman to acknowledge her.

"Henry, please," Jane murmured, finding his blatant begging a partner for her humiliating in the extreme.

"Come, come, sister." Henry patted her wrist with maddening

condescension. "You cannot spend the evening dancing only with your brother. Lent is upon us and you won't have another chance till April."

Jane wished the floor would open and swallow her up. She had hoped for some sign that James had retained feelings for her, but he was as severe in manner as in dress. Her eyes now rested on his much-inspected toe caps.

"Good lord, you two are killjoys! I'll go find myself a merry partner and leave you to your gloomy corner." With a slight bow, Henry retreated, doubtless pleased with himself for dropping his sister into a socially impossible situation. He ever rejoiced in such small victories over her.

Jane took a step back. "I apologize, sir. I did not ask my brother to force you to dance, as you are obviously so unwilling to do so. I bid you good night."

The toe caps closed the distance she had opened up between them.

"No, he is right. It is our last chance. I would find the experience"—James paused, seeking the right word—*"enlightening."*

"How so?" Jane couldn't help feeling a tingle of pleasure as he took her hand and led her on to the dance floor to join the procession. He was even more handsome than she remembered—his face firming into that of the man he was becoming rather than the youth she remembered. His hair curled at the temples and hung to his ruff, defying any attempt to order it, but his beard was close clipped and velvet smooth.

"I'm intrigued to find out if you still think yourself so far above us poor Laceys, madam." The dance separated them before she could frame a reply. He returned to steer her through the next figure. "Ah, but of course you do: you are a marchioness now—a rung above my brother, the earl, and so far above me it hurts my neck just to catch a glimpse of your exaltedness. You must be very pleased with yourself."

It was worse than she had feared: *bitter* was too mild a word for what he felt towards her.

"I can explain, sir. I never considered myself superior to your family, far from it." Jane tried a conciliatory smile, but it slid right off his defenses.

"I'm delighted you see the truth, madam. You may have won the title, but you never had the nobility."

With that insult, the music changed to the faster, cheerful third section that concluded the allemande, giving Jane no opportunity to respond. She felt as if he had just slapped her. He'd unjustly lashed out, not giving her the chance to explain what had really happened between his brother and her all those months ago. A fury such as she had not felt in many years rose in her as he swung her cynically through the final measure, his eyes hard, his smile without mirth. The musicians struck the final chord and the dancers faced each other.

"It's been a pleasure, my lady," James drawled.

"You, sir," Jane said, quivering with anger, "are an arrogant swine!"

She did not even curtsy as she left, swishing her skirts as she passed as if to sweep him away like so much dirt. So much for her glorious reunion with the man of her dreams.

CHAPTER 4

JAMES CURSED UNDER HIS BREATH as Lady Jane dismissed him, leaving him stranded in the middle of an emptying dance floor. He should never have taken up the invitation to partner her. He had done so because she had looked so humiliated by her brother's crude handling of their encounter that he'd felt compelled to take pity on her. Then he had compounded the error by letting his annoyance at his weakness prick him into insulting her. Out of loyalty to Will, he should either have refused to dance with the jilt or kept silent throughout, but his damnable fascination with her had lured him into speaking his mind. Now she'd given him the cut in front of the whole court and they would be gossiping about it for days. A number of people had doubtless overheard her final remark, which would add to the storm of speculation.

He took refuge behind the dais where the Queen sat, barricaded from view by the legion of courtiers fawning over the monarch. If it had been in his power, he would've left immediately for his bed, but he had agreed to return with Raleigh, so was stuck at the festivity until the favorite was ready to retire—which from the looks of it might not be for some hours.

"My penance," James muttered, signaling a servitor to bring him some wine.

Jane looked very fine, he admitted to himself, gulping down the indifferent vintage. She was wearing a cream-colored dress with fiddly decoration on the stomacher—pretty and probably very expensive. He knew nothing about fashion—in fact could not care less about the subject—but even he acknowledged that she had a style all her own. Regal, if that was not blasphemy in Elizabeth's presence.

A new dance began and James made sure he caught no one's eye as a prospective partner. Jane was among the dancers, being squired round the floor by Lord Mountjoy. James tried to stop watching but found he couldn't tear his gaze away. He had half feared he had fallen in love with Jane that spring when his brother had courted her; if the truth be told, her breaking off the match had been a big relief, as he did not have to find excuses to keep away from home any longer. So why was he still angry with her? He had taken the rejection personally, while Will had shrugged it off without so much as a bruised feeling to show for it. Then Jane had gone and proved her shallow nature by marrying that old stick of a marquess—James had not been surprised, really, just disappointed. She was like her brother: out to climb the social ladder and improve her family's standing at the expense of any finer feeling. Being the Queen's lady was doubtless all part of the plot, a rung up to influence as one of the gatekeepers to Her Majesty.

James raised his goblet in a silent toast. Good luck to her. Her business was just that: hers. He would make sure he kept his distance in the future.

Raleigh found him an hour later.

"Why the sour looks, Lacey?" he asked breezily. "The ladies have all been asking where you've run off to."

James gestured to his spot in the shadows. "I prefer to observe rather than participate this night."

"A certain lady ruined you for others, eh?" Raleigh rubbed his hands together, rings flashing. "A luscious piece, our lady marchioness. And a widow now." He tapped his mustache, lost in private memories. "That makes her fair game."

James's temper immediately soared, an arrow loosed from a tight-strung bow; the look in the man's eye was predatory. "And one of the Queen's ladies," he said severely. "Our sovereign does not like poachers on her preserve."

"True. But the risk adds to the thrill, don't you think?"

James did not want to think anything of the sort. "Are you ready to leave, sir?"

"Aye, the Queen is tired and has gone to bed. I'm free to go." Raleigh clicked his fingers to his manservant. "Have the barge brought up to the landing stairs, Meadows."

James caught a glimpse of Jane talking to Lord Mountjoy, her face lacking the radiance it had held when she had first greeted him. Had he done that to her? He wasn't sure if he should be proud or guilty. One of the twisted aspects of his self-hatred was the impulse to make others taste the bitterness of life—but when he did so he always regretted it.

"Or perhaps you wish to stay and hunt?" Raleigh asked shrewdly.

"No, sir. There's nothing for me here." James left the hall without a backward glance.

The morning following the masque, Jane woke up with a headache and a foul temper. After snapping at her maid and generally making a nuisance of herself, she decided she wasn't fit company for the other ladies and had to get some air. Most of all she would have liked a good heart-to-heart with Milly, but she was on duty in the afternoon and would not be able to get permission to be absent in the city. The nave of Westminster Abbey would provide a protected walk from the cold drizzle falling from the winter skies, so she headed in that direction, asking her manservant to wait at the door while she walked the gray stone aisles in peace, reading the inscriptions with faint interest. The weak light filtering in through the high windows made the church feel as if it were underwater and the tombs she was looking at were the debris of past shipwrecks.

Jane was just bending over to inspect a frieze at the bottom of one monument when she felt an icy touch on her shoulder.

"Mother dear." Richard Paton stood feet apart, arms on his hips, like the portrait of old King Henry. ﹡

She straightened up quickly and turned to face her stepson, the new Marquess of Rievaulx. In his late forties, he was heading towards a barrel-shaped trunk with spindly legs, not shown to any advantage in the current fashions for tight hose. Jane wished she could find something to like in her stepson, but he only shared his father's hazel eyes and not a jot of his gentle nature.

"Lord Rievaulx," Jane replied coolly, folding her hands in the enveloping sleeves of her furred coat to hide their nervous trembling. She never felt safe with Richard, knowing he wished her ill.

"I saw you at the masque yester eve. I trust you are well?"

What was this? An overture of peace?

"I am. And you?"

"Plagued by lawyers and debts."

"I see. I am sorry to hear of your difficulties."

"Are you? Then you can help me by dropping your claim to the dower interest in the Rievaulx estate."

Jane gave him a tight smile. "I'm not that sorry."

Richard glanced over his shoulder, signaling his two brothers, Otho and Lucres, to approach. Otho sauntered over, thumbs tucked in his battered leather belt; Lucres moved more gracefully, with the smoothness of a snake about to strike. She looked for an escape. A priest was walking across the nave; perhaps she could catch up with him and ask him a spiritual question or two until her stepsons had tired of their pursuit?

"No, no, my lady: you will not slip away from us," Richard said, his gaze following hers. "We insist you listen to us—you've avoided this conversation for too long." He gave a nod and Otho and Lucres linked arms with her, half carrying her as they abducted her from the abbey out a side door.

"Put me down!" Jane protested. "This is a sanctuary—you can't do this!"

"You have no need of a sanctuary to keep you from your family." Richard glanced around the covered porch into which they had emerged to find a private spot. "Over here."

Jane found herself backed into a corner between the tomb of a knight and a stone bench.

"Ready to listen?" asked Richard, leaning one hand on the wall by her head, his face so close she could feel the warmth of his breath on her cheek. Rain dampened his hair, making it lie flat and greasy against his scalp. He blocked her in completely; all anyone passing would see was the bell of her skirts pressed against stone.

Jane swallowed.

"Good. Then, my lady, you will give up your lawsuit and return the jewels your late husband gave you in his dotage. Don't think a six-month bride—not even a bride, as he never touched you—can walk away with my inheritance."

Jane wondered what she could say. Jonas had only bequeathed her what any widow was owed: maintenance while she lived. It was what he had wanted for her. And the sole jewel that had come from the Rievaulx family was her wedding ring, which for sentimental reasons she had no desire to return—the others had come with her as part of her dowry. To return the ring would be akin to agreeing that her marriage to Jonas had not been real.

"You father wanted me to have your full respect as his widow," Jane said at last.

Richard snorted. "What, you? A chit of eighteen whom I would not stoop to marry myself? My father's judgment was severely impaired in his last days—a point the court will be hearing in full."

"I loved your father—"

He cut across her with a swipe of his hand. "Oh, spare me the false grief, lady. I can see that our entreaties make no difference to your brazen heart. I will have to take back what you will not give."

He slid his hand down her left arm to manacle her wrist. Before Jane could guess his intention, he made a grab for her ring. Quickly, she made her hand into a fist and tried to pull free.

"Let go of me!" She struck out at him with her other hand, trying to push him away, outraged that he would dare assault her. She got in a good blow to his nose, making his eyes water.

"Not till I get what I want!" he growled. "Hold her, won't you?"

Otho seized her right hand and pinned her against the wall. She screamed in frustration as Richard peeled her fingers straight, but Otho clapped a smothering palm across her nose and mouth. Lucres circled, keeping watch.

"I'll break your fingers if I have to!" warned Richard, bending her wrist back so that it burned with red pain.

In danger of suffocating, Jane bit Otho's palm; he let go with an oath and she hauled in another breath to scream.

Boots rang on the pavement; she heard a grunt as Lucres was thrown clear.

"Gentlemen, are you mad? Assaulting a lady in broad daylight—in a churchyard, of all places?"

Richard froze, feeling the point of a rapier prod him between the shoulder blades. Jane closed her eyes, head dropped back against the wall as the ache throbbed up her arm. They must have made a strange tableau—three men against one lady. How heroic.

"This is none of your business," hissed Richard.

"Oh, but I think it is. Step away from the lady."

Jane realized she knew that voice. Of all the cursed luck: her rescuer was none other than James Lacey. When he saw her face, he'd probably tell them to carry on.

Richard was not going to be made to back down so easily—he still had two brothers against the interloper's single blade.

"Sir, this is a family matter. I advise you to leave well alone." He tightened his grip on Jane's wrist, making her gasp.

"Even so, I hate to see a lady abused. Call it a quirk of character." The blade pressed a little harder, passing through the first layer of clothing to the doublet beneath.

"Brother, leave it for another day," warned Otho, looking nervously around. A party of gentlemen had paused by the fence to the graveyard, watching the scuffle.

Richard released Jane's arm and stepped to one side.

Just kill me now, God, why don't you? Jane cursed her rotten luck. She didn't bother to open her eyes. Why look when you knew that you'd see a sneer?

"My lady, are you unharmed?" James's tone betrayed his surprise to find her in this position. His question was not exactly hostile, but neither was he oozing concern.

She cradled her injured hand to her breast and pushed away from the wall that had been supporting her for the past few seconds. "I'm . . . I'm quite well, thank you, sir."

"What has the lady done to deserve such treatment from you?" asked James, glowering at the three much older men.

Oh yes, it had to be something she had done. He couldn't conceive of this being none of her fault.

"Our stepmother refuses to return a family ring which is mine by right," spat Richard. "Not that it's any concern of yours, young man."

"Stepmother?"

The condemnation packed into that one word was quite enough for Jane. She pushed past Richard, not looking at James. Her stepson caught at the back of her coat, but the flat of a rapier knocked his hand free.

"I think you have *persuaded* your stepmother enough for one day. My lady, I will walk you back to your rooms."

Jane could hear him follow her. "No need, sir. I left my man at the west doors."

"No, I insist. You are as white as a sheet." He touched her arm, but, bruised from wrist to elbow, she flinched away. "I meant only to offer my support. You look ready to faint."

She gave a harsh laugh. "I am in no danger of fainting. Throw a few things at choice targets, perhaps, but not faint."

"I take it you and your stepsons do not see eye to eye?" He cupped her elbow gently, their quarrel of the night before temporarily called off. For the moment, she was just a lady in distress, and Jane sensed he had never walked by on the other side, even if he was not clear of the rights and wrongs of the case.

"My stepsons have no love for me, sir. Their father warned me to expect this from them. It is why he wanted me to seek the protection of the Queen's household." Shock had loosened Jane's tongue; it was rare she confided in anyone apart from Milly.

"And the ring?"

Jane held out her hand, annoyed that it was shaking. "My wedding band—a ruby. The estate can have it back when I die, but I will not shame my vows by handing it over without a fight. Jonas would be disgusted with me if I did that."

James looked down at the ring she had tried so hard to defend and felt his stomach lurch. Her fragile wrist was flaming red, already bruising; she had a cut on her palm where the band had been driven in by Richard's clasp. He felt a sudden desire to race back and beat the stuffing out of the new marquess.

"My lady, you are hurt."

Jane flexed her fingers tentatively. "Nothing broken, I think. Still, I would have been much more hurt if he'd managed to get the ring off my finger."

Her flicker of a triumphant smile was what did it for James. He couldn't help himself. Lifting the injured hand, he kissed her knuckles.

"You, my lady, are a tigress. You had no need of my poor services, did you?"

"Oh, I don't know, sir, you make a very good rescuer. I was fortunate you came by just at that moment."

He sheathed his rapier through the loop on his belt. "Not luck, my lady, but thanks to the fact that they chose to attack you on the path to the fencing hall. If not me, some other practitioner of the art would've come by at any moment."

"I always thought my stepsons were idiots; they can't even stage an ambush right," Jane muttered.

James surprised himself by laughing. The young marchioness had always had a vinegary sense of humor, adding relish to any situation that other ladies might make bland with vapid remarks. It was one of the things that had attracted him to her before; he had never understood why his brother had thought her insipid and too proper. For his part, he'd always suspected her of being as tempestuous as he was. Events had proved him right.

They found Jane's man snoozing on a bench by the western doors to the abbey. James gave him a shove.

"Do your job, man. While you were sleeping, your mistress was accosted."

The servant stammered his excuses.

"Next time, keep her in sight at all times." James bowed to Jane. "I'll leave you here."

She dipped a curtsy. "Thank you, sir."

James waited on the steps until he had watched them arrive safely at one of the doors to Whitehall Palace. He shook his head, puzzled by his actions and hers. The day before they had been throwing insults at each other; now, they were acting very much like friends.

CHAPTER 5

Silver Street, London

MILLY READ THE LETTER FROM JANE several times, trying to make sense of it. It had clearly been written in two parts: the first, spitting with fury at the unmannerly conduct of her James; the second, recounting a quite different treatment at his hands. Her poor friend had it bad: she did not seem to realize that her strong swings of emotion betrayed her deeper feelings. What remained a mystery was exactly what he felt towards Jane.

"Mistress, there's a young man to see you," Henny announced, hovering in the doorway to the upstairs parlor, wringing her hands.

Milly tried not to be irritated by her servant's nervous habit—and failed.

"What manner of man is he?" she asked, threading her embroidery needle with azure silk. "Not the bailiff, I hope? I thought all my accounts were settled."

"No, no, not him." Henny tugged her black apron straight. "He's one of those blackamoor fellows like you see in the households of the great lords. Dark as the devil himself."

Milly put her work aside with a huff of displeasure. "I beg you not to speak so."

Her reproof sailed over the head of London-born Henny, who shared the prejudices of her fellow citizens. They were accustomed to thinking anyone different—Jew, Moor, Spaniard, Russian—the spawn of Beelzebub.

"Shall I send him up, mistress?"

What else would Milly ask her to do with him? *Patience, Milly, patience*, she reminded herself.

"Please."

"And Old Uriah too?"

"Whatever for?"

"Well, he might turn nasty on you."

"Henny, go downstairs this instant and show our caller up with all the politeness you are capable of displaying. I will not require a guard. I expect he brings us business from his master or mistress, not threats."

Milly checked that all was in order in the room, making a final inspection of her own person to ensure a neat, efficient appearance. She stood by the window, waiting for the visitor to arrive.

"Go on up, um, sir. First door on the right," Milly heard Henny say cautiously, as if she were baiting a lion, throwing meat scraps to stop him from turning on her.

The man's steps were light and fast on the stairs. The door opened, the draft making the flames in the fireplace leap up the chimney.

"Diego! My goodness, it is you!" Milly was shocked that she recognized the caller. It had been three years since they had last met.

He had served her father as a groom and page boy for years until Porter had fallen into disgrace. When Diego had been sold off with her father's horse, Barbary, she had lost track of what had become of him.

Diego grinned and made a flourishing bow. "Mistress Milly."

Questions crowded into Milly's brain like groundlings rushing to grab the best places to see the play. "How are you? Where are you living? How did you find me?"

He laughed, seized her outstretched hands and twirled her around. "You look well, mistress."

"I am—but I refuse to let you call me that: I have to be Milly to you or it feels all wrong." So many memories danced between them: around the same age, they had become friends when her father had ordered Diego to teach her to ride. Milly suspected Diego found the many-layered class distinctions of England incomprehensible and amusing, observing them when he had to but ignoring them when it suited. He was one of the few who had not been scared to offer her comfort when her father was dragged off to the Tower. They had kept in touch for a while, but his messages, sent in the form of bead necklaces and bracelets, all handmade with loving attention, had ceased after she had moved for the fifth time. She guessed she had just become too difficult to track. "Please, how did you find me?"

Diego laughed at her curiosity—she was never one to let a secret rest. "I remembered, Milly, that you were friends with Lady Jane. I came across her two years ago and asked her maid if she knew where you were, but that girl was not helpful." His brown eyes twinkled with humor, suggesting that the reception of his request had met with a much less polite response. "When I saw the lady was at court, I tried her new servants, and they were much kinder. They said their lady had called here." He squeezed her hands and let go. "You have done well for yourself, Mistress Porter."

Few others would think the fall from gentlewoman to needle-worker a good thing, but Diego never saw matters in the usual light. Milly clasped her hands together in delight, this unlooked-for visit making her giddy with happiness, as he brought a reminder of the many good times of her childhood. With Diego, she had always felt somehow more vibrant, more herself.

"I'm so fortunate you took the trouble, Diego. Oh, I have so much to tell you! I thought I had lost sight of you completely. I imagined you were caught up in the household of some great lord, an ambassador, perhaps, traveling the world in his entourage."

Diego picked up some half-finished embroidery and inspected her work, running his fingers lightly over the fine stitching. "You mostly have the right of it. I serve the Earl of Dorset and his brothers." Milly's squeal of surprise made him flinch and grin. "By the toes of the great crocodile, mistress, I had forgotten you did that."

She giggled. Diego had always teased her with outlandish oaths. "By the tears of the white elephant, it is an incurable disease with me, I vow. But the Earl of Dorset—how did that come about?" How strange that three of her friends had become entangled with the fortunes of that noble family.

He laid the embroidery carefully back on her worktable. "I went with Barbary. My lord the earl was in need of a horse and your fa-ther's was up for sale. You see it is simple, really. I am with Master James Lacey for the moment."

"But of course—that's how you know Lady Jane is at court." She gestured to him to sit. "How long do you have for your visit?"

"Long enough. My master is closeted with Master Raleigh and his friends. They're planning a voyage."

Milly threw a shovel of coal on the fire, not wanting Diego to feel cold. She remembered he hated the English winters. "Oh? Where are they going?"

"The Americas." Diego pulled a skeptical face. "These Englishmen, they are strange people. They think to take the land for themselves. Is not this country enough?"

Sitting opposite him, Milly shook her head. "Come now, Diego, we English aren't as bad as the Spanish and Portuguese, with their huge empires. We have to keep up with the neighbors."

"But why do they think these lands theirs?" Diego seemed genuinely puzzled. "They go to the other side of the world and steal gold and silver, then squabble over it like a pack of dogs and a bone. Why can we not all stay where we are and be content?"

Milly shrugged. "I don't know, but it seems in man's nature always to want more. I know I'm always thinking of the next thing—a successful business, friends, happiness, family one day." Her eyes flicked up to meet his and dropped almost at once. "I want to sew my own little embroidery empire. Don't you want more than you have?"

Diego did not answer immediately. Instead, he gave her a penetrating look, his gaze traveling from her eyes down to where her hands rested in her lap. He cleared his throat. "Aye, I have always wanted more, but I am afraid to ask."

Milly wondered what he was trying to tell her—and was a little scared to guess, if the truth be told. He had always treated her more like a sweetheart than his master's daughter. Their stations in life had set them miles apart then, but now that she worked for a living they were very much on a level.

"I never thought of you being afraid of anything," she said, blushing. Silently, she cursed her redhead's pale skin for making her so obvious with her embarrassment.

"Oh, but I am."

A loud rap at the door broke the moment. Christopher Turner burst into the room, already in midflow.

"My jewel of the Thames, you must help me!" he exclaimed dramatically. "I have a poem to write, but my muse has refused to visit me. I am desperate, nay, thirsting like a man in the midst of a desert, for an idea." A little late, Christopher noticed she had a guest. Undeterred, he spun round to sharpen his wit on Diego. "Master Moor, at your service. Forgive my rude interruption; bear with me and I will try not to bore."

Diego had risen to his feet, as uncomfortable as a cat doused in cold water. "Sir Player."

Milly rushed in between her two guests. "Kit, this is an old friend of mine, Diego—he . . . er . . . served my father once. Diego, Christopher Turner, as you guessed, a player, neighbor and very good customer."

"And who do you serve now, my blackberry of the English hedgerow?" asked Christopher with his customary sparkle.

His teasing fell flat with Diego. "I am part of the Earl of Dorset's household, sir."

Christopher stiffened, his warm manner frosting over like a window on a January morning. "Indeed? You have my pity."

"My master is most generous," Diego said staunchly. "I have no need of your pity."

"Then I'll have it back." Christopher snapped his fingers. "See, 'tis gone."

"Mistress Porter, I take my leave," Diego announced, turning his shoulder to the interloper.

"Oh, but I thought you were able to stay for a visit!" she protested.

"I will call another day. I see you have more pressing demands on your time."

She tried a smile, but the harmonious mood had gone. "You're quite wrong. Master Turner can wait, can't you, Kit?"

The player was silent, staring at Diego with dislike.

"Kit?" Milly prompted.

"It is always my pleasure to wait for you, my dear," he said with unnecessary warmth, sending out quite the wrong signals to Diego as to the nature of their relationship.

"Mistress Porter, good day." Diego bowed and hurried out.

Angry with Christopher, Milly threw a cushion at him. "Urgh, you infuriating creature! You scared him away!"

The player slumped into the chair Diego had vacated, unconcerned. "No good can come of any dealings with the Dorsets or their servants, love. Here speaks bitter experience. Best for you that he leaves you alone."

"You, sir, are insufferable! I'm not your love—and I don't need you patrolling the boundaries of my friendships."

Christopher clapped his hand to his forehead. "That's it! A beautiful image—the scornful woman, the boundaries of love—I can see the sonnet now." He leapt up and smothered her hand in kisses. "Thank you, thank you, sweet Milly. You've saved my bacon."

Milly found it hard to remain cross with Christopher for long. He had a deep, sometimes irrational, prejudice against anything to do with his father's family, but otherwise meant well.

"Oh, I'm so pleased I could be of service," she said sarcastically. "Almost worth you running off one of my best friends to make you a few pennies."

"My heart and my purse are yours, dear one!" Christopher called over his shoulder as he made his exit.

"Shame both are usually empty!" she shouted after him.

"Brilliant!" Christopher's laughter floated up the stairs. "I'll use that image too, O muse of the gold-thread heaven."

Diego marched back to Durham House through the streets of the city, for once oblivious to the interest his unusual coloring attracted from the pallid Londoners. Milly Porter had for a long time been his ideal girl. He remembered the extraordinary copper sheen of her fine hair when she had worn it down as a child, the lightness of spirit she always displayed, her sweet and very kissable lips. He knew that he was not thought unhandsome by English girls—he had dallied with enough to know that his dark skin was not scorned by them at least—but Milly had always seemed impervious to his charms, persisting in seeing him just as a friend.

But then, they had been very young when they had parted, thirteen or fourteen. She had never understood that his handmade gifts were courting presents in the traditions of his country. He had come to her workshop with high hopes that she might now be ready to recognize what lay between them—hopes that had been dashed by that ridiculous long-legged chattering monkey in his too-loud clothes.

As he walked, lost in thought, a man staggered backwards out of an alehouse, knocking Diego into the path of an oncoming cart.

Diego quickly rolled out of the way and got to his feet only to be swiped by the carter's whip.

"You stupid foreigner! Got a death wish?" the oaf bellowed.

Diego wished him a speedy passage to the Christian hell and walked on, trying to wipe the muck from his livery. He hated Londoners—apart, that was, from one particular citizen. For her, he would make an exception.

CHAPTER 6

"DAUGHTER!"

Jane stopped, caught on the stairs leading to the river where she had intended to take passage to Milly's. It was her day off duty, but she had heard from Henry that her father had come to court. Thus far, she had managed to avoid him. Now, her plan to hide out in the city thwarted, she turned and curtsied.

"Father, how fare you?" *Let's try to keep this civilized,* she thought. She signaled to her servants to wait.

Thaddeus Perceval, Lord Wetherby, stood arms akimbo on the top step looking down at his daughter. A stout man with coarse manners, he had a crop of bristling white-gold hair, harsh lines bracketing his mouth and hard eyes a paler shade of blue than Jane's. He had not bothered to refurbish his wardrobe before presenting himself at court, so was clad in a russet tabard coat and mud-colored doublet and hose a decade out of fashion, proclaiming him every inch the country nobleman.

"I'm well. I left David and your aunt in good health," he replied gruffly.

Jane played with the creamy silk lining on her long sleeves. "I'm glad to hear that."

Her father gestured to the boat waiting at the bottom of the steps. "Where are you off to, Jane?"

The last thing Jane wanted was for him to know she was still in touch with Milly Porter; he had made it quite clear that she had to cut all ties with "that traitorous drab" when Milly's father was sent to the Tower. The fact that a man the Earl of Wetherby had previously extolled as a fine soldier and better hunter could prove to be guilty of so serious a crime had meant Thaddeus took the revelation as a personal affront.

"I was thinking of visiting Goldsmiths Row," Jane invented quickly.

"What, so rich now are you, daughter, that you can spend your money on luxuries?"

Jane just smiled tightly in reply, knowing there was no good response to that question.

"Still, I think that errand can wait when you've not seen your old father for almost a year." He beckoned her up the stairs.

Jane really had no choice but to obey the summons and get it over with. The prickly kiss he gave her suggested all was well between them—at least as far as he was concerned. Was he so dense as to have forgotten the bitterness with which they had parted? He had volubly resented Jonas's forcing a marriage contract on him that ensured Jane retained control of her own dowry should she be left a widow. Thankfully, he had no power over her now, other than the social expectation that children show their parents respect and honor. They both knew that if she stood up to him she would suffer widespread condemnation.

So be it, thought Jane, steeling herself. *I refuse to be bullied.*

"Has Henry spoken to you?" her father asked, walking her back into the palace and seating her on a bench in an alcove near the great hall.

Jane glanced longingly out the window at the little garden of sandy paths and box hedges, knowing she could not yet escape. "Yes, sir."

"Fine lad, Henry."

Jane held her peace, watching a gardener painstakingly rake the paths smooth.

"He's found a good match for you, second son of a Frog duke—a sound man. Shipping and wine interests—big estates near Bordeaux. Eldest son's a bit feeble, so he's likely to inherit."

"Good for me or for you?" Jane asked quietly, plucking her sleeves nervously.

Thaddeus grinned, mistaking her intent. "Both. He'll help us develop the French market for our broadcloth."

Jane searched for ways to turn down this interference in her life but could come up with nothing but a straight refusal.

"My regrets, sir, but I am not willing to wed again so soon after Jonas's death."

"Good God, girl, it's been months! I can't believe a young woman like you wants to waste the bloom of her beauty on widow's weeping. You made a excellent match—well beyond my expectations for you after you-know-what—but no one expects you to pretend to grieve beyond the month's mind."

Jane would have protested his cynical estimation of her, but there was no point. He had never believed her capable of emotions he did not feel himself. "Still, sir, I must refuse your kind offer to matchmake for me."

Thaddeus sprang to his feet, dropping the act of concerned

father for his more usual one of irate parent. He ground his fist into his palm. "Henry warned me you were still as stubborn as ever! You don't know how lucky you are, girl, being brought up with every luxury. Time you repaid your debt by doing my will for once in your pathetic life!"

Jane closed her eyes, mentally summoning up the image of all her gold stored safely away, a bastion against her father's attacks. He could lob as many insults at her as he liked from his trebuchet of a tongue, but they would merely rebound from her walls.

"As it is my marriage we are discussing, sir, I do think my wishes must be taken into account."

"Pah! You are a wicked, disobedient girl! What do you want to do? Hide behind your widowhood, taking lovers and bringing shame on the family with your loose antics!"

How he had concluded that she was about to launch herself on a career of lewd behavior when she had been the very soul of propriety since coming to court, Jane could not guess.

"That is not my intention, sir. I seek only to serve the Queen."

Thaddeus looked as if he would very much like to beat her. "Henry's already told me people are whispering about you behind your back—scenes with your lovers on the dance floor—brawls on holy ground—I could have you shut away as unfit for decent company! Your stepsons are already claiming you are guilty of witchcraft, bewitching their father and swindling them out of their inheritance!"

Jane could not sit still any longer. She leapt up, going head to head with the man who had made her life a misery for so long. "And you'd use their prejudiced estimation of me against your own flesh and blood? Be very careful, sir: if you go down the path of supporting them in their wild claims, you risk losing every penny I have. They're intent on stripping my fortune from me—even the dowry you gave Jonas. Do you really prefer the Patons to have it than your own daughter?"

It appeared to be a close run thing in Thaddeus's mind, as he hesitated before answering.

"What I'd prefer, Jane, is a dutiful daughter who lets her father manage her wealth and marries the man I select. How can you—a chit of eighteen—know what's best for you?"

"Jonas believed me capable of making decisions for myself."

"Your husband was in his dotage—how could he judge?"

They were in danger of arguing in circles—it had to stop. Jane dipped a curtsy.

"Excuse me, sir, I recall an errand I must run for Her Majesty." She brushed past him, her skirts catching on the buckle of his shoes. She wrenched free rather than stoop to untangle them.

"This isn't over, Jane," her father warned.

Jane raised her chin in stubborn defiance and left without deigning to reply.

"If the winds are favorable, I look to the *Dorothy* and the *Bark Raleigh* making the crossing in two months." Raleigh tapped the chart spread on the table. "We must ensure enough supplies for the expedition to manage until it reaches the Caribbean. I refuse to let the endeavor founder for want of salt pork or fresh water."

James stood back from the main group clustered around the maps. Most of the gentlemen were wearing thick fur-lined coats for the meeting, making them look something like a gathering of woodland creatures. His eyes drifted to the window, where he could see the Thames and the myriad boats plying between the north and south banks. Raleigh's circular study might have been cold, but it had one of the best views in the city over to Lambeth marshes and the countryside beyond.

Dr. Dee, the Queen's astrologer, turned back the baggy sleeves of his black robe and thumbed through a thick book full of his tiny scribbles. His long white beard bobbed in front of him like a heron's beak.

"Late April—the twenty-seventh—that would be the most auspicious day to begin this enterprise, according to the stars," he announced in his reedy voice.

And who were they to argue with him? Dr. Dee had decided the very day of the Queen's coronation, and his prediction of a long and glorious reign looked to be coming true—that was if they could stop Spain from crushing their little Protestant nation on the fringe of Europe. James shivered, the lick of river breeze on his face from the cracks in the casement taking him back once more to the cold Low Countries.

"Lacey, are you with us?" Raleigh's voice cut through his dark memories.

"At your service, sir." James pushed off from the wall to join the men at the table.

"You are still intending to go on this voyage?"

"Indeed, I can hardly wait," James said drily.

"For your survey of the terrain for defensive purposes, what equipment will you need?"

James tried to drum up the necessary enthusiasm to answer. "A couple of good men to help with the measurements, someone capable of recording our findings—a mapmaker, preferably."

"I'm sending a draftsman—I've used his skills before: he's very good."

"Then that will suffice. I take it we are not expecting to make a start on fortifying the site we choose for the colony?"

"No, no, I have no wish of making the mistakes of other expeditions."

Like the ones led by your deceased half brother, James added silently.

"Preparation is the key," continued Raleigh. "Your role is to find out what we will need, then come back and dispatch our colonists ready to build a defensible home. We'll be sending farmers and craftsmen, men and their womenfolk when we finally are ready to put down roots in America."

"Then I have all I require." Indeed, he barely needed anything these days but to rid others of the burden of his presence.

"You'll take a manservant with you?"

"Aye."

Raleigh made a note on his list of personnel intending to travel. "I'll put you in the *Bark Raleigh.* Helped design it myself, you know."

"That makes me feel so much better, sir."

This time Raleigh caught the irony. He glanced up at James and grinned, his handsome face taking on pixielike mischievousness. "I'm sure it does. Risked myself in her a number of times—she's a faithful vessel to the honest seaman."

James quirked an eyebrow, amused by the man despite himself. "And are you honest?"

Raleigh laughed. "Sometimes. At sea, always. I know better than to try to cheat that mistress."

The meeting disbanded and James returned to his chamber to find Diego scrubbing what looked like the contents of half the London sewers off his hose.

"What happened to you?"

"A drunkard and a cart horse happened to me, sir." Diego beat the hose with a tablet of soap.

"We have laundry maids to do that," James said reasonably, recognizing that he had walked in on a rare show of temper from his man.

Diego rolled his eyes. "You have maids—I have insults for asking for their services."

James scratched his head. "Why? What have you done to set them against you?"

Diego gave him a look that suggested his intelligence hovered somewhere in the region of "village idiot." "I have not done anything, my lord. In case you have not noticed, Londoners do not like me."

James stripped off his leather jerkin, thinking it was about time he changed for dinner. "More fool them. You're a likeable fellow, Diego."

"I could be as charming as our host, my lord, and still they would hate me. The only black fellows like me they see are either devils on church walls or villains in a play."

James stopped in the middle of unhooking his doublet. This was the most Diego had ever confided about his feelings in the years they had been together. He had become so used to his servant's appearance, he had forgotten how Diego suffered for it. Truth be told, he'd shared those prejudices when he'd first met Diego; only closer acquaintance had taught him to look beneath the skin. He approached Diego and took the soapy hose out of his fingers.

"As I said, more fools they." He walked to the door and bellowed into the corridor. "Ho there!"

A maid came scurrying up the stairs and bobbed a breathless curtsy. "My lord."

"See that my man's livery is cleaned immediately. I do not want to hear a whisper that any of you have scorned him in any fashion—not by a word, not by a look. Do I make myself clear?"

The maid gave Diego a frightened glance. "Aye, my lord."

James thrust the hose into her arms and turned his back on her, closing the door.

"Thank you, master," Diego said quietly, still with an edge of resentment in his voice.

"Lord, man, don't thank me. I'm only asking for what is your due. If they mock you, my servant, they insult me."

Diego let slip a grin, more at ease with the idea that James did it for selfish reasons. "And we cannot have that, can we, O most proud and powerful lord?"

"No, we powerful lords can't. Now, I don't suppose I have any clean hose myself, do I?"

Diego dug a patched blue pair out of James's trunk. They both looked at the sorry sight with something like hopeless acceptance.

"Oh well, at least you fill them out well, according to the ladies," Diego offered.

James snorted, hoping Diego was right. He rather liked the idea of Jane admiring his legs—not that it would lead anywhere, of course. They had made a truce, and he would settle for a brief interlude of friendship. He owed it to her, and to all who knew him, to get out of their lives as soon as was practicable. He was the blight, and Jane the rose that should flower unblemished by his touch.

The Queen had chosen to dine with a select company that night, telling her ladies that she thought banquets were a waste of time during Lent. No one could enjoy a prolonged meal with the cooks trying to make fish and white meat palatable when everyone really hankered for a good piece of venison, beef or suckling pig. Jane sat at her end of the table, enjoying her almond-flavored chicken, thinking that she could live quite happily without red meats despite the Queen's pronouncement. She kept quiet, though, having learnt early on in her service that the sovereign only allowed a very few to challenge her in argument—Raleigh; Lord Burghley, her chief adviser; Mistress Parry—but certainly not a young dowager marchioness. The Queen had been known to box ears when angered. Scooping up another bite, Jane wondered how much her relish for the fare was influenced by the company. Fate had been kind and placed her next to James and far from that snake-in-the-grass Raleigh.

"I never had a chance to ask you, my lord, how is Lady Ellie—I mean, Lady Dorset?" she asked shyly, her eyes lingering on the little dip in James's chin not quite hidden by his neat, close-clipped beard. She could imagine pressing it lightly with her finger.

"Delivered safely of a son and heir for the earl," James replied. He rubbed the spot she had been looking at, as if feeling her gaze.

"Oh, that is wonderful news." She smiled down at her plate,

gilded by the light from the branched candlesticks set along the table.

James studied her profile. "You mean that, don't you?"

"Why should I not? Ellie is . . . was my friend."

"I thought you despised her and my brother."

Jane blushed. "Never. You mistake the matter."

"But he said you told him so when you rejected him." James mopped up the juices on his plate with a crust of bread.

"If he recalls the conversation properly, I actually did not *say* anything of the sort."

James was quick to understand her implication. "Just allowed him to think it?"

"Well, yes. I never did get an opportunity to explain that."

"Master Lacey, I hear from my cousin that you are involved in this scheme of Captain Raleigh's," interrupted the lady on James's other side, her glare at Jane indicating that she disliked the way Jane had been monopolizing the young nobleman's attention.

James politely turned to the questioner, giving a brief description of what was being discussed at Durham House. Jane listened in, alarmed to hear that James intended to go on the voyage himself.

As soon as he could extricate himself from the simpering lady, he turned back to Jane.

"You were about to explain something, I believe?"

Jane was momentarily unable to recall what she had been on the point of confessing, so disturbed was she by the revelation that he was going to risk his life on a shot in the dark—a voyage to the other end of the world.

"You're going on Walter Raleigh's expedition?" She gripped her knife, her knuckles white. "Why?"

James glanced down at her hand. "The thought distresses you?"

"Yes, it does. You'll very likely not come back. What need have you of such mad adventures?"

"I'm a second son, my lady: it does not matter what I do."

"Of course it matters!" Jane's anger grew. He appeared to be careless of his own life, as if it were nothing to gamble it away.

"Lady, do not concern yourself with my fate. I really am not worth it." He smiled at her as if this would make all things right. "Now, I want to hear what you have to tell me about your decision not to marry my brother. It has been a mystery to me—one I would be grateful to you for solving."

Jane wanted to hit him for his casual disregard of his own well-being, but now was neither the time nor the place to continue that argument.

"I stopped the match going forward because I knew he wanted Ellie." Jane reached for her goblet and took a sip, delaying the moment when she would have to look at him, fearing to see disbelief. "She needed him more than I did."

"Why not tell him so?"

"Would the earl have been able to reconcile his duty to his intended bride with what he owed to the one he really loved? I feared that he would never break it off if left to his own devices. He would have condemned us all to unhappiness."

James stared at her as if seeing her for the first time. "You did it for Will and Ellie?"

She gave a soft laugh. "And partly for myself, I admit. How

would you like to be wed to someone who was in love with one of your best friends?"

"But we thought . . . I believed you . . ."

"Yes, yes, I know: you thought me a coldhearted harridan. Strange how so many people come to that conclusion." She leant towards him confidentially. "What am I doing wrong?"

Her smile told him she was teasing.

He replied in kind. "You look too perfect, for one thing. People find perfection disconcerting—we immediately assume we must have done something wrong, and that can be annoying."

"I am far from perfect." If only he knew, thought Jane. She'd never really forgiven herself for her ill-advised passionate encounter with Raleigh two years before. Not only had it been against her moral code, it had been stupid, which in many ways seemed the worst sin.

"All right then, tell me something about yourself to prove you fall short of perfection."

"Like what?"

"Do you snore?"

She wrinkled her brow, pretending to consider. "I don't know—you'll have to ask my maid."

"Perhaps you have an annoying habit, like cracking your knuckles?"

"I've never done that in my life!"

"You are not winning the argument, my lady."

"Oh yes, I see. Then stop distracting me. I'll confess. It's something very serious and you'll never look at me in quite the same way again."

"Go on."

"I can't sing," Jane whispered.

"Really?"

"Not a note. Donkeys bray more tunefully."

"Excellent, i'faith." He slapped the table. "You have toppled from your pedestal and now are flat in the mud with us ordinary folk."

Jane laughed. "And that is where I have always been, sir. It was you who thought me perfect. Jonas always called me—" She broke off, fearing to disrupt the playful mood between them with a reminder of her husband.

"Go on, my lady."

Jane twisted her wedding ring around her finger. "He called me his little bird. It was a joke, because I sang like a duck, not a nightingale."

"You miss him?"

"Every day. He . . . he was the kindest man I've ever known."

James brushed crumbs from his sleeve. "Did you love him?"

"Yes."

First checking that they were not being overheard, he cleared his throat. "Then I should tell you that those stepsons of yours are making a great noise about you never having been fully his wife."

This was possibly the last subject on earth she wanted to discuss with James Lacey, of all people.

His cheeks reddened, his embarrassment matching hers. "I see I've made you uncomfortable. Forgive me."

Jane gathered her courage. "No, I want you to understand, sir, that Jonas and I were dear friends and companions for each other. I did honor him and he cherished me. Our marriage might not have been conventional, but it contained more love between the two parties than many others I have seen."

"I can believe that." James touched the back of her hand gently. "One of the parties was very deserving of all possible affection. He was a fortunate man."

"No, sir, it was I who had the good fortune. He saved me in more ways than I can tell you."

He gave her a stunning smile, more striking because his face had of late been so sad. "I will stick to my view of the case, my lady."

CHAPTER 7

DIEGO TAPPED NERVOUSLY ON MILLY'S DOOR, uncertain of his welcome after business hours. From the other houses, he could hear the sounds of people sitting down to supper, laughter, a baby crying in an upstairs room. A cat tiptoed across the street—darker shadow against the night, eyes shining with a devil's glow. Diego touched his amulet. He had to be a little mad to come on his own, but he had not been able to stay away.

"Aye?" A gruff old man with hair like a wire brush peered at him through a crack.

"I am here to see your mistress."

"Who's calling? Can't see you—step into the light."

Diego let the light from the lantern he was carrying fall on his face. The old man's eyes widened. "Just tell her Diego is here."

Grumbling, the servant shuffled off. Diego hunched on the doorstep, not liking being left exposed on the streets this late. Cheapside was usually safe during the day, but after dark back streets like this one were notorious for pickpockets and worse. It awakened the same fears in him as the dark jungle ravines far from his village, places his father had warned him never to venture—traps where vines curled round feet, snakes slithered and wildcats prowled.

"Hey-ho, my fine young man," called a woman approaching him from the north end of the lane. She lifted her skirts above her ankles to show her red petticoats. Her lank yellow hair straggled like vipers from under her cap, her lacings loose as if her clothes were only barely staying on, like a reptile's skin about to be sloughed. "Want some company?"

"Thank you, madam, but no," Diego replied, giving her a pleasant but cool smile. When traveling with the army, he had spent time with some of the camp followers in the Low Countries—the laundresses who made money on the side in less reputable ways—and he had come to appreciate the appalling lack of choice that led them to their way of life. Women would not have been allowed to fall into such dire straits in his home country, but here it was considered a cruel fact of life. London was so strange.

"Shame—you look a nice armful. Never 'ad a blackamoor," the drab replied cheekily, not at all abashed by his refusal.

"Sadly, most gracious lady, that is an experience that will have to wait."

A thin stick of a man approached from the far end of the lane at a fast pace, chin jutting forward like the prow of a frigate.

"Wot's goin' on, Mary? Get yer carcass up to Cheapside and earn yer keep."

Mary rolled her eyes at him. "All right, all right, Jed, I was just goin'. Good night, sir." She gave Diego a toothy grin.

The man now noticed Diego waiting on the step. "Bleedin' foreigners." He spat at Diego's feet. "Tryin' to get a free tumble, eh?"

"No," Diego said curtly, willing the old man to hurry back and let him in. The last thing he wanted was to bring trouble to Milly's doorstep.

The man sized him up, clearly thinking he could take the young stranger in a fight, possibly cut his purse into the bargain. "Don't want you pawing our girls, understand?"

A pair of tough-looking men, followed by two more drabs, came up the lane towards them.

"What's afoot, Jed?" one asked. Diego was alarmed to see that the newcomer was built like a rhino. While he knew a few moves to deal with a single attacker, the odds were now radically against him.

"Black boy here cheekin' Mary," growled Jed.

"He did not!" Mary protested.

"Shut it!" Jed slapped her hard, sending her ricocheting into the wall.

"Bloody hell, Jed, why'd you go and do that?" she shrieked, clasping her head. "You tryin' to bleedin' kill me?"

"Leave her alone!" shouted Diego, rushing forward to put himself between her and the man's raised fist.

"Keep yer hands off her, you black devil!" squawked one of the other women, stepping in his path.

Diego realized he'd made a terrible error leaving the step: he was now in the middle of the hostile gang, his only ally sprawled on the ground nursing a head wound from where she had clipped the wall.

"Go back to where you came from!" bellowed the rhino, pushing past the woman and launching a right hook at Diego's chin.

Diego ducked, only to be jumped on from behind by the stick man. The impact took him to the pavement. He got in a few good punches until his right arm was pinned by the rhino and one of the women sat on his legs. Hands tugged at his clothing, seeking his purse. He kicked her off and curled up, trying to protect his head and middle from what he knew was going to come.

Old Uriah hauled himself up to Milly's parlor in his own good time to announce that she had a caller. His words were rendered redundant by the sounds of a scuffle on the street outside. Milly rushed to the window in time to see Diego being set upon by three ruffians and their doxies. She shoved the window open.

"Leave him alone!" she shouted. "Uriah, do something!"

The old man peered over her shoulder. "But, mistress, there're three of 'em!"

"By all the saints, don't just stand there—fetch the watch, the neighbors—I don't care, just get help!" She grabbed a ewer off her washstand and threw it over the brawlers as if they were a pack of fighting dogs. "Help! Help!"

Shutters were thrown back at windows up and down the lane. Heads poked out.

"Mistress Porter, whatever is the matter?" called her neighbor, Master Rich, the tailor, napkin still thrown over his shoulder from his evening meal.

Milly pointed frantically at the street below. "My friend—they're killing him—please, help him!"

Rich went back inside, summoning his apprentices. The door to his shop opened and four young men issued out, eager for a scrap. Milly tried to keep an eye on what was happening to Diego, but he was lost in the middle of the battle. To her relief, she saw Christopher Turner emerge from his nearby lodgings with two friends in tow; they approached the fight at a run.

"Thank God—Kit—it's Diego—he's in there somewhere! Save him!"

Christopher tapped his fingers to his forehead in a salute to indicate he'd heard her plea. Throwing his red cloak to one of the drabs with a wink and promise of reward if she kept it safe for him, he dived into the midst of the skirmish. Milly then caught a glimpse of Diego, back up on his feet, exchanging blows with a great hulk of a man. Foreseeing the inevitable outcome of such a battle, Christopher seized Diego by the back of his coat and dragged him clear, Diego valiantly flailing punches left, right and center, confused as to who was a friend, who an enemy. Milly rushed downstairs and opened the street door just as Christopher shoved Diego through. Flipping a half-penny to redeem his cloak, Christopher swiftly followed, slamming the door shut behind him.

"Oh Lord! How can I get them to stop?" groaned Milly, worried now for Master Rich's apprentices and Christopher's friends.

"Not much fuel left for that fire, my sweet," Christopher replied. "Don't worry yourself."

Sure enough, with a few exchanges of insults that turned the air blue with their coarseness, the scuffle subsided to a war of words as the two sides parted, both feeling they had come out on top.

Diego had fallen to his hands and knees, nose dripping blood on Milly's rush mats. He looked like a wild beast brought to bay, quivering with the aftermath of a struggle for life. Milly hurried to his side.

"Oh, Diego, you're hurt." She gently brushed the tightly curled hair on the top of his head.

He sat back on his haunches, his livery ruined, his face battered. He wouldn't meet her eyes. "Nothing to speak of. Do not concern yourself."

But Milly was already halfway to the little kitchen to dampen a cloth for his nosebleed. "Don't you tell me not to worry, Diego; I just saw you almost torn apart by those mindless mastiffs. If they want to bait a bear, they should go to Bankside."

"What started it?" Christopher asked, leaning back against the pattern table, taking care not to crush the expensive fabrics spread out for the morrow. He crossed his ankles and examined his fingernails. "Fights don't erupt without cause."

Diego stood up stiffly, holding the linen rag Milly had given him to his nose. "They took exception to my face, sir. That was the only cause they required."

Christopher reached into a workbasket to toy with a pair of scissors. "I regret to hear that, but you must realize, Master Moor, that your presence outside Mistress Porter's shop at such a late hour will do her reputation no good. If you were her friend, you would leave her alone."

"Oh, tush!" interrupted Milly. "Why can he not visit me when he likes? I have Uriah and a houseful of girl-apprentices of my own to keep everything decent—stop being so silly. And what about you? The late hour has never stopped you calling by for supper and a gossip, has it?"

"But I am not a foreigner, Milly; I'm a neighbor," Christopher said patiently, annoying her with a tone that suggested he was explaining something very simple to a slow child. "Master Diego's presence will be remembered, discussed, and his connection to you chewed over by the unkindest scandalmongers in Cheapside. Business will suffer. You are still new here—still on trial."

"In that case, I had better go," said Diego bitterly.

But Milly wasn't going to let him be run off again by interfering players who should know better.

"No, you will not. *You*"—she poked Diego in the chest with the tip of one finger—"are going to come upstairs to my parlor and have supper. *You* are going to stay until I've treated your injuries. Henny and Old Uriah will join us so that no one can speak ill of your visit—God knows they both gossip enough as it is; they might as well spread a helpful rumor."

Diego dabbed his nose, which was no longer bleeding. "Are you certain, mistress?"

"Yes. Come along."

With a defiant glare at Christopher, she conducted Diego to the stairs. "Go on—I'll be up when I've warmed some pottage for us all. I swear you are swaying like a drunkard—you must be seeing double too." She turned back to the player. "You are welcome to stay, Christopher. And thank you for your assistance earlier out there." She gestured in the direction of the street.

"You're being foolish, Milly. No good can come of this friendship," Christopher warned. "He'll be off in a trice on the whim of his Lacey master, leaving you with his mess to clear up."

Milly drew herself up to her full height, still a foot shorter than the player, a ruffled hen daring to cluck at the fox. "So you won't be staying, I see. Good night, then."

The force of her disapproval drove him as far as the step. "Milly, listen to me. See sense before it is too late—"

"Good night, Master Turner." The door clapped shut in his face.

James left the palace feeling as though he had just discovered that the Earth had left its usual place in the heavens to circle the moon. Striding through the streets separating Whitehall from Durham

House, his way lit by a torch-carrying linkboy, he had plenty of time to mull over the fact that everything he had thought about Jane for the past eighteen months had proved wrong. She had given up life as a countess for the sake of her friend. He had believed it as soon as he heard her confession—indeed, the truth had been obvious once she had provided the explanation—and now he only had himself to blame for persisting in thinking ill of her for so long. If he had gone to her after she had rejected Will, he could have heard the story from her side; perhaps then things would have developed differently—she would not have married her marquess and he . . .

I probably would not have gone to the Low Countries, James admitted to himself. He had taken the commission in a fit of temper, soured for the alternative of court life by his ill feelings towards Jane, the consummate court lady.

But he had gone and now he was not fit company for anyone— outside he knew he seemed very much the same, but inside his soul had crumbled into pieces. If old King Henry had not gotten rid of the monasteries, he would have been tempted to lock himself away from the world in one so he did not inflict his presence on others.

Tipping the linkboy, he roused the doorkeeper to Durham House, who ushered him in with a respectful "Good even, my lord." His boots making staccato strikes on the stone stairs, he bounded up to his room, loosening the tight grip of the ruff on his neck. Pins fell from their anchorage, but he did not bother to look for them— his chamber was lit only by a single candle on the cold hearth, as Diego had asked for the night off to visit a friend. James cursed, having forgotten to order his fire lit by one of the maids before his return. He threw his cloak onto a bench by the door and stooped to light the kindling.

It had just caught with a voracious flare of flame when a voice by the window spoke out.

"About time, my lord. I was freezing over here waiting for your return."

James leapt to his feet, drawing his rapier and dagger. He didn't recognize the interloper and had no intention of making his further acquaintance.

"Get out!" he ordered.

The young man had one leg braced across the embrasure, the other on the floor, his head supported by the arm resting on a raised knee—the picture of indolence. James glanced behind him, fully expecting to see an accomplice coming at his back. He had to be a thief—James had no political importance that made him worthy of assassination.

"I'm alone, my lord," the man said, as if amused by James's suspicions. "Quite alone."

"Get out."

The man slowly got to his feet, moving a step out of the shadows. He was about James's age, tall and clean shaven, with a curling mop of black hair. A pearl earring swung from one lobe. Oddly, James found himself thinking of his brother Tobias. There was something about the dark eyes that reminded him of the scamp.

"My lord, I would ask you to forgive my intrusion, but I know a Lacey never forgives what they see as an insult." He bowed. "My name is Christopher Turner." He paused as if waiting for a response.

"What's that to me? I am not usually on first-name terms with thieves and vagabonds who come to rob my chambers. Put back everything you've taken and get your misbegotten carcass out of here."

"Misbegotten?" Christopher gave a sour laugh. "That's true— thanks to your esteemed father."

"What's that about my father?" James realized that whatever reason had brought this man to his room, violence did not appear to be part of his plan—his stance was relaxed, showing him to be more at ease with the situation than James was. James lowered his weapons but kept them in his hands; the tip of the rapier now rested on the floor.

"Christopher Turner," the man repeated. "Does that mean anything to you?"

James took a wary step closer to the hearth, where the fire was now quickly consuming the kindling. He put his dagger back in its sheath and used his free hand to lob a couple of logs onto the blaze.

"I'm afraid you have me at a disadvantage: I'm not aware of having heard that name before in my life, though I can tell you fully expect me to know it."

"Well, if that doesn't take the prize." Christopher gave a self-mocking laugh. "Here I was, all ready for the grand reunion, and you don't even know I exist. Puts me nicely in my place. I will begin again." He drew himself up and gave a court bow, deep and accomplished. "My lord, Christopher Turner—not a thief, but I admit to being a vagabond under the Queen's laws. Player at the Theatre. Resident of London. Writer of indifferent sonnets."

James snorted, deciding the fellow was actually quite amusing, for all his sneaky turning up in the chamber uninvited. Raleigh's house was well known as a gathering place for gentlemen hangers-on; no doubt it had been an easy task for the player to talk his way in with the hope of gaining an audience. The court was plagued with rhyming fellows offering their pens for hire.

"Good lord, a poet—that's all I needed to make my night complete. You're in the wrong room—if you want patronage for your verses, try Raleigh. The day I send a lady a poem is the day I will ask to be taken out and shot." He sheathed his sword and leant against the mantelpiece, not yet trusting enough to sit in the man's presence.

"But I've left out the most important part, my lord. My mother was Judith Turner." The player paused again, but got nothing more than a raised eyebrow in reply. "She . . . I regret to say, was mistress to your father. I am your brother . . . half brother."

James was dumbstruck. He had not thought his father a saint, but he had never before come across a bastard of his get; still, as he had already noticed the resemblance to Tobias even before the man had spoken, he was minded to believe him.

"I . . . er . . . I am pleased to make your acquaintance, sir," he said stiffly, wondering what was the correct response in such circumstances.

"No, you're not." The player appeared quite philosophical about the embarrassment he represented to the family.

James wished he felt more alert to deal with this new relation—he hated messy scenes, and this looked like one in the making—the abandoned son confronting his legitimate brother, probably with a set of demands James had no means to satisfy. "Why have you not made yourself known to us before?"

"Ah, but I am known to some of the family at least, sir. I received a small stipend from the estate until our father's death, administered by the steward: one Turville, if I remember rightly. Paid for a smattering of learning, but sadly dried up when I was about ten, and I was obliged to take to the stage to earn my living." He spoke lightly, but James recognized an underlying seam of bitterness mined over years of neglect.

"Your mother?"

"Dead, my lord, these ten years."

"My condolences." James turned away to light the candles standing at either end of the mantelpiece, giving himself a moment to come to terms with this surprise. He wasn't sure what he should feel on discovering he had another brother, particularly one close to him in age, if Turner had truly been ten on the death of the old earl. Would his mother be offended to know that her husband had kept a mistress? The Dowager Lady Dorset was no fool; she might well be aware of the fact. No. He qualified that idea immediately: it was inconceivable that she would allow her husband's child to be cut off so abruptly—she was too kindhearted to take revenge on a boy for the father's failing. She had to be ignorant of the affair.

"Why have you come here this evening, Master Turner?" James asked, gesturing to a chair opposite him. "I know I speak for my older brother when I say that we will wish to assist you as far as we are able."

Christopher rejected the offer of a seat. "I'd prefer to stand, sir. Please be assured I have not come to beg from you or force you to acknowledge me—God knows the time for that is long past and it is best we go on as before."

"So what do you want?"

Christopher rubbed the back of his neck—a gesture James recognized with a disconcerting flash of insight as one of his own. "I want to ask you to rein in your man."

"My man? What, you mean Diego?"

"That's the fellow. He's courting a friend of mine and I want it to stop."

A coldness seized James's chest. "Why?"

"She's a lovely girl—brave and talented. She deserves better."

"You object because he is a blackamoor?"

"I object because he's in your service."

Anger rose, memories of Diego's ill-treatment on the street and under this roof rushing to the fore—the need for diplomacy with this neglected relation swept away. "Diego is a loyal servant and a good man. Any woman should be honored to receive his attentions. Methinks, sir, that if you want this girl for yourself, you should make your advances to her, not try to stab your rival in the back by running to his master."

Christopher's fury mounted in proportion to James's. "You don't understand; you don't know what it's like for those of us who tangle with the Laceys! I wager you won't be staying in London long. You destroy lives and sail on unharmed, leaving nothing but shipwrecks behind. I don't want that for Milly Porter. He'll ruin her business—he'll ruin her!"

"You carry your resentment against my family too far, Master Turner. Now you know we were ignorant of your birth, I would expect you to temper your prejudice with understanding of the reasons for our neglect."

"Not all were ignorant, sir. The last payment came two months *after* our father's death; your brother at least must know."

"He was but fourteen at the time of our father's death. No, our steward, Turville, must know, not the earl, and I intend to question Turville closely about this, make no mistake." James ran his hand through his hair in exasperation. "But as for Diego, if he likes this girl, I say good fortune to him. I have no intention of interfering."

Christopher shook his head, lip curling in disgust. "How like a Lacey: washing your hands of any responsibility."

"You couldn't be more wrong. You don't know me or my brother, so are in no place to judge our motives." James had had enough: newfound brother or no, the man was displaying a glaring absence of respect for his social superior, ordering him around as if he were the servant, not the nobleman. He'd showed enough forbearance. "If, when your temper cools, you wish to make yourself known to my brother, the earl, I am sure he will welcome you. But I warn you, do not stand in the way of my man's happiness—he is part of my household and therefore part of the family. I will defend his rights as forcibly as I can."

Christopher laughed darkly. "See, with one hand you claim I will be treated as family, and with the other you put the claims of a servant over mine."

"Do not be absurd, sir." James found Christopher's sense of grievance overplayed, like that of an actor addicted to bombastic speeches. Turner was wrong to expect him to cast aside years of loyal service from Diego so lightly to please a half brother he did not know.

Christopher tugged hard at the cords securing his garish red cloak round his neck, betraying how furious he still was despite his devil-may-care pose. "Perhaps you'll give my views more weight when you hear what became of your blackamoor this night."

James felt a lurch of alarm. "What's happened?"

"His presence provoked a brawl outside Mistress Porter's door."

"Is he injured?"

Christopher shrugged. "Slightly damaged—nothing life-threatening."

"Is this the truth? Is he still out there? Where did you leave him?" James gestured in the direction of the city as he picked up his cloak, determined to go and find him.

Christopher watched his preparations for departure with wry amusement. "He's under Mistress Porter's roof. She is seeing to his hurts."

As if on cue, there was a tap at the door. James strode across and opened it to find one of Raleigh's men standing outside.

"Yes?"

"Message from the city, sir. Your servant has met with a mishap and, according to his rescuer, is somewhat confused in his wits thanks to a head injury. The messenger asks if you will indulge your man with a further leave of absence until he has recovered. The person caring for him does not think him fit to make his way home this evening."

James turned to his visitor. "This is Mistress Porter's doing, I take it?"

Christopher lounged on the window seat, arms crossed. "Aye, this would be like her."

James addressed the servant. "Tell the messenger I will come to fetch my man on the morrow and to thank his kind rescuer."

The servant bowed and went off to deliver his message.

The interruption had taken some of the heat from the confrontation in the room. At a loss as to what he should do about his half brother, James closed the door and went back to his post by the fire, maintaining the distance between them. It had been a strange evening—first he had been shaken by Jane's revelations, and now it was ending with a new blood relation and a servant in trouble. He was the worst member of his family to have to deal with this prickly half brother—Will had the firm kindness needed to put Christopher in his place, Catherine the motherly warmth to embrace, Tobias the spirit to humor, Sarah the charm to beguile him. All James had to offer were failure and hardness bred into him by a season of warfare. But he had to tender some kind of olive branch.

If he had no other gifts, at least he could be practical.

"And you, sir, do you need a lodging for the night?" James asked. "I can request this of my host if you do not wish to venture on the streets so late."

Christopher rose and settled his cloak round his shoulders. "I take it that this is my dismissal. *Exit stage left.*"

James rubbed his chin, perplexed. Could he say nothing right to this stranger? "I meant only what I said. I have no desire to run you off, having just met you. We may disagree about what lies in the best interests of the lady, but need that stand in the way of us getting to know each other as brothers?"

Christopher bowed. "Aye, it does. It always does come down to the best interests of the lady in the end—the Lacey way is to ignore them, leading to disaster, and I want no part of that. I'll take my leave."

It was hopeless, James realized. Christopher stubbornly persisted in seeing his legitimate brothers as reflections of the father who had abandoned his bastard child. He was not going to be persuaded otherwise on so brief an acquaintance, and James wasn't sure he could be bothered in his current frame of mind to make the effort required to bridge the gap.

"Then farewell, Master Turner. I will tell my family about you and ask what happened to your stipend."

"I won't hold my breath. Good night." Christopher turned at the door and gave another of his flourishing bows, more mocking than respectful. "Thank you at least for not running me through."

"Oh, there's still plenty of time for that, brother," James growled. "You and I seem destined to strike sparks off each other."

Christopher's laugh carried back up the corridor as he disappeared down the stairs.

CHAPTER 8

AS HER FRIEND HAD REQUESTED, Jane arrived outside Milly Porter's house early the next morning before the shop opened for business. Milly's midnight note had been most enticing—an incident was alluded to, some difficulty involving a dear friend, a plea for Jane to advise her on how best to handle a ticklish situation. Intrigued and rather pleased to be needed, Jane had hurriedly obtained leave from court and ridden pillion behind a single attendant to Milly's door.

She was waiting for her groom to descend to help her from the saddle when James Lacey appeared at her side, hand extended.

"Lady Rievaulx."

What was he doing outside the very same shop in Cheapside?

"Sir." Jane accepted his hand and slid off the saddle into his arms. The brief brush of bodies sent a thrill through her, a lick of fire's warmth after a frosty ride.

"I'm surprised to see you here," remarked James. Not only had he stolen her line, he was still holding her hand. His black leather gloves were well worn, almost as soft as skin. "You have some purchases to make?"

Feeling annoyingly addled by the smile in his dark eyes, Jane shook her head. "No, sir. I have a friend to visit."

He cocked an eyebrow. "Here?"

"As you see, sir."

"Then allow me." He turned to the door and knocked.

An old man opened the portal.

"My lady, my lord, please enter. My mistress will be down anon." The doorman gestured them inside to the workroom. Two leather-cushioned chairs were positioned by the window, refreshments on the little table between them. Milly had obviously been expecting them but was in no hurry now that they were here. Jane began to have suspicions—Milly did not know she had already had a chance to explain the past to James at dinner last evening; this was doubt-less her friend's way of helping her.

"Lady Rievaulx, would you care to be seated," James said with a twinkle in his eyes that undermined his formal tone.

"Thank you." Jane arranged the skirts of her wine-red riding habit to fall as neatly as she could manage after the disturbance of the ride. She feared her petticoats must be horribly muddied, and she hated to be at a disadvantage. "But why so correct, sir? Last night, I believe you were calling me Lady Jane?"

"Indeed, that is how I first knew you, and it is hard to break the habit. But after last night I wish to make amends for the lack of respect I have repeatedly shown you." He took a seat, stretching out his long legs encased in dark leg hose, which, unlike her clothes, did not show up the dirt. "I know now you are a lady deserving of all honor, deserving of the high title your marriage brought you."

She smiled and poured two glasses of small ale, feeling a crin-kle of pleasure inside rather like the tingling sensation of biting into strong cheddar. Finally, they were able to be amicable once more, misunderstandings cleared out of their path. Could the way to something more also be open? She risked a glance at him to find him studying her face. "So to call me Jane is an insult to my honor? I am saddened—I thought it rather a mark of our friendship."

"It is—I mean, I hope you took it that way."

"Then please do carry on doing so when we are among friends. There is another Lady Rievaulx—my stepson's wife—an old harpy of a woman, and each time you call me that I immediately think of her."

"I don't think of a harpy when I think of you—far from it." He took the proffered glass and raised it to her.

Jane nodded at the compliment. "And as for being called the Dowager Lady Rievaulx, that makes me feel quite in my grave, even if it is correct."

"Indeed, you are not yet twenty."

"Eighteen, sir. The same as you." She liked the feeling that this created a little bond between them.

"Then Lady Jane it is. What shall you call me?" His long lashes veiled his eyes for a moment—he was planning some mischief, she could tell.

"What do you suggest? What do your friends call you?"

"Dolt? Halfwit? Idiot? These are but a few of the names my brothers give me."

"Oh, I couldn't call you those."

He bowed in acknowledgment.

"I would only think them, of course."

He gave a bark of laughter. "My lady, you are a pearl." He took her hand and brushed his thumb over the knuckles. "Please, call me Jamie, if you do not mind the familiarity."

"When we are among friends then."

"Yes, among friends."

After a restless night on a pallet bed in Old Uriah's small chamber—by the Nile crocodile, did that man know how to snore!—Diego pulled on his mended doublet, intending to report to his master. His rapid exit was blocked by Milly. She stood in the way, ear pressed to the door as she eavesdropped on the conversation being carried on in the front room.

"Milly?"

"Shhh!" She flapped her hand at him.

"What are you doing? My master has come for me—I saw him ride up five minutes ago."

"Wait!"

He put his hands on her waist, intending to lift her out of his path. "He is not a patient man."

Milly turned in his grasp and smiled up at him, her clever face glowing with pride at her own ingenuity. "He'll be patient this day—indeed, he'll thank you for any delay you can dream up."

Diego resisted the temptation of closing the gap between them and covering her lips with his, though their stance was ideal for just such an advance on his part. He tapped her nose instead.

"What mischief are you brewing, Mistress Porter?"

She grinned, then ran her tongue delicately over her lips, a cat lapping cream. "I . . . er . . . I invited Lady Jane to call on me this morning."

"Aye, I saw her dismount outside too. Had you better not go and welcome her?"

"And spoil everything?" Milly shook her head, a stray loop of hair flopping down over her eye. She blew at it to get it out of her eyes. "Bother, my hair is a mess this morning—it's all your fault."

Diego very much wanted to hear what he would spoil, but also felt compelled to ask how he was to blame for the delicious descent of her fiery hair. "So what have I done now?"

She tucked the lock self-consciously beneath her coif. "I sat up half the night trying to make near-invisible mends on your livery and was too late to plait my hair properly this morning before Lady Jane arrived."

"Oh, really? Your hair is loose under there?" The temptation was too great to resist. Diego tugged the coif from her head, releasing the glorious fall of hair over her face. She gave a squeak and tried to catch it, but he just laughed and backed her against the door, holding her hands still.

"I think you will have to start again." He lowered his face to nuzzle the top of her head, letting his lips slide against the fine silken strands.

Silence fell between them as both realized this had moved from play to something far more seductive—the hidden note in their relationship for once sounding clear. Diego held his breath, fearing she would reject him. She should reject him. Look what had happened only last night! He would bring her nothing but trouble. But she did not push him away.

"I have always loved your hair," he said softly. "It reminds me of watching the sunset on the beach near my village—the great circle of our father, the Sun, slipping under the horizon, flooding Mother

Sky with molten fire." His fingers caressed her wrists. His heart missed a beat when he encountered a bracelet he had made on her left arm. He rubbed it lightly against the soft skin of her inner arm, hearing her breath catch in her throat.

"You . . . you like my hair?" she asked tremulously.

"No, Milly, I *love* your hair." *And I love you,* he thought.

Milly became predictably flustered under his admiring gaze. "Oh, well, thank you. I . . . I know I am no beauty, so that is a very pretty compliment."

He brushed the hair off her face gently. "To me, you have always been beautiful, both inside and out, from the top of your head to the tips of your toes." It was no good—even if he was damned for it, he had to kiss her. He bent his head and lightly pressed his lips to hers. It felt better than he had imagined—her mouth soft and yielding under his like orchid petals. He had had so little that was truly lovely in his life he wanted to preserve the moment for all time. He released her lips, keeping his forehead against hers. "Forgive me."

Milly had closed her eyes; she was now pressing her fingers against her mouth. Diego felt a burst of anger against himself—he had insulted her, taken a liberty with his dearest friend.

"Please forgive me, Milly. It will not happen again."

Her eyes flashed open, bright with curiosity. "It won't? Was I that bad at kissing?"

What was this? She was not upset?

Diego pulled her closer, one arm round her waist, the other cradling the back of her head. "Oh, Milly, you are a joy to kiss. I was afraid I had offended you."

She wrinkled her nose in a frown, her dusting of freckles

disappearing down the creases. "I will only be offended if you refuse to kiss me again, as then I'll be convinced I'm a failure at it."

He smiled but answered solemnly. "We cannot have that."

"No, we can't."

He took her lips again in a long, exploring kiss, full of tenderness for this fiery miracle in his arms. When they broke apart at last, he asked breathlessly:

"How was that for a delay?"

She rested her head on his chest, her finger tracing the darn she had made in his livery. "I'm sure your master will be very grateful."

James poured a second small glass for Lady Jane and himself, wondering if he should go in search of Diego. Mistress Porter appeared to be taking a fearfully long time to come and greet her guests; did that mean Diego's wounds were worse than reported? James felt he did not deserve to sit at peace with Jane while others were suffering.

"Sir . . ." Jane corrected herself. "Jamie, you seem ill at ease."

He smiled at the familiar use of his name. "It's my servant, Diego. He was set upon last night in the street outside. That's why I'm here—to collect him and ensure that he is unharmed. Do you think I should go in search of him?"

A funny expression crossed the lady's face—wry amusement, he would have called it if the subject had not been so serious.

"No, I do not think that will be necessary. In Milly's note, she mentioned the incident and said that her friend had emerged largely unscathed. If she keeps us waiting much longer, I'll go and hunt her down for you."

Silence fell between them, a little awkward on his part. He took the chance to examine her face as she brushed nonexistent crumbs off her lap. He wanted to tell her that she need not worry about her appearance for his sake, as she had always appeared perfect to him—a little too perfect, if truth be told. A few crumbs, a little mussing, and she would be more approachable. He wanted to run his fingers down the smooth curve of her neck, loosen the heavy gold braids she had coiled on her head, to which was anchored a jaunty felt hat with an extravagant plume. Her skin looked like cream, a hint of a blush on her cheeks. Edible. Entirely edible—he just wished he had the right to feast.

"Jamie, you aren't paying attention." Jane's eyes glittered with laughter.

"I was, but not to your words. Forgive me."

Her blush deepened. "I was asking how the plans for your voyage are progressing. Is there any hope you can be persuaded to stay on dry land?" She dropped her gaze. "Is there anyone who can change your mind?"

"I thank you for your concern, my lady, but there is no need for it." The sooner he took himself off, the better for all. He did not want Jane to have time to nourish hopes of more from him—his external charm could not make up for his inadequacies.

"You said that before. You seem to regard yourself as entirely expendable now your brother has his heir."

He toyed with a basket of trimmings lying on the bench beside him. "There is some truth in that. I can see you are worrying about me but, really, I'm not worth it. And just so you understand why my brother insists I take the risk, you should know that

Will's sending me on this expedition in the hope that I can find both fortune and my old self—he believes it's a medicine I need to take."

Jane frowned. "You've . . . you've been ill?"

James pulled a self-mocking face. "Sick of heart, my lady."

She swallowed and glanced out of the window. "Oh, I see. Did the lady reject your suit, then?"

He smiled. "Your mind is swift to think of love when I had another kind of heartsickness in mind."

"There's another kind?"

He wondered why he was telling her so much. He guessed it was because she was in danger of entertaining tender feelings towards him—a regard that she would not maintain if she knew the truth. He owed it to her to reveal a little of that ugliness and dispel her illusions.

"Since we met at Lacey Hall, my lady, I've served in the Low Countries."

She looked confused at his change of subject, not realizing that it lay very much at the heart of what was wrong with him. "I see. Congratulations, I know you always wanted a military career."

He gave a grim smile. "I did, didn't I? I was arrogant. Oh, I'm a passable fighter when I have to be, but I did not take into account my weak stomach for the realities of war. I returned much chastened, believe me, madam."

She placed her hand gently over his. "Jane, remember?"

"Jane." He wondered ruefully if he should have encouraged such intimacy—her name was a gift he did not deserve.

"There is no shame in hating to see bloodshed or to be sickened when you are forced to take a life. Not to feel would be the worse crime."

He curled his hand into a fist under hers. "But I should've had a tougher hide. I could not bear to stand by and watch others suffer, but that was what was asked of me. You see before you a coward and a failure."

"How so? Did you neglect your duty?" Her tone was brisk but she kept her palm wrapped round his fist, not pulling away from him as he had expected at his admission.

"No, I did my duty to my commanding officer."

"But you feel you failed someone else?"

He closed his eyes, aware only of the warmth of her hand on his. "There was so much evil abroad—it was not what I expected. No honor in it." He cleared his throat, the confession tumbling out. "I remember a village—a massacre—children, women, old men—all cut down for no reason."

"You were there?"

"I watched from the forest."

"I see." And he felt that she really did. "There were how many soldiers? One? Five?"

"Fifty, or thereabouts."

"Oh, so you think you, a single English gentleman, could have saved the village on your own?"

He shook his head. "No, no, not really. But I didn't even try."

"And now you can't forgive yourself? Yes, yes, I see how that makes you a coward."

Her repeating his insult came as a shock. He was so used to people—his brother, other officers, even his servant—telling him he was not to blame.

"You think me a coward?" If she condemned him, then he would know his self-hatred was fully justified.

Jane faced him, her blue eyes blazing with a fierce light. "Not for standing back, no, I don't. That was the only thing you could do. No, you are a coward for not accepting your decision and facing up to the consequences. What you did was right. What the Spanish soldiers did was wrong. Your task is to bear witness to that outrage and fight to prevent other villages suffering a similar fate."

James knew she spoke only common sense but could not bring himself to admit it. He could not pardon himself so easily. Instead he turned it into a jest. "Good heavens, madam, you are terrifying—an Amazon, like our Queen." He reached for the glass, annoyed that his hand was so obviously shaking.

She stilled his arm with a single touch. "I'm sure, Jamie, that it is far easier to see the truth from a distance. And, no, I don't really think you are a coward—I only said that to shock you into listening. I think you are wounded, not on the outside but in the heart, as you yourself said. I would . . . I would like to help heal you, if you would permit it."

James stiffened. "I am not a charity case, madam."

"It's Jane. And I offer this not out of charity, not unless you mean *caritas*." Her eyes dropped to her lap. "Or love."

She was making him an offer he was so far from deserving that he wanted to weep. He could only respond with a clumsy retreat.

"I see you are a Latin scholar, Lady Jane, another trait you share with our sovereign. Now, where's that man of mine got to? As pleasant as your company is, madam, I have much to do this day."

Rising quickly, James marched over to the door to the stairwell and wrenched it open. Milly and Diego spilled into the room, locked in an embrace.

James could have kissed his servant himself for providing the diversion from his awkward moment with Jane. He stood, thumbs hooked in his belt, as he watched the pair struggle to their feet.

"I see your injuries are well on the way to mending with the application of the lady's physic, Diego."

He had to hand it to his man; he dealt with the embarrassing situation with aplomb. Diego did not release the fair one's hand but brought her forward.

"My lord, may I present Mistress Porter?"

The poor girl was blushing a bright red that clashed with the remarkable color of her hair. She bobbed a curtsy.

"Master Lacey."

"She is my betrothed."

"I am?" squeaked Milly.

"She is?" asked Jane at the same instant. "Is this true?"

Diego gave the lady a charming bow. "I have been courting your friend for many years, Lady Jane. She wears my gifts." He brandished her wrist as evidence, displaying the intricate bead bracelet. "In my homeland, that means we are promised to each other. All I need do now is discuss with her father how many head of cattle I must pay for her."

James recognized that Diego had gone off on one of his occasional stampedes, trying to force the world he was in onto the path of the one he had been forced to leave behind.

"Um, Diego, the lady herself must agree, you know. And I'm not sure what her father would do with these chimerical cows of yours— unless he's a farmer, that is." He addressed the latter to Milly.

"He's a soldier, sir." She was worrying her bottom lip, clearly of two minds as to what she should say to this unorthodox proposal.

Not a proposal—a claiming, James thought.

Jane stepped forward and disengaged Diego's hand from Milly's wrist. "Your servant is an unusual man, Master Lacey. He springs out of nowhere and demands to marry her merely because we witnessed the folly of a kiss. I can forget it if you will."

"Of course. I saw nothing. Come, Diego, you can return later when your lady has had a chance to consider your offer. And I want to hear about last night. Your adventure brought a most interesting visitor to my door and I wish to know how that came about."

Still looking at Milly as if she were the last oasis in a desert, Diego nodded. "I come, my lord."

James snapped his fingers. "Now, not in the next millennium, Diego."

"Aye, sir. At once."

Seeing that Diego's feet were still firmly planted, James swore under his breath and pushed open the shop door to summon his horse from the boy he had left holding it on the street outside.

"You will have to walk," he called back over his shoulder. "Ladies." With a final bow, he left, relieved to depart from the scene of so many messy emotional entanglements, not least his own.

CHAPTER 9

JANE WATCHED HER FRIEND EXCHANGE a few whispered words with the blackamoor servant before he ran off to catch up with his master. Once Milly returned from seeing him out, Jane arched an inquiring eyebrow.

"Well?"

Milly clapped her hands to her cheeks. "How red am I?"

"Strawberry."

"Oh heavens! And your James saw me like this! I'll never be able to face him again."

Jane hooked her arm through Milly's. "I would worry more about him seeing you rolling around on the floor with his servant. What was *that* about?"

The shop door opened and two women entered, baskets over their arms and their eyes bright with avid interest in the comings and goings over the past twelve hours. Milly immediately assumed her business manner.

"Ladies, good morrow. I will send my assistant to you at once. I must escort the marchioness upstairs for her fitting."

The gossips curtsied and muttered to each other in low voices, clearly overjoyed to share the chamber, if but briefly, with one of the most exalted in the land.

Milly deposited Jane in her upstairs room and dragged Henny away from her breakfast in the kitchen, her rapid-fire conversation clearly audible in the stairwell.

"Two women in the shop. Keep them occupied and say nothing about what's happened!"

Henny giggled. "You really getting married, mistress? Me and Uriah heard everything."

Milly clapped a hand to her forehead. "Give me strength, Lord. I can't talk about that now, just do as I ask and *don't gossip!*"

Jane thought there was less chance of Milly's being obeyed than of men voyaging to the moon. Her poor friend had dropped herself into a deep ditch with her antics in the doorway. In Jane's experience, people usually preferred to see you flounder in the mud than to offer a hand to help you out.

In a wistful mood, Jane drifted to the casement and stood to watch James ride out of sight, Diego jogging along at his stirrup. Her soul still felt bruised from James's rejection of her offer. Was her love really so objectionable that he could dismiss it with a jest? Had she been wrong to think they had more than friendship between them? Had she made a complete fool of herself? She rubbed her arms. Milly's position was enviable—at least her lover had boldly claimed her, riding roughshod over the many obstacles in the way of such an unlikely match.

"Jane, are you still speaking to me?" Milly asked from behind her.

She turned and smiled. "Yes, of course."

"Are you surprised?"

"I admit I am. I've met him before at Lacey Hall, but how do you know him? I take it that kiss was not the result of a few hours' acquaintance?"

Milly was avoiding her eye. "His name is Diego. I've known him for years. He served my father and was my friend when we lived on the Earl of Leicester's estate."

"Yet you never mentioned him to me? I thought I was your friend at that time too?"

Milly fiddled with a scrap of cloth lying over the back of a chair. "Yes, you were. But he was a servant and I a lady. We were all so young then. You would not have approved."

That was true. Jane knew that she would have thought it beneath her schoolroom friend to have a sweetheart among the lower classes. Time had mellowed her somewhat, but not to the extent of throwing out all social expectations. They could not ignore the fact that he was African.

"He is . . . well, he's different, Milly."

Her friend laughed. "Is he? What can you possibly be referring to? The fact that he's got dark skin and thinks he can buy me with a herd of cattle?"

"I mean no disrespect to the man. He is very handsome, if a little short." She meant the last as a purposeful tease. Diego was short only when standing next to his master.

Milly blushed. "Not too short for me."

"True, you must make him feel like a giant. No wonder he loves you."

Milly groaned and slumped in a chair. "Do you think he does?"

"Oh yes. But it won't be easy for either of you, you know. You might be closer in rank these days, but he is still so obviously a foreigner. Many will object—think it unnatural."

"Do you?"

Jane folded her hands together and took a seat on the windowsill. Did she? There had been something shocking earlier about seeing the fair and dark entwined together, but also something strangely beautiful. It was new, but she thought she could become used to the idea over time. What was a man if not his heart? True worth lay inside, as she had discovered with Jonas. She might not be completely reconciled to the notion of a marriage between an African manservant and an English girl, but she owed it to her friend to support her, whatever her decision.

"I will judge Master Diego on his merits when I have the chance to get to know him, not on his origins," Jane promised. "I can see that he is hopelessly in love with you, which already puts him in my good books."

"Oh, thank you, thank you." Milly let out a sigh of relief, the tension easing from her shoulders.

"Will you accept him?"

"I think I want to, but there is so much that stands between us. My father is not going to be pleased."

"Not even with all those cows to soften the blow?"

Milly threw a ball of wool at her. "Diego doesn't have any cattle." She frowned. "At least, I don't think so. He's a servant, after all."

"But if he's the one for you, then you must make it happen, persuade your father. You will have my support."

"And the Dowager Marchioness of Rievaulx is a force to be reckoned with."

"She is indeed," Jane agreed.

Whitehall, Westminster

James took Diego to the fencing hall in Whitehall Palace, thinking it would be good for the both of them to have some physical activity to straighten out their overheated brains. A whitewashed chamber empty of all ornamentation but the pillars supporting the roof, the hall echoed with yells and the clashes of blade on blade. Stripping down to shirts and trunk hose, James selected two rapiers and daggers so they could fight Italian-style, the daggers acting as a block when crossed with the swords.

"Come on, you lovesick loon, let's knock some sense into you," he told Diego, tossing him a set of leather padding.

With a grin, Diego strapped himself into the protective clothing and took up his weapons. They had learnt the art of two-handed combat together during their time in the Low Countries. The servant was well matched with his master, having a streak of cunning that counterbalanced James's reach.

There was no need for further words as they went through their usual patterns of defense and attack. Their concentration was accompanied by the squeak of their shoes on the boards and the rhythmic ring of blades. Around them, other fighters were going through their exercises with noisy protests or groans; James and Diego moved like two dancers perfectly in tune with each other, surrounded by a bubble of silence, oblivious to all else.

When they finished their pattern, James was surprised to find they had attracted an audience. Jane's brother, Sir Henry Perceval, led the "bravos" and a smattering of applause. A little farther off stood the three Paton brothers, watching him with unfriendly intent.

"Your man has taught you well," Sir Henry declared, slapping Diego on the back.

James vowed to repay Diego for his smirk later. "We learnt together, sir. We were trained by an Italian gentleman in Antwerp."

"Forgive me." Perceval's apology sounded insincere. "Then I must beg you to lend me your sparring partner one morning. My skills in the duello are sadly lacking. A good English broadsword is more my style."

"Nothing wrong with the old ways," complained one mustachioed gentleman with a rubicund complexion, glaring at the Italian-made weapons.

"Still, I always look to improve. One never knows what an enemy might attempt."

"Then it would be my pleasure to make Diego available," James replied with matching insincerity. "But unfortunately we have other business this day."

"But of course." Perceval gave a nod of dismissal and moved off with his companions to engage the Patons in conversation. Bearing in mind the state of relations between Jane and her stepsons, James wondered what they had to talk about.

"Thank you, O glorious master, just what I always wanted—an hour with that cockatoo," muttered Diego, putting the weapons back on the rack.

"Don't be foolish, man, I was thinking of you. If you want to marry that fiery-haired maiden of yours, you will need some other means of supporting her than a servant's wage." James rubbed the sweat from his face and chest with a linen towel. "Perceval will pay you—as will any other gentleman who asks for your services as a sparring partner. You stand to make a decent purse if you play your cards right."

"You would allow me to keep the money?"

"Of course. I'm not an ogre, Diego."

Diego's face lit up with delight. "Then it is safe to tell you, O most generous lord, that I have already been earning a little extra—but only when not needed by you, naturally."

James rolled his eyes. How had he missed that? "Naturally. What have you been doing? Understand, as long as it does not involve dabbling in crime, I'm unlikely to mind."

"I have been giving riding lessons. I have money already saved."

James laughed. Diego was famed in army circles for his skills on horseback. "You sly fox! Enough for those cows you mentioned, I hazard?"

"Yes, I can pay her bride price as long as it does not amount to more than twenty pounds."

James tossed Diego the towel for disposal. "Ods bodikins, man, you've more money than I have. What have I been doing wrong?"

Diego laughed at James's country bumpkin oath. "You need to find yourself a rich wench, master; then you would sniff at a mere twenty pounds."

"You have the right idea, I see. The lady's business must be worth a modest fortune."

"If she will have me."

"She was wrapped around you like ivy on a stone wall."

"That does not mean she will welcome my suit. It takes a brave girl to risk marrying a foreigner, especially one like me."

James was grateful that his man had cooled off now and could see the potential problems in the way of his marriage. There was no need, therefore, for him to be the one pouring cold water on the idea. Indeed, it left him the far more pleasant role of encourager.

"If she can see past the disadvantages of your rank and other things, then she is a very sensible girl and you deserve to find happiness with each other. The Lacey family will back you both to the hilt and use our influence to smooth any objections from other quarters." James thought briefly of Christopher Turner; he would not be pleased by this development and could make trouble for Diego. "No matter who protests—friend or family—both the earl and I can stand behind you and bear witness to your many sterling qualities."

"That is very generous, master." Diego did not seem quite sure what to do with such a glowing report. "I thank you. If Milly does accept me, we will need your support. Merely waiting at her door last night brought citizens out against me. I do not like to think what they will say when we give notice that we intend to wed."

"These citizens, who were they?"

"Three bawds and their doxies."

James laughed. "Oh well, then, what can the Earl of Dorset and his poor brother do to outweigh the influence of such fine upstanding members of the London populace? You're doomed!"

Diego shook his head, smiling sadly. "They are not alone in regarding a foreigner as the work of the devil."

"Then we will have to charm them into thinking that you were sent by an angel. Was not one of the early followers of Our Savior an Ethiope? And the Queen of Sheba must have been a dusky maid, and she was a fabled beauty."

"First a warrior, now a theologian—you are a wonder, O most learned lord."

"And you, Diego, are an impudent servant and a lucky dog to have such a lady."

"I know, sir."

"If you do marry, then I hope you will stay in my family's service and come to Lacey Hall. Both of you."

"Thank you, my lord. All I have to do now is persuade the lady."

Jane waited outside the Queen's bedchamber while Blanche Parry and the other ladies in the inner circle helped the sovereign change robes for greeting foreign guests at the afternoon's reception. Jane's role as the newest Lady of the Privy Chamber was to pass any urgent messages within—never let it be said that any male, even the lowliest errand boy, caught a glimpse of the Queen without her full armor of stunning dress, burnished wig and mask of cosmetics.

Watching the flames leaping in the hearth as she stood by the door to the inner sanctum, Jane grew increasingly proud of her prickly mistress as messengers came and went, revolving round the Queen as moths do the candle. According to Mistress Parry, Elizabeth with her long red Tudor hair had been something of a beauty when she ascended the throne in her twenties, and while no longer in dewy youth, she still made good use of her assets as a woman. She commanded her court with steely femininity, outwitting the male courtiers at almost every turn.

Jane's attention was caught by a brief challenge over by the door from the audience chamber. Then the guard stepped back, allowing Walter Raleigh into the room. The three other ladies-in-waiting, intent on their embroidery by the hearth, stood up, all of them preening themselves surreptitiously to look their best for the reigning favorite. Jane stood stoically motionless, not even checking the lay of her pearl-edged headdress as her fingers itched to do.

"Ladies, good morrow!" called Raleigh cheerfully. He was resplendent today in pale-green velvet doublet and hose, pinked and slashed over every inch, gold sarcenet peeping through the gaps. He looked like a daffodil about to burst from its bud. "I understand your mistress is within?"

"Aye, sir," simpered Lady Mary Burnett, fluttering her brown eyes at him like a lovesick cow facing the prize bull. "She bade you wait for her here."

Raleigh held her gaze and smiled into her eyes. "And that," he said in a rumbling voice, "will be entirely a pleasure." He kissed her knuckles.

The girl blushed a fetching shade of rose before subsiding back to her stool and picking up her needlework from the chair nearest the fire. Raleigh did not take the hint to occupy the empty seat beside her but instead prowled the chamber, inspecting the hangings with a mocking eye, flicking at the depiction of Adam and Eve in the Garden of Eden with something like distaste. Jane sensed he knew very well she was standing guard at the door to the Queen's bedchamber by the very fact that he was trying so hard to pretend he hadn't yet seen her.

Sure enough, when he reached her on his circumnavigation of the room, he feigned surprise.

"Ah, Lady Rievaulx, I heard you were at court." He bowed. "Congratulations on your appointment."

"Sir." Jane inclined a regal head, her rank allowing her to give him the barest recognition. It was hard to forget that the last time they had enjoyed any private conversation had been on the memorable occasion when she had surrendered her virtue to him, thinking he was in love with her.

He pulled a sad expression. "I understand that condolences are due also for the death of your husband the marquess." He tried to take one of her hands to give it a comforting squeeze, but Jane quickly clasped them behind her back. "A fine man."

"Your condolences are noted, sir."

Raleigh took a step closer as if examining the tapestry just behind her head, grasping her elbow to point out some detail that had piqued his interest. He lowered his voice.

"Why so formal, my love? I would've thought we were well past that point."

Jane cast an anxious glance across the room to find, as she had suspected, that they were the center of attention for all three ladies by the fire.

"I regret our interlude," Jane whispered furiously, "and beg you, as a gentleman, not to refer to it again."

Raleigh caressed her inner arm through the satin of her white gown, letting the material slide sensuously up and down. "I have no regrets, my love. You were delightful in your passion—so honest and unfettered. Would you not wish to experience the like again? As you are a widow, there will be none to condemn you."

None except herself, Jane thought. She wanted to shout at him that if she had been honest in her passion he most certainly had not; he had known she expected a proposal. But then, what would be the point? Raleigh was too slippery to allow a girl to trap him into a less-than-brilliant marriage, so ruthless as to make use of any admission that he had successfully fooled her. Far better for her to appear unaffected by his wooing: that was the best blow she could deal to his vanity.

"Indeed, sir, I have gained plenty of experience since then," Jane lied, letting her voice drop to a husky come-hither whisper, "and will no doubt gain more in the future." She let the pause stretch, seeing the hope blaze in his eyes that he would be allowed back into her arms. She gave him a cold smile. "But not with you. I thank you for inducting me into the mysteries of Venus, but my taste now runs to lovers of greater skill and subtlety."

She almost laughed when she saw an angry muscle clench in his jaw. He dropped his hand from her arm.

"I see."

She could tell he was itching to ask who numbered among the legion of lovers who far outdid him in bed. Let him guess and wonder. Each time he saw her, his confidence, and other things, would shrivel with inadequacy.

"I see that you do, sir," Jane replied pertly.

The door to the bedchamber snapped open, making them step quickly apart. Elizabeth sallied out, pulling an exquisite pair of white kid gloves over her beringed fingers, adjusting the slashes in the leather to allow the stones to poke through and be admired.

"Master Raleigh, accosting my ladies again, I see?" the Queen asked with an edge to her humorous tone, her eyes flicking to Jane.

"I fear, Your Majesty, I was merely boring Lady Rievaulx with my opinion on Flemish weaving," Raleigh said hurriedly. "Your Eve looks like she could do with a good meal or two." He pointed to the character on the tapestry, who was sadly lacking in the bosom. "And Adam needs a visit to a barber."

The Queen wrinkled her nose at the pair. "You are right, Raleigh. I had not noticed. But we cannot afford to lavish money on new arras while England's coffers stand almost empty."

Raleigh heard the cue. "Then let me give you a new hanging for this chamber. I have one I think you will like—Solomon building the temple for the Lord as you, madam, build our nation."

The Queen smiled knowingly at the flattery. "That will be most acceptable."

She swept on. Raleigh lingered a moment to murmur to Jane.

"See what you've just cost me."

Jane bit her lip to stop her laughter. "It was you, sir, who chose to accost me, not the other way round. You have a jealous mistress."

He harrumphed, seeing the humor in the situation. "True. You are no longer the naive girl I knew in Yorkshire, are you, Lady Rievaulx?"

"Indeed, no. And you, sir, for all your faults, have always been discerning."

He laughed at that. "Excellently done, i'faith, a compliment with an insult. Welcome to court, my lady."

CHAPTER 10

FROM HER POSITION BESIDE THE THRONE in the drafty great hall, Jane watched as the little parade of the foreign dignitaries came forward to be given a coveted introduction to Elizabeth. Rarely had so much fine fabric and so many jewels and furs been gathered in one place. Even Jane's father had found a new black silk doublet from somewhere, managing not to disgrace the earldom of Wetherby by his appearance.

"Your Majesty, may I present Clément Montfleury, son of the Duke of Valère, from the Bordeaux region of France?" Jane's father knelt in his place as petitioner before the Queen, praying for a sign of royal favor. His grizzled head, so rarely bowed before anyone, was lowered, giving a glimpse of the thinning patch on top.

At the Queen's nod, Jane's father's protégé came forward with the light-footed step of a morris dancer, twirling a silk handkerchief to make more of a flourish with his bow. He too sank to his knees, waiting to receive the royal command to rise. Jane gaped. Surely her father had to be jesting with his intent to pair her with this popinjay—he was barely five feet tall and outrageously effeminate. She suspected that if she came within range, the perfume on his much-groomed black beard would be suffocating.

Not having to worry about being forced to marry the man, the Queen could afford to be entertained by the newcomer. Those familiar with Elizabeth's expressions could see the smile hovering.

"Seigneur Clément, welcome to our court." She extended her hand, allowing him to rise and kiss her signet ring, which the French noble did, letting out a surprisingly high-pitched giggle of nervous laughter, quickly smothered. Elizabeth arched an amused brow.

"I trust you left your family in good health, sir?" she asked in fluent French. "I met your father once, methinks, some ten years ago."

"He counted it a . . . a great honor, Your Majesty." Clément's voice was somewhat squeaky. "He speaks of you often and prays for the felicity of your happy realm."

Jane sought out her brother standing at the edge of the room. He was watching the introduction with a calculating look, weighing the Queen's mood and what it meant for their family's aspirations. He must have felt her gaze, because he met her eyes for a moment and smiled, nodding towards the Frenchman. Jane replied with a scowl and a slight shake of her head.

"And what brings you to England, *monsieur*?" the Queen asked politely, this time in her native tongue, to include Lord Wetherby in the exchange.

"Lord Clément and I are partners in a business venture, Your Majesty, which we hope will prove most advantageous to both countries." Jane's father rose from his knees on the Queen's nod. "He also comes, on my suggestion, to meet my daughter, the Dowager Lady Rievaulx. We are intending, with your most gracious permission, to make a match between our two houses."

Jane sensed the attention of the court shift to her. She mastered her anger to keep her expression serene; she was not going to provide any more ammunition for her enemies.

The Queen beckoned Jane forward. "Lady Rievaulx, know you of this match?"

Jane approached and knelt at the Queen's side. "The notion was explained to me by my father a few days ago, Your Majesty, but I told him at the time I still consider myself in mourning for my late husband."

Elizabeth waved her away. "I will consider the matter, Lord Wetherby, Seigneur Clément, and give you my answer. For the moment, I am loath to lose my newest lady before I have even had a chance to become accustomed to her presence in my household."

Jane stifled her sigh of relief; if Elizabeth prevaricated, as was her usual practice when she did not want to make a decision, Jane might never have to refuse the Frenchman outright.

The Queen dismissed the two petitioners and looked to the next party waiting for her attention. Horrified, Jane watched the three Paton brothers approach and kneel. The stars must surely be against her this day.

"My lord Marquess." The Queen acknowledged Richard with a cool incline of her head. Her secretary bent to her ear and whispered a reminder of the Patons' business with her. "I have received your letter appealing against the dower settlement on your stepmother. But is this not a matter for the courts to decide? What mean you by bringing it to my attention?"

Richard cast Jane a vicious look. "As our stepmother now serves in your household, we felt it only right to alert her mistress to the situation she has brought upon us."

"I see. Then I thank you for your consideration." Elizabeth

beckoned Jane forward again with a wry smile. "It appears that you are a person of great interest to many this day, Lady Rievaulx."

Jane did not share the Queen's amusement. "Indeed so, madam."

"Yet you have not yet brought your side of the dispute to me, as I would have expected from one in your position so close to my person. Why is that?"

It quickly went through Jane's mind that the real reason was that she hardly knew the Queen and had had no idea how Elizabeth would view the matter; but if she had guessed that the Patons would move so quickly to appeal to the sovereign, she would have pleaded her case immediately. Neither of those facts, however, would sway the Queen in her favor. Youthful inexperience seemed her best tactic.

Jane kept her eyes demurely lowered, fixing them on her wedding ring, hoping Richard was choking to see it still on her finger. "I am but newly widowed, madam, and have no experience of the law. I look only to respect the dying wishes of my husband and had not anticipated that anyone would object to them."

"But they do object, child," Elizabeth said gently, nodding to Richard Paton.

"Indeed we do!" spluttered the marquess. "Sadly, I have to conclude that my father lost his wits in the last months of his life and married this scheming girl before we could stop him. He didn't even bed her—his doctor swears that he was incapable of doing so—I dispute that she was his wife in truth!"

Mortified, Jane wished the floor would split and swallow her whole—better yet, gulp down Richard and spit him into hell.

Elizabeth frowned. "We do not think this a subject suitable to a public gathering, my lord marquess, and your tone is unmannerly. If the marriage was not complete, then the church authorities must be consulted. Pray, do not speak of this again."

The Queen dismissed him with a flick of her wrist, but it was too late. The whispered gossip about Jane had now been stated before the entire court; she had never felt so humiliated. While many tried to keep the smirks from their faces in her presence, she knew they were speculating about her and itching to chew over her reputation in the corridors and antechambers.

As soon as Jane was able to retire from her post, she took her chance and fled back to her room. The other ladies had been too polite to raise the subject of her supposedly virgin widow status—or the French suitor—but no doubt they were relishing the scandal now that she had left the field. The thought made her boil with rage.

Once in her room, Jane grabbed the first object to hand and threw it against the wall. The pitcher smashed, splashing water everywhere.

"Damn him, damn him!" Jane screwed her hands into fists. Quite whom she was consigning to hell—Richard Paton or her father—was debatable—both, most likely.

"My lady, whatever is the matter?" Her maid appeared, hovering fearfully at the door.

"Leave me!" Jane ordered, desperate for a moment alone to regain control of her temper.

"But, my lady . . ."

"Out!"

The servant snapped the door closed and ran off.

Well, wasn't that the crowning achievement! She had just managed to offend her maid and now the girl would spread the news of her reaction to the scene at court belowstairs. Her temper had always been her downfall when dealing with servants.

Temporarily defeated, Jane slumped on the bed, kicked off her shoes and curled up. The silent room reminded her how isolated she was now that she had lost Jonas and had no friend at court.

But that was not so, she reminded herself; she had one ally. She gazed at the empty pillow beside her, imagining James Lacey lying there to comfort her. He would put his arm round her shoulders, pull her head to his chest and tell her not to worry. No Frog duke's son would come between them; no rapacious Patons would steal her dowry, ring and dowager rights with him to defend her.

It was a lovely fantasy, but only that—a fantasy, Jane acknowledged. James might be a friend, but he did not seem to want her enough to stay in England to help her.

Durham House, Westminster

After a poor showing in the first round, James regretted that he had accepted Raleigh's invitation to join in the archery competition in the gardens of Durham House. The young gentlemen attending the event were betting high, so he could not match them with the scant contents of his purse; his performance on the field also did him no favors with his peers. His skills lay with blades rather than bows, but no true Englishman would like to admit that, so he doggedly continued, annoyed to see his name hovering in the lower half of the scoreboard.

Raleigh clapped him on the back. "Bit rusty, Lacey?" His own quiver of six arrows had landed in the center of the target, one right in the bull's-eye. He was coming second after Lord Clément Mont-fleury—the Frenchman providing the biggest surprise of the competition by being revealed as an excellent shot, his slight frame concealing a wiry strength that enabled him to bend all but the largest of the bows.

"So it would seem," James replied coolly. With his height and power, he had no problem drawing back the string of the tallest of the longbows, but his arrows all flew to the left. One had even ignominiously missed the butt entirely and buried itself in the wicker fencing behind.

Raleigh rubbed his hands together. "I should warn you: the Queen is coming to award the prize to the winner and doubtless shoot a few arrows herself—she has a passion for the sport. If you wish to impress her, I suggest you correct your aim. We can't have the Frog winning, can we? Remember Agincourt—the English archers triumphing over the French!"

"Sage words, sir, but easier said than done. I think our hopes for national glory rest on others."

"Indeed." Raleigh laughed, enjoying James's discomfort.

The Queen's party arrived at noon at the riverside stairs. James hung back as Raleigh conducted the sovereign and her attendants into the garden, seating them under the special canopy erected for the occasion. White canvas painted with gold stars protected the sovereign from the faint drizzle in the air. James immediately noted Jane was among the ladies, dressed in a fine black fur-edged coat over a cream gown. She looked beautiful, like a slender lily next to the full blossomed rose of the Queen in scarlet.

On Raleigh's signal, servants bearing refreshments appeared from all points of the garden. Hot punch in pewter tankards came as a welcome respite to the chilly day. James warmed his fingers around his drink, breathing in the clove-scented steam. Musicians, hidden behind the Queen's shelter, began to play a selection of lively folk tunes, adding to the impromptu festive atmosphere. Lent might be a sober time of year, but Raleigh had cannily found a way of getting around the formal gloom of the season of the Great Fast. No churchman would protest the necessity of loyal men practicing the art of archery.

Charles Blount, son of Lord Mountjoy, strolled over to greet James. A popular courtier hampered by a spendthrift father, he, like the Laceys, knew the problems of maintaining a decent appearance at court on very little.

"Lacey. Not your sport, I see?"

"That obvious, is it?"

"Well, I've heard rumors of your prowess in the fencing hall, so I am rather relieved to find you have an Achilles' heel."

"Not my only one, I confess."

The two men watched the bustle around the Queen in friendly silence, Blount running his fingers up and down his bowstring as if about to strum it like a harp.

"Stunning girl, that Lady Rievaulx, don't you think?" Blount remarked, seeing where James was looking. Jane had refused all refreshments and was trying to stay out of everyone's way at the back of the tent.

"Indeed." More than stunning, she was perfect.

"Did you hear what happened yester eve?"

What was this? He fumbled his tankard, sloshing a drop on the ground. "No, I was not at court."

"Ah, then you've not heard the most delicious bit of gossip

about her. Two bits, in fact." Blount grinned in anticipation of serving a feast of scandal, unaware of the feelings he was stirring in his companion. "Her father is trying to wed her to that Frenchman." He nodded discreetly to Montfleury, who was preening himself in the midst of a circle of male admirers. "If that peacock has any desire to bed a girl, then I'm the Pope in Rome. I assume Wetherby doesn't want grandchildren—or not legitimate ones, at any rate."

James clenched his jaw, tempted to march over to Montfleury and snap his bow in half.

"If that was not amusement enough, the Patons mauled her reputation in front of the Queen. The marquess blurted out that Lady Rievaulx is a virgin—therefore no true wife of his father—and thus he disputes her dower rights." Blount gave a man-of-the-world's knowing laugh. "Now all of us are queuing to relieve her of the proof of her innocence to protect her from her loving stepsons—that's if someone hasn't done it already. There are other rumors circulating that she has been a little too friendly with a certain person in the past."

"Who?" James asked through gritted teeth, filled with an irrational desire to punch anyone who dared so much as lay a finger on Jane.

"Oh, it's just some servants' talk that she is not a maid—doubtless scurrilous. You are considered the front-runner in that race, my friend."

"Me?" James rocked back on his heels, genuinely astounded by the answer. "Why do they think that?"

"Passionate arguments on the dance floor, a private conversation at the banquet—you act as if you know each other very well."

"I do not *know* the lady in that fashion, sir," James replied stiffly. "I have no reason to think her anything but a virtuous girl."

"Shame." Blount winked. "The *un*virtuous ones are so much more fun."

Refreshed from her river journey, the Queen rose and led her ladies out on to the archery field. "Bring the hunting bows. The ladies will battle for the honor of competing against the winner of Master Raleigh's competition."

Elizabeth's own attempt was not to her usual high standard, for which she blamed the damp weather. Her attendants were clearly torn between letting her win and making a decent showing, until the Queen scoffed at one lady's purposely erratic shot.

"Ladies, do not mind me. I am not so fragile as to disapprove of another triumphing on occasion."

After that the standard rose immeasurably. James was delighted to find that Jane was skilled at the bow, proving to be one of the most accurate. He joined the other gentlemen who had elected themselves to the privilege of returning the arrows to the fair competitors after each round.

James bowed and handed Jane her scarlet-fletched darts. "You continue to surprise me, my lady. Where did you learn to shoot like that?"

Jane fitted an arrow to the string, raising the feathers to brush her cheek as she lined up her shot and released the bow. The shaft flew sweetly to hit the very center of the butt. "When you have a brother like mine, sir, you soon learn the desirability of being able to knock him off his perch."

Jane was declared the winner of the ladies' competition amid much cheering. It was only then that she learnt against whom she would be competing in the final round, occasioning many jests about Cupid's arrows going astray. James could tell she was finding the whole match an excruciating experience—singled out again in front of the court with her completely unsuitable suitor. She looked very alone standing by the fifty-yard mark, trying to pretend none of this bothered her. The Frenchman, by contrast, was delighted by the coincidence, fluttering his wretched handkerchief at her in some misbegotten attempt at wooing her with his display. James had seen enough. He strode forward to take the quiver from Jane's shoulder.

"If you will allow, my lady, I will hand you your arrows."

Jane's expression changed to relief that she now had a buffer between her and Montfleury. "Thank you."

He winked at her and whispered: "Knock the Frog off his log."

Montfleury switched from the more powerful longbow to a hunting one like Jane's. He tucked his handkerchief away. "Ladies first, *ma belle.*"

Jane lined up her shot, aware that all eyes were on her. The result was a perfect hit. She stood still while the Frenchman huffed over his new weapon, testing the tension on the string. His missile drifted to the outer ring.

His complaint was immediate. "*Sacrebleu!* It is not well balanced and I have not used this weapon before."

"Then, by all means, take another shot." Jane smiled sweetly at him. "That can be your practice."

"*Non, non,* I will keep to the terms of the competition. No one will say that I, Clément Montfleury, am a cheat!"

"What manner of man is this?" James whispered as he passed Jane her next arrow.

She raised the bow. "A man much enamored of himself, I would hazard." Her second attempt landed right next to her first, eliciting much applause from the onlookers. Montfleury's reply was a great improvement, landing in the inner circle.

"I narrow your advantage, my lady." The Frenchman mopped the rain from his fingers with his handkerchief. "The doe flees, but the hart doth pursue."

"I do not run, my lord, I lead." Jane released her dart to land a third in the center of her target with a satisfying thud.

"I vow you are imagining his face as the bull's-eye." James passed her another missile.

Jane smiled cheekily up at him. "Not his face, sir."

That was the moment when James realized he had fallen in love with her for a second time, his warrior maiden standing up in front of the cruel gossips of the court, shooting down in flames the pretentions of her suitor. When she was declared the victor by ten points, the crowd cheered, rejoicing that England's reputation for superior archery had been saved for that day. Montfleury feigned magnanimity in defeat, though James could tell he was peeved with his prospective bride. James could not have been prouder of her.

"You are a marvel, Lady Jane." Handing over the bow and quiver to a servant, he offered his arm to escort her back to the Queen's side.

Jane shook her head. "I was lucky. Montfleury is in truth a very good archer—he was hampered by the change in bow."

"But any soldier or sailor will tell you that good fortune always plays a vital role in a campaign. I know men who refuse to sail with a captain they consider unlucky."

She laughed. "But I am not considering setting myself up as one of the Queen's rovers, Jamie."

"For shame: you'd make a very good one—a rival to Sir Francis Drake, no less."

"I will bear it in mind—I might need another life should the one at court get any worse."

They were almost at the tent. James discreetly squeezed her arm. "I have heard the talk about you, my lady. Consider me at your disposal to assist in any way I can."

Jane toed the damp ground with her shoe. "But you intend to go adventuring. You will not be here to defend me."

James released her arm reluctantly. "Aye, but I do intend to come back. I have to do something with my life, my lady. I cannot remain a cipher, of no use to anyone."

"I don't consider you a cipher."

"But I do—and therein lies the problem. I'm not a fit companion for anyone in my present state. I have to earn my place."

"But you are good enough as you are. I don't need a herd of cows to prove to me your worth."

Wrong-footed by her words that suggested they were discussing courtship, James was momentarily speechless.

Jane flushed, realizing that she had rushed her fence and been pitched from the saddle on the other side. "I see you were not on the same stave of the song as me, Master Lacey. I apologize."

They had been talking privately for too long. James needed time to regroup, a space to regain his footing in this relationship, which he had foolishly allowed to drift too far off-balance. "Lady Jane, pray do not be embarrassed that you mentioned such a subject. I would that I could sing the same stanza, but so much stands against that event. It is natural, where there is friendship between a man and a woman, to speculate that it might lead to more." The Queen was staring at them, her face set in a frown. "We must discuss this properly—I want you to understand why I cannot be the one for you. Please, will you meet me later? In the knot garden after supper?"

Jane smiled bravely, racking up his guilt that he had let her assume too much about him. "Until then, sir." She took her leave, returning to the Queen's party to receive her congratulations and prize.

James watched the little performance, feeling disgusted with himself. He had spoiled her moment of triumph by his handling of that conversation, making it a hollow victory for her. He could tell that she was mistaken as to the reasons why he had rejected her tentative proposal; Jane did not understand that it was no reflection on her worth, but that he considered her far too good for him. He had been serious in his views on luck: he was nothing but a curse on those around him and had no intention of inflicting himself on such a shining lady as Jane. If they married, he would soon dull that glow, be a parasite living off her fortune. He would lose any self-respect he still had—not that there was much left after the Low Countries.

CHAPTER 11

JANE DRESSED WITH GREAT CARE for her meeting with James that night, ordering her maid, Margery, to brush her hair with a hundred strokes until it curled like silk over her shoulders. Margery then braided it in a crown and pinned Jane's favorite black velvet cap to the top. Not quite happy with the effect, Jane tugged a tendril loose so it hung artfully to her ruff, teasing her cheek. That should get his interest. Finally, the maid applied a light touch of cosmetics, just a hint to accent Jane's eyes.

"You look very well, my lady," Margery announced as they both gazed critically in the mirror.

"You may go." Jane waited for the girl to depart, then took a deep breath to gather her courage. At first Jane had been dismayed by James's reaction at the archery competition to her confession that she had thought of him for a husband; she had been despondent for several hours, only to recover her spirits in an imagined conversation with him in the privacy of her room. She pointed out to the chair that took his role that her money was of no use if it could not buy her happiness. She knew she was not good enough for him, be-smirched as she was by slander, but she would work hard to earn his high opinion. He might think he was below her in rank, but did he really want to see her married off to a man like Clément Mont-fleury? And as for the Patons, he would prove an invaluable bulwark against their bullying, so he was not useless—far from it: he was essential to her well-being.

The chair had agreed and let her sit on its lap. Now she only had to persuade the man.

The little garden was deserted when Jane arrived. February was too cold for most people to venture outside after dark, so she had the smooth raked paths to herself. She pulled a fur-lined cloak around her, hood over her head. The enclosure was surrounded on all sides by buildings, passageways between hall and private chambers. Needing no more fuel for the gossip about her, Jane sought out a place where their tryst would not be visible from the windows. She found what she needed in one corner: a bench shielded by an evergreen shrub, so deep in the shadows that only the most eagle-eyed spy would note that it was occupied. She had chosen a russet kirtle and cloak of deepest blue and left off all jewelery, so knew she must be almost invisible sitting in the farthest recess of the arbor.

She heard James's footsteps before she saw him. He strode into the very center of the garden, stepping over the low hedges to reach his goal. Scanning the grounds, hands on hips, he looked very disappointed not to see her there. Allowing herself the pleasure of watching him unobserved for a few moments, Jane then put him out of his misery.

"Over here!"

With flattering eagerness, James jumped over the box border to reach her. He seized her hand and pressed a kiss on her fingers.

"Thank you for coming, my lady."

She patted the bench beside her. "Please—I've something I want to say to you."

James sat, keeping a few inches between them, body angled towards her. Jane launched into her little speech as practiced before he could intervene, not daring to meet his eyes until she had stumbled all the way through.

"So, you see," she concluded bravely, "I see no impediment to our . . . closer acquaintance."

She looked up to find James smiling sadly into her face. He reached out and traced the line of her cheek, trailing a fingertip to her chin. "No, you wouldn't: you are too good to see me for what I really am."

"You're wrong. I've known what you are since we first met at Lacey Hall. We suit, Jamie, don't you see that too?"

He leant forward and stole a kiss from her lips, so earnest and serious as they tried to persuade him of his worth. Her breath was warm and sweet, her mouth yielding beneath his. When he moved back, her eyes were closed, her expression full of wonder.

"If I had one wish, Lady Jane, it would be that I was the man you deserve."

Her eyes flicked open, the expression in them moving swiftly from confusion to frustration. "But you are!"

"No, I really am not."

"Stop saying that!" Winding an arm round his neck, she pulled him to her and kissed him full and hard, her desperation to convince him in her touch. Something seemed to give way inside him; the wall he had erected between them crumbled and he allowed his desire for her to run free. His hand stole under her cloak to clasp her waist, the other pressed between her shoulder blades to bring her against him. The embrace lasted for many minutes, deepening and intensifying until neither could remember what had brought them here, what lay unresolved between them. Finally, breaking apart to catch their breath, they gazed at each other, both stunned by the lightning bolt of passion that had seared through them.

"Who would've thought?" James murmured, nibbling her ear, unable to stop touching her.

"Thought what?" Her voice was faint as she lost herself in the delight of his caress.

"That we are powder and flame when brought together. The perfect lady and the flawed adventurer."

"Please don't count me as perfect. I've made too many mistakes." Jane wished sincerely she could be the girl he thought she was—untouched and pure. If only she had waited for someone like him, not fallen for the first smooth-talking courtier to cross her path, then she would have felt stronger. But she had too much pride to confess that fault to him and she feared to lose his good opinion forever.

"Your mistakes must be mere molehills to the mountain range of mine." James kissed her lightly, a farewell of sorts as his resolve to deny himself any happiness until he had paid for his sins reasserted itself. "This mustn't happen again."

Infuriating man! Jane was tempted to thump him. They made progress and then he rapidly drew back. "Why not?"

"For all the reasons I've said—I have to go away—you deserve better."

"But if I decide you are the one I want, can you not accept it?"

He didn't answer but stroked her face. "You are so beautiful."

Temper flaring, Jane pushed his hand away. "And you are so stubborn!"

He had the gall to laugh. "That's right, my darling, don't let me off easily."

Jane plucked a handful of ivy leaves and threw them at him. "Why can't you just love me?"

He brushed the leaves from his hair and shoulders patiently, not rising to her bait to lose his control. "Because I can't allow myself that pleasure."

"Aargh!" Jane pulled her cloak around herself tightly and jumped up. "I don't understand you! I've told you how I feel—and you—you seem to like me enough to kiss me—why can't we be together? It's just your mind telling you this—there's no real reason, no impediment."

He hung his head, not meeting her eye. His silence was more damning than anything he could have said.

Jane felt her hope pass from fresh green fruit to a withered Lenten apple, too long in store. "You really have made up your mind on this, haven't you?"

"I have."

"And I'm . . . I'm not enough to make you change."

He made no reply.

"I see." Weary of yet another hurt, Jane began to retreat. She had risked her heart by laying herself open to him and he had rejected her offer as not good enough. "Then I bid you Godspeed with your adventuring, Master Lacey." Clinging to her ragged composure, she dipped a curtsy and turned to leave.

"Jane, wait."

She stopped, swallowing down tears. Please let him have realized he was wrong—please!

He held empty hands out at his side. "Forgive me. I wish I weren't as I am."

The last flicker of hope snuffed out, Jane made herself walk away. One foot in front of the other—for her self-respect she had to do it. But her ankles felt weighed down with chains as if she were a prisoner in the Tower walking out to the block.

Milly invented an excuse to come to Whitehall so she could share her news with Jane. Finding her friend alone in her chamber, she dumped the parcels she had brought as cover for her true errand and rushed to hug her.

"Oh, Jane, I am so happy!" Milly squeezed her tight, feeling Jane's stiffness melt and an answering embrace envelop her.

"I'm pleased for you." Jane gently eased herself away. "Now tell me exactly why you are so pleased with yourself—as if I couldn't guess." She waved to a chair by the window, bidding her guest to be seated. From the dent in the cushion, it must have been the one Jane had been occupying until Milly arrived—strange because the place by the window was distinctly drafty and not as cosy as the one by the bed.

Milly bounded over to the chair and sat down, only to jump up again immediately, her happiness impossible to contain. "Diego came back yesterday. We are betrothed!"

"Congratulations."

Milly paced the floor between window and hearth. "Now there's only my father to persuade. Diego said that his master would offer us a home at Lacey Hall if my neighbors are hostile to the match, but I hope we can carry on living in London. There's my business to consider—and Diego has hopes of earning his way, offering gentlemen riding and fencing lessons. We should do well enough." She smiled down at the bracelet on her wrist. "Oh, Jane, he's so wonderful! He really loves me—says he has done so since we were children. He even thinks my wretched hair beautiful." She laughed and twirled on the spot. "He insists on no dowry—thinks he should give my father his savings for marrying me—that was our first argument!" She couldn't stop grinning as she remembered how they had made up. "We're going to get married as soon as we can."

Milly stopped spinning like a top when she realized Jane wasn't saying anything. Her friend was silent and pale; her blue eyes had shadows under them like fading bruises.

"Jane, whatever is the matter? Do you . . . do you not like my news?"

Jane tried a smile—not a success. "I really am happy for you, Milly. It's not you. James Lacey and I, well, we had a disagreement yester eve, that's all."

Flush with love, Milly could not imagine unhappiness for another. "Then you must go see him—sort things out! As soon as I saw him, I could tell he would be perfect for you."

"It's not that easy." Jane rubbed her arms.

"But you love him—and he certainly cares for you." Milly pounced on one of her parcels. "Here, I have a rather fine new hat for you that will make you look simply ravishing. Put this on and go find him—he won't be able to resist."

Jane took the hat and tried it on to please Milly. The round brim of the velvet cap circled her face, making her eyes seem enormous. With a smile, it would be dashing; today, it merely framed her sadness.

"Thank you. Please add it to my account."

Milly sighed. Part of her did not want to spoil her own joyous mood by understanding the source of Jane's melancholy, but friendship deserved better than that.

"How bad is it, Jane?" She unpacked the other garments she had brought, leaving them on the bed for Jane to admire later.

"Completely awful." Jane ran her fingers down the cold stone of the window frame, her back to the delights spread out on the quilt. "For knotted reasons of his own, he doesn't want me and, believe me, I've made my interest clear, so it is not a misunderstanding. I'm simply not what he wants."

"What does he want?"

"Ah, there's the question. Absolution for what he sees as past sins? Or maybe punishment for surviving when others did not?"

"Diego thinks he is troubled by a haunt—an unquiet spirit. I thought you would . . . I don't know, maybe cheer him up, make him snap out of this mood?"

Jane traced a raindrop running down the rippled pane of glass. "So I hoped. But I'm not enough."

Milly came up behind her friend and gave her another hug, gentle this time. "I love you, Jane. And he's an idiot."

"Then I'm the worse fool for falling in love with him."

CHAPTER 12

JAMES WOKE UP IN A COLD SWEAT and found himself sprawled on the floor, his knife buried in the belly of his pillow, feather-guts spread across the boards.

"My lord?"

Pulling himself up on to his knees, James met Diego's startled eyes, the whites standing out against the dark of his face. Disorientated, he groped for the side of the bed. His servant made to get up.

"Leave it. I'll manage. Go back to sleep."

"But the pillow . . ."

"You can clean up in the damned morning, can't you?"

"Aye, my lord." Lids lowered, veiling his expression, the manservant lay back down on his pallet bed at the foot of James's four-poster. James doubted Diego would return to sleep as quickly as he pretended, but he for one was thankful for the illusion of privacy in which to tackle the aftermath of his nightmare.

Dragging a quilt off the bed, James wrapped it around his nakedness and ducked under the drapes so he was concealed in the window alcove. The night was freezing, a chill damp breeze coming off the oily waters of the Thames, but he welcomed the discomfort as his due for his weakness. The dream had come again—the one where the bodies of the Dutch children fell around him, broken puppets on cold snow. He'd attacked the soldier murdering the innocent, only to find he was stabbing at an inoffensive pillow. And Jane asked why they could not be together? What if she had been beside him—would he have attacked her and only realized too late what he had done? It was not an idle question. He sometimes worried about having Diego in the same room at night, but the servant had always refused to lie elsewhere.

"God, you're a mess, Lacey," James murmured, scrubbing his face with one hand. "Do everyone a favor and get yourself off to the other side of the world."

Contrary to what he had told Jane, part of him did not expect to come back. He certainly wouldn't return if the journey did not cure the strange black mood he had been in for so many months. He'd throw himself over the side of the ship first if he thought he still posed a risk to those he loved.

James was still standing in the alcove when dawn broke. He heard the scuffle of sheets as Diego rose to light the fire, the sounds of the city waking, boatmen shouting, birds singing as they made brave attempts to attract a mate in anticipation of spring. Good luck to them.

"My lord." Diego handed him a tankard of warmed ale. The spicy tang of nutmeg filled his nose and turned him from statue to human again. He took a sip.

"Thanks."

"Your shaving water is ready." Diego drew back the curtains, revealing a room already straightened, evidence of the pathetic pillow fight removed.

James dropped the quilt, comfortable to walk around unclothed in front of his manservant. He pulled on his shirt and woolen hose, fingers stinging as warm blood circulated once more, his nails losing their bluish tinge.

"I've decided we'll go and join the ships in Plymouth." He lathered his face, then sat back for Diego to shave him. "I'm doing no good here."

Diego thoughtfully prepared the razor on the strop. "I see, sir."

"Pack up. We'll hire a couple of hacks. We should be there at the end of the week."

"My lord, I . . . I do not wish to go." Carefully, Diego smoothed the blade over James's cheek, trimming off the excess hair to shape the beard so it followed the line of his jaw and didn't invade the rest of his face.

James studied his man's expression. "What's this? Mutiny?"

"No, sir: love."

He grimaced. "I had forgot. The pretty copper-headed maid. She's agreed to wed you?"

Diego nodded, turning his attention to the other side.

"I'm pleased for you. Then I'll go alone. There's bound to be a suitable replacement for hire at the port, and I'll save on the second horse." Despite his prosaic tone, James realized he felt relieved: it had not sat right with him to drag Diego along on what was likely to prove a dangerous voyage. Only the desperate should consent to such an adventure. Separating himself from the last person who cared for him felt right, akin to renouncing worldly goods in preparation for death. He had no intention of hiring another man—no one should see him in his nightmares. He'd move heaven and earth to get a cabin alone.

"If you're sure, sir?"

"I've never been more certain. Get wed. Be happy." The trim over, he rubbed his face dry and threw the towel at Diego. "Then name your first son after me."

The court was preparing to move. The privies at Whitehall had reached their capacity, the taint in the air unpleasant, so the order went out for transfer to Greenwich to allow the palace to be sweetened. Jane's maid packed her wardrobe and other personal effects from her chamber—several trunkfuls, by the time she had finished.

"I'll see to these, my lady." The maid bristled with annoyance at having her work overseen by her mistress. "Can't trust those boatmen—they're not above misplacing a cargo or two." The girl had been cold towards her ever since the episode when Jane had practically thrown her from the room. The application of the soothing balm of a half-crown had done little to soften her disposition.

"Thank you, Margery." Jane smiled at the maid, but her overture was met with a stony look. She sighed inwardly. "I will meet you at Greenwich this evening."

A tap at the door turned her thoughts from the fractured state of affairs with her maid.

Margery answered the summons. "What's your business here?" Her curt tone told Jane that it was someone of low status.

"I have come to ask a favor of your lady, maid."

Margery gave a snort. "She won't want to be bothered by the likes of you. Get thee gone before I call the guard."

"Enough, Margery!" Jane stepped into view of the open door. "I know this man. Diego, please come in. Have you a message from Milly?"

With an amused glance at the maid's crestfallen face, Diego advanced past her and into the chamber.

"No message, O most beautiful lady. I am here to cast myself on your mercy."

Delighted to be of assistance to her friend's betrothed, Jane gestured him to a seat, which he refused, insisting on standing respectfully in her presence. "Just ask, Diego, and if it is in my power I will happily oblige."

He tapped his chest with a fist and bowed. "I would ask to serve you, my lady."

"But you serve Master Lacey."

"He has gone to join the ship for America."

So soon? a small voice wailed inside Jane.

"I have begged leave to stay with Milly, which he has graciously granted. Until such time as I marry her and can take her back to Lacey Hall, I am on temporary leave from my Lord Dorset's household."

Aware of Margery's avid interest in this conversation, Jane tried not to give away her consternation at the news that James had left without even a farewell. She forced herself to focus on Diego's predicament. "So you need a place while you remain in London?"

"Aye, my lady."

The request was simple enough, and she was not short of money to pay for ten more servants, let alone one. "Then of course, you may enter my service for however long you require—on the understanding that the Laceys do not object. I do not want to be accused of luring away one of their best men."

"Master James will not mind—he holds you in very high regard."

But that was not the kind of regard she wanted from him. "When would you like to start?"

"At once, my lady. My master left early this morning."

Already? "I see. A sudden decision?"

"Aye, it was."

Jane could not come to terms with what this meant before two witnesses; she would have to leave the matter for later. But with the household on the move, this meant much later.

"Then, Diego, you may accompany me now. I have the day free, as the court is leaving for Greenwich, and we will only be in the way if we stay here. Come."

Diego gave Margery a wicked grin, enjoying his little victory over her attempt to bar him entry. "I follow, my lady."

Jane led the way to the palace stables, where she had sent orders ahead for her horse to be made ready. The yard seethed with people and vehicles as the complicated business of removing the Queen's household got under way. Carts lined up for the heavier items that were to be taken by road over London Bridge; porters swore color-fully; court officials issued threats liberally as priceless goods were levered aboard. Few noted the lady with her blackamoor attendant slipping between the throng. Seeing that the horse had been pre-pared with the pillion saddle, Jane dismissed the manservant she had sent down earlier to convey her orders to the stable and told him to stay and assist Margery.

"You can ride pillion, Diego, I trust?" she asked.

"Indeed. I have some small skill with horses, my lady." Diego went to the hack's head and whispered in his ear. The gelding im-mediately quieted and lipped his new rider's outstretched palm, captivated by the stranger.

"Small skill, I vow," Jane said wryly.

Diego handed her up onto the rear seat before mounting smoothly in front.

"Where to, my lady?"

"Guess." Jane prodded him between the shoulders.

"Will I like the destination, O most kind mistress?" Diego kicked the horse into motion, heading for the gate.

"Indubitably."

She did not have to say any more. Diego twitched the reins and set course for Cheapside.

Diego enjoyed Milly's surprise when she saw her two favorite people in the world, as she called them, arrive together. She flew about her upstairs workroom to make them comfortable, moving her latest commission from a chair and fussing about whether or not she had suitable refreshments for them. Deciding in the negative, she despatched Henny to the cookshop with strict orders to buy the freshest batch of sweet rolls.

"There's no need to go to all this trouble," Lady Jane protested, trying to prevent the whirligig of activity. Diego knew better than to try to stop his Milly when she had an idea in her head. He stood back to watch and enjoy.

"You should have sent word! Oh, look at the mess!" Milly stuffed her embroidery silks back into the basket on the table.

"I did not mean to stop you from working." Lady Jane picked up the smock Milly had removed, admiring the flower motif on the breast. "Perhaps we should help—you have a business to run, after all."

Diego smothered his laughter when he saw Milly's aghast expression. She was frantically trying to think how to turn down the offer without causing offense.

"Not that I'm very skilled at this work," Jane continued, a twinkle in her eye. "But I'm sure I could stitch something given half a chance."

His new mistress was teasing Milly. Diego turned to the window to hide his grin.

"But, um, Lady Jane, I don't really have that much work on at the moment," Milly lied in desperation. "There is no need for you to help me."

Lady Jane threw the smock to Milly. "Got you! You should've seen your face."

In a flash, Milly's expression went from worried to relieved. "You wicked creature! You had me thinking you were serious!"

"I did, didn't I? You were always pathetically easy to gull, Milly. You need someone hard-headed to keep you safe from tricksters like me."

Diego raised his hand. "I volunteer for the position, my lady."

"Excellent. I'll sleep better knowing that."

Milly glared at them, hands on hips. "Oh, you two! I can't have you conspiring against me."

Jane laughed. "Only for your own good, my dear."

Henny returned with a tray of sweet rolls glazed with cinnamon-sprinkled icing.

"Those smell wonderful." Lady Jane took a seat at the table for a second breakfast.

"Best in London," Milly promised. "You won't taste anything finer at court."

Even with Henny dismissed, Diego refused to sit at the table with them, taking his share to eat at his post by the door. Though he paid little heed to the distinction of rank, he suspected his new mistress did; the informality between the old friends was not something he felt able to share while engaged in Lady Jane's service.

The girls worked their way through two rolls apiece.

"Did you leave your man below?" Milly asked, licking her fingers.

Lady Jane shook her head. "He's right here."

Milly's eyes widened. "You mean Diego?"

"I have left Master James's service, and her ladyship was kind enough to take me on until we can be married," Diego explained.

"But why leave him?" Milly put down the last half of her roll and pushed the plate away.

"Master James has gone to Plymouth and is bound for the Americas. I wanted to stay with you."

The two girls exchanged looks—Milly's questioning, Jane's resigned to disappointment.

"Oh, Diego!" wailed Milly. "What about Jane? What about her hopes?"

Diego's heart sank at Milly's distress. He had thought to please her by staying, but she was not taking the news in the way he had anticipated; she appeared more worried for Lady Jane than happy for them. He had long known of the attraction between his old master and new mistress, but Milly was clearly party to far more confidences than he.

Milly turned pleading hazel eyes on him. "But I thought you'd promised the earl you'd stay with his brother?"

He had, hadn't he? But circumstances had changed; he had

exercised his freedom of choice and followed the path he preferred, the one that would lead to happiness. What did he owe these Laceys, who only employed him because he was useful to them? Why should he risk everything by following his master on a voyage he did not really understand and knew would be dangerous?

He countered her charge by making it personal, dodging the issue of the promise. "Do you want me to go, then, Milly?"

"Of course I don't want you to go!" Milly took Lady Jane's hand and gave it a squeeze. "But you know better than most how your master is at the moment. Doesn't he need a friend with him on this voyage?"

Diego crossed his arms. "I am not a friend."

Milly rose and went to him, cupping his cheek tenderly in her palm. "Aren't you? I know you are far apart in rank, but you have done so much together—and look how worried he was about you when he thought you in danger!"

Her argument struck home. He had brushed over the burr of James's loyalty to him, but it stuck in the way of pretending his detached stance was smooth and untangled. At Lacey Hall he had thought himself apart from these English people; now that he had fallen in love with one, he was being drawn into ties he had not had since leaving his village in Africa.

"But what can I do to help him, Milly?" He turned her palm to plant a kiss in the center. Lady Jane tactfully pretended to be occupied with a pattern book to allow them privacy. "He has to fight his own battles."

"But none of us should have to do that alone." Milly's eyes filled with tears—his wife-to-be was so softhearted it was a wonder she had survived thus far in this cruel world. "You told me yourself he suffers from terrible nightmares—that he can't bear to share a room with others in case they see him in that state. Think what it will be like for him in the close confines of a ship."

"He'll get himself a new man. Servants like me are ten a penny."

She shook her head. "That's not true and you know it. You were with him in the Low Countries; you understand. He won't find another person who can look after him like you can." She lowered her voice. "Lady Jane loves him. I want them to have their chance, as we have ours, but they won't get it until James Lacey is . . . is . . . healed, I suppose you would say . . . healed in mind and spirit." She pressed the tip of her finger into his breastbone. "Remember that we are only able to be together thanks to their generosity."

Diego reflected ruefully that sometimes it was a burden to have a betrothed who was so much nicer than he. "So you think I should go after him?"

Milly closed her eyes briefly, then nodded.

He leant forward and kissed the tip of her nose. "Consider it done."

"I love you," she whispered.

"Love you too, Milly-mine."

She thumped his chest. "And don't you dare not come back!"

"I will command the waves to be smooth just for you."

She rested her head on his breast and sighed. "I'm going to regret this."

He nestled his cheek against her hair. "No, you will not. You must always remember, whatever happens, that you are right. I was blinded by my desire to be with you, but I am sure that we must not start our life together with a failure to do our duty to others." He winked. "Particularly when we want to continue in their service for the rest of our married life."

"How long will you be away?"

"Only for the summer, if all goes to plan."

"Then we marry at Harvest?"

"Aye. If your father agrees."

"How can he not when I am betrothed to a heroic explorer?"

"Hmm, we will see."

Hand in hand, the pair turned to Lady Jane. Diego gave her a bow.

"My lady, it seems that my service to you is to be very brief. Milly has reminded me of my duty to Master Lacey. I must hurry if I am to catch up with him in Plymouth."

Lady Jane dropped the pattern book back on the table. "So you will go after him? But what about your marriage?"

Milly squeezed Diego's hand. "That's only delayed by a few months, Jane. We'll cope, but I very much fear your James won't if he doesn't have a friend beside him."

The lady sat back in her chair and gave a deep sigh. "I cannot tell you, Diego, how relieved I am to know that you'll be with him. He's seemed so alone, not at all his old self. He needs you."

Diego was flattered by the faith the two girls had in him, even if it was undeserved. "I will do my best."

Jane felt in her purse. "Such loyalty must not go unrewarded. Here, take this—two sovereigns—these should see you to Plymouth."

"And beyond, mistress." Diego pocketed her generous payment, relieved that the practicalities of chasing after his master had been solved. "I will be able to equip myself for the voyage in style thanks to you."

166

"I regret that your service is so brief, but I . . ." Her voice broke with emotion. She regained control and continued. ". . . I will never forget what you are doing for James. I will look after Milly for you while you are away, and try to smooth the path with her father too."

"Then I will be more than repaid for what is merely my duty."

Dashing away a tear and smiling over-brightly, Jane stood and went to the door. "I will go below to give you a chance to say your farewells in private."

Diego swept Milly into his arms and hugged her tightly until she gave a little squeak. "I am going to miss you," he whispered.

"And I you."

"Do not worry. My talisman will protect me."

Milly fumbled for the cord, then kissed his necklace. "What is it made from?"

"A few things, including a lock of your hair, shamelessly stolen when you were not looking."

"I'm glad—and I give it freely. Travel safely and come back soon, my love."

Diego set her back on her feet. "Will you do one thing for me, Milly?"

"Anything."

"Do not let that player near you. He is too charming. I do not trust him."

She giggled. "You have to understand, Diego, I am immune to him. But I'll keep him at arm's length, never you fear."

"Make sure it is a very long arm."

CHAPTER 13

The Red Lion, Plymouth

JAMES FINISHED HIS LETTER to Will with a drop of wax on the fold, to which he pressed his signet ring of a knight on horseback to make a seal. The image blurred, the hapless hero squelched off on one side, but it would do. Brushing aside some hazelnut shells left over from a midnight snack, he stood the letter upright against a candlestick to remind himself that he had to send it on the morrow. What would Will make of the news that they had another brother— an actor with a disposition like that of a bear at the baiting ring? He would put his money on Will's taking a trip to London in the very near future to meet Christopher in person; his older brother was in essence the kindest of men and would hate to think one of his blood had been so neglected, even if it had been through no fault of his own.

His duty by his half brother done, James threw himself on his lumpy bed and stared at the ceiling, hands linked behind his head, wallowing in his loneliness. There was no one in this city who knew him, no one who cared whether he went out or stayed inside. He felt as rootless as a dandelion seed spinning in the wind. Out of doors, life carried on without him. The Red Lion, on Exeter Street, was one of the better establishments near the harbor in Plymouth, but even it could not remove itself from the noise that went with being one of England's busiest ports. James, who had thought he had little to learn about low life after being in the army, had garnered a few new curses listening in to the exchanges on the street below, thanks to the drabs that earned their living from the tides of sailors that flowed in and out of the town. The girls' tongues were as sharp and colorful as their clothes.

A tap at the door interrupted his solitude.

"My lord?" The landlord stuck his head into the room, hesitant to disturb the moody occupier of his best chamber.

"What is it, Jarvis?"

"There's a blackamoor below—claims he's in your service, sir."

"What?" James sat up. Diego here? Was there bad news? Had something happened to Jane—or to his family?

The portly landlord tucked his thumbs in the strings of his apron and nodded sagely. "So you don't know him, then. Thought as much. I'll send him off with a flea in his ear."

Moving quickly to dispel the misunderstanding, James got to his feet. "No, no. He's my man. Send him up."

A few moments later, Diego arrived outside the door, taking in the messy lair in which James had been brooding for two days now like a lion nursing a sore paw.

"I see you did not engage another man as yet, my lord." Diego ventured across the threshold and picked up a shirt lying in a rumpled heap on top of a pair of muddy boots. "Or, if you did, you must sack him at once—he is not worth his wage."

James smiled, swamped with relief to see his man's familiar face back where it should be—at his side. He hadn't realized how much he had missed his closest companion. "It was such liberation to be rid of my last plague of a servant that I thought I would shift for myself."

"And that was such a good plan." Diego put the boots outside the door for a serving boy to clean.

James thought that Diego did not look like a messenger bearing bad tidings, but that still did not answer the question of what he was doing there. "You bring news?"

"No, sir."

"Then why are you here? Did you fall out with your lady love?"

Diego touched his talisman—the one round his neck that he refused to take off even when bathing. "No, sir. It was she who sent me to you. With the Lady Jane's blessing and assistance, for you forgot to pay me my earnings for the last quarter."

James thumped his forehead, cursing himself for being ten types of fool. Of course Diego hadn't come for him. "I left you stranded in London and you've come to collect what I owe you. You should've gone to the earl—he'd've seen to your pay without putting you to the trouble of crossing half of England."

"I did not come for my wages." Diego opened the window and shook out James's cloak, which was covered in horsehair and straw.

James scratched his head. "Diego, I am not a wizard skilled in reading the minds of stubborn African servants."

Diego stopped his tidying and turned to face James, his expression taking on a steely cast, as if he anticipated an argument. "I came because it is my duty to accompany you on this voyage. I promised your brother I would do so."

James felt queasy from the pitch and toss of hope and

disappointment, like a landlubber on his first rough sea. Though he wanted the companion, he couldn't take Diego with him just because the servant felt obliged to his family—that would not be fair. "And I released you from that promise, remember? You have a duty now to Mistress Porter."

"I also came because Milly brought me to my senses. I want to be with you on this adventure." Diego picked up a discarded doublet and brushed off the dust. "We have been together for the last year, and I . . . You have my loyal service, my lord."

Being a man of action and plain dealing, James did not claim great skill at reading the meanings hidden behind surface words as a subtler mind could do. Yet, if he was not mistaken, Diego had just confessed that he felt a kind of friendship towards him. For what was camaraderie between men but a mutual promise to stand shoulder to shoulder? Having felt so worthless, James was moved that Diego, who knew all his weaknesses, could still feel that way about him.

"I should refuse to take you with me."

"But you will not, my lord, because you recognize that you need a servant with you on this journey—one who understands you."

James flexed his fingers, annoyed at how thankful he was that he was no longer alone. "Oh God," he groaned, "I just know I am going to be selfish and agree to take you with me."

"And that is what I want, sir. You should understand that it is also what my lady love desires. And yours." Diego held out a pocketful of coins.

"What's this?"

"Funds for our expedition—courtesy of the Lady Jane."

James swallowed, his throat closing with emotion that he was not comfortable in displaying even before Diego. He turned away to the window. Jane should have sent him curses, not money and a companion.

"Now, my lord, we must think how best to make ourselves ready for our adventure, and that includes what we can do to make sure we will come back. My Milly thinks the only way to persuade you not to do anything reckless is to tell you that she fully expects you to return me to London safe and sound."

James raised an eyebrow at being lectured, albeit at a distance, by a seamstress.

Diego smiled knowingly at his expression. "You have only met her once, my lord, but my lady in a temper is quite a sight. It might involve scissors."

For the first time in days, James laughed. "'Swounds! That I would like to see."

"Like the wildcat of my homeland, she may be small, but she packs in a lot of power, my lord. I would not stand in the way of her claws."

James grinned. "Sound advice about any irate female, I would say."

"I am glad you say that, for I have been promised similar retribution from the marchioness should I not bring you back in one piece. I trust you will not abandon me to that lioness's paws."

James dropped into the chair by the fireplace and kicked up his heels to rest on the low bench. "So we are to be governed by the ladies in this?"

"Aye, my lord. You had better submit gracefully."

James threw his arms wide. "So be it; I submit, Diego." Before adding in a serious tone: "And thank you. I am more grateful than I can say."

The two captains of Raleigh's tiny fleet greeted James and his servant on board the *Dorothy* the following day. The ships bound for America were currently bobbing at anchor in Sutton Harbor in sight of the city of Plymouth, with its thicket of roofs and steeples. As they discussed the voyage over the best charts available, Arthur Barlowe impressed James with his calm demeanor and obvious experience—James rather hoped he would be spending the voyage on the vessel Barlowe commanded. Philip Amadas, by contrast, was a small firebrand of a man, spitting with temper and barely suppressed violence. He had already made an enemy of both James and Diego by pushing the servant out of his way with unnecessary force as they came into the cabin. Angry and impatient with life, Amadas would surely make for a capricious captain in the long days at sea.

"We leave as soon as our last stores are aboard," Barlowe explained to James. "We should make landfall in America two months later."

James studied Barlowe's weatherbeaten fingers tracing lines on the maps as if he could see the ships crossing with similar ease. The captain had square nails; one thumb was tinged with a bluish cast where it had got trapped in a hatch. Such workaday hands inspired confidence, proclaiming that this was a man who knew every inch of his vessel and was not above turning his skills to the necessary duties. "You have a full crew, captain?"

Barlowe's face cracked into a wry smile. "Not yet, lad—I mean,

Master Lacey. There aren't many tars in Plymouth keen to sail anywhere near the Spanish Americas—they've heard what has happened to others who've fallen into the hands of the Inquisition—not pretty."

James knew all about the Inquisition from its work in the Low Countries; his sympathies were entirely with the reluctant sailors. "But you're not worried that we won't be able to man the ships?"

Barlowe rolled up the chart. "Have no fear, sir. About a week before we depart, I'll start a rumor in the alehouses of Spanish gold—that's the medicine to purge the Inquisition rot. We'll have Englishmen lining up on the shore to be taken aboard."

"They should come for England's honor!" Amadas threw the remark over his shoulder as he rummaged through the chest of charts to find one of the Caribbean.

Barlowe clapped him on the back with the ease of long familiarity. "But, Philip, not everyone has your high principles. At least we know where we stand with the men if good old honest avarice can be relied on to keep them happy in our service."

The tour of the ships was brief, as they were each no larger than a tennis court. James was pleased with his accommodation, a small cabin near the captain's berth on the *Bark Raleigh*, which he would share with Diego. The bunk was too short for him, and he could touch both walls if he stood in the center and stretched out his arms, but he knew it was palatial compared to the accommodation given to ordinary seamen.

Diego sniffed. "At least you will not be able to make much of a mess, sir. Less work for me."

"Watch yourself!" growled James good-humoredly, rather enjoying the less servile attitude his servant had acquired since their brief separation in London. He felt he was for the first time really seeing the man behind the servant; Diego was no longer hiding so many of his thoughts from his master. "If you don't behave, I'll leave you with the Indians."

Diego scoffed at that, but continued with his exploration of the meager storage space allowed them.

"You have more experience of long voyages, Diego: what do you think we will need?" James asked, ceding the reins to him on this matter.

"Stout shoes, heavy coats—and a lot of luck."

"We can buy the former and pray for the latter."

Diego toed the vile chamber pot back under the bunk. "Oh, and, sir, I think I should remind you of something."

James flicked through the moldy-looking bedding on the bunk, making a mental note to bring his own. "Foul—I swear I can see the lice. What's that?"

"I get seasick."

James raised his eyes to heaven, only now recalling the hellish crossing of the Channel in Diego's company. Wonderful. "Then let's also pray that, on this voyage, I don't."

Greenwich Palace, south bank of the Thames

Life was most definitely not fair. Not only had Jane just said farewell, perhaps forever, to the man she loved, she was now being ordered to pretend to be enamored of an unlovable Frenchman.

"He's a fine man!" her father blustered once he had cornered her in a corridor of Greenwich Palace to give her a piece of his mind. "Most girls would jump at the chance to wed him."

Jane tapped her foot irritably, making the pearls dangling from her ears judder. "I am not 'most girls,' Father. It seems my standards are somewhat higher." She curtsied and attempted an escape.

"Come, Janie, can't you even pretend to a semblance of liking for the man, enough to accompany him to the Easter Day celebrations?" her brother cajoled, cutting off her retreat on the other side so that she was herded into the doorway to her chamber. She stayed where she was, preferring to remain in the public areas of the palace with her loving family, knowing they were not averse to resorting to violence to get their way.

"Henry, I can think of no redeeming features upon which I can build even the faintest pretense. It would be a mere snowflake, melting on the first breath of laughter. No one would believe it."

Henry glanced across to the flushed face of their father—the earl looked on the point of a seizure, so angered was he by a daughter who exercised her own judgment. "Father, give me a moment with her alone."

Thaddeus reluctantly withdrew farther up the corridor, muttering vile threats against rebellious Eve's daughters.

"Janie, my sweet, I've been talking to your maid," Henry began casually, leaning over her with his hand planted on the wall beside her head.

Jane snorted. "Debauching her, more like. No wonder she's been so hostile of late."

"She's a talkative little thing abed."

Jane rolled her eyes. "Really, Henry, I think you would have the decency to spare me the details."

He gave a lupine smile. "She mentioned your habit of disappearing into the city for the flimsiest of excuses."

The blood drained from Jane's face.

"First I speculated that my not-so-proper sister was concealing a lover—I'm still not sure that isn't the case—but consider my wonder when I discovered an old acquaintance had taken up residence in Silver Street. How is dear Milly, Janie?"

"You . . . you remember Milly?"

"Who could forget the little redhead and her disgrace of a father? I recall also that you were particular friends but were ordered by our worthy sire to sever all ties."

Trying to dampen down the flare of panic, Jane twisted her hands together hidden in her long sleeves, squeezing them tightly to keep control of her reactions. "I'm an independent lady now, Henry. I can do as I wish—consort with whom I like."

"Not . . . quite," he replied, his eyes hard.

"Please, Henry, leave it alone!" Stupid, stupid to appeal to his mercy—he had never possessed that quality.

"It made me wonder what you might have done to help her into her present employment. Did your doddering husband approve of your friendship, or maybe he was too senile to realize what you were about? What would Richard Paton find if he examined more closely the family holdings in London, I wonder? I can't imagine that a new business like Mistress Porter's would survive if ejected from its tenancy so soon, before it had a chance to establish itself properly."

Jane closed her eyes. "What do you want me to do?"

"Marry the Frog. We don't even ask you to bed him—Lord knows I doubt him capable of handling a girl like you—but you've been a virgin wife once, so that won't be so distasteful, will it?"

She could feel the prison bars descending around her—marriage this time would not be an escape but a trap.

Henry brushed her cheek with sickening tenderness, his cold blue eyes warmed for once by his sincerity. "You don't understand Father and me—we don't want you to be unhappy, Janie. We only want you to do your part furthering the family's interests."

That was his perspective, not one she could share when she was the chosen sacrifice. "You would condemn me to this barren mockery of a marriage?"

He chuckled. "Come now, we are not so cruel. No one will mind if, after a decent interval, you look for solace elsewhere. Even a bastard son will be better than nothing—I'm sure Montfleury will not mind. Look at the great families—all of them have a few cuckoos in the nest."

"You want me married and at the same time preach the virtues of adultery?" Her brother's cynicism still had the power to shock her.

He shrugged. "The rules aren't quite the same for men like Montfleury. No wife of mine would dare stray, but the Frenchman will regard your lapses philosophically, even welcome the fact that some other gentleman is seeing to your pleasure."

She shoved him in the chest to gain breathing room. "You disgust me."

"I take it you will submit to your family's will?"

In the darkness engulfing her, Jane grasped at the single glimmer of hope. "You forget the Queen. She has not approved the match."

"Ah, that is where you come in, my dear sister. If you show yourself ready and willing, she is unlikely to stand in your way. The prerogatives of the crown only stretch so far; she will not risk offending the nobility over so slight a matter."

"But I'm not willing."

He sighed. "Then I fear dear Milly is out of business."

"I hate you."

"I can live with that. You yield?"

Jane couldn't bring herself to speak the words, so she nodded instead, thinking to buy herself the time to avert the danger to her friend. She would go along with this pretense only so far; even saving Milly's livelihood was not enough for her to enter into this marriage.

Henry patted her cheek. "Good girl." He stepped back. "Father, Jane has agreed—as I told you she would. Let's take her to Montfleury before she has a chance to change her mind."

Thaddeus beamed at his son, his pride and joy. "That's grand, lad. The Frog's waiting in my chamber."

"Wait! What's going on?" Jane tried to resist as they dragged her, one on each arm, to the Earl of Wetherby's apartments.

Henry nodded to an acquaintance as they passed through the courtyard. "Smile, my dove—we wouldn't want anyone to whisper you were coerced, now would we?" He squeezed her arm. "You see, Janie, your life is going to change this day. Overcome by the violence of his passion for our English rose, the gallant French suitor is going to declare his love and enter an impulsive engagement. Your aged parent will find you in a compromising embrace that makes the need to wed imperative to preserve your good name. Both of you will then throw yourselves on the mercy of the Queen, pleading the impetuosity of youth as your excuse."

"No, stop! I need time! Stop!"

"Time to wiggle out of our agreement? I think not."

Her father shook her. "Just do as you are told, daughter, for once in your ungrateful life!"

Reaching his rooms, Thaddeus bellowed to his servants: "Out!"

The attendants scattered, leaving the apartment clear of witnesses. Montfleury rose from his chair by the fire, delicately dabbing the last crumbs of his breakfast from his upper lip.

"You have found my beloved?" He smiled and bowed with a flick of the same napkin he had just used. To be fair, Jane could allow that Montfleury had his own style, a courtly elegance in his movements when he was not nervous, but he was unthinkable as a husband.

"As you see, my lord. We'll leave you to do the rest." Thaddeus turned back to his daughter, ringing her neck lightly with his hands and squeezing. "Do not fail me, Jane!"

Henry released her arm. "Remember Silver Street."

The two Percevals quit the room, leaving the field clear for the lovers.

Jane's wits were in a flutter of panic—she needed more time; she had to think her way out of this situation.

"My lady, you are more beautiful each time I see you." Montfleury kissed his fingers and sent the salute wafting towards her. "I am not unhappy to be your chosen one."

Chosen one? Jane felt like a player thrust on stage in a play where he had not had time to learn the lines. She struggled to muster her dignity. "Sir, I know that my father is eager to see the union of our two houses."

Montfleury skipped towards her. "As am I, madame. Passionately eager."

Unlikely. "But I beg your indulgence. I need more time to consider your kind proposal. I am scarcely out of mourning my first husband and loath to take another so soon."

Montfleury grasped her wrist and raised her hand to his mouth. Before Jane could stop him, he began peppering her skin with wet kisses. "You will be an ornament to the house of Valère. *Mon père* will be most pleased with you."

Jane tugged her hand free. "But it is you who will have to wed me, sir. Forgive me, but I am under the impression that a wife will not add to your happiness."

"*Au contraire,* I am ravished by your beauty and feminine accomplishments." The little nobleman made a grab for her waist, pulling her towards him. Jane had forgotten how deceptively strong he had proved himself at the archery tournament. It all felt horribly false—he was no more attracted to her than to a stone.

"Please, sir, unhand me."

"And your dowry sweetens the medicine, *n'est-ce pas?*" He maneuvred her towards the earl's bed until the mattress hit the back of her legs.

"Stop this!" Jane tried to bat away his hands, which were now busy disturbing her clothes to make it look like they were caught in the throes of passion.

"As soon as we have accomplished our purpose here." He fell forward on her, pushing her back on the bed.

"No, stop!" Jane heaved in great breaths of his cloying perfume as she wrestled to get herself free, her skirts rucking up in the struggle. It would almost have been funny to have such a reluctant ravisher if his purpose had not been so serious.

The chamber door crashed back on its hinges.

"What is this? Oh, merciful heavens, what naughty behavior confronts a loving father's eyes?" declaimed the earl. "And before so many witnesses."

Jane struggled all the harder, guessing that her wretched situation was being paraded before half the Queen's household. This was insupportable!

"Father, do not look—it will be too much for your poor heart. My sister—discovered on a bed with a man! Oh, rue the day! I fear she is compromised beyond all chance of redemption." Henry picked Montfleury up by the back of his doublet, hauling him off Jane. "Sir, you may be a lord, but you must answer to the lady's family. She is not without protectors."

The Frenchman knew his script even if Jane did not. He struck his breast dramatically. "Sir Henry, be not alarmed. The lady has just done me the great honor of agreeing to be my wife. You interrupted us when our mutual delight overflowed into an exchange of passionate kisses—we cry you mercy."

"Ah, then all is changed. You display a forgivable weakness in the circumstances." The earl clasped Montfleury's arm in two hands and gave it a hearty shake. "My horror turns to joy to know I am to gain such a noble son-in-law. Jane, come kneel for my blessing."

Jane was lost for words. Trying to put her disheveled clothing to rights, she got to her feet. Could she repudiate the match before these witnesses? Her father had gathered a flock of his northern cronies, dour barons and sharp-tongued ladies, long necks craning over shoulders like inquisitive geese, all ready to fall into line with the powerful earl's interpretation of the ridiculous scene.

"Kneel before our father, Janie," murmured Henry, guiding her with an uncompromising grip to a spot on the floor in front of him.

Jane decided that saying nothing at all was the best she could do in the circumstances. Her knees reluctantly folded as she knelt before her sire. His hand rested on her head, heavy with authority. He had her just where he had always wanted her.

"Bless you, my child. May this union prove a happy one for both England and France."

Inside, where none could see, Jane wept.

CHAPTER 14

St. Paul's Cathedral, London

THE ONLY PEOPLE LESS PLEASED THAN JANE with the announcement of a match between the houses of Valère and Wetherby were the Patons. If Jane's marriage settlements encompassed the money she had brought with her to the Rievaulx estate and she maintained control of her dower properties for her lifetime, Richard Paton would be much impoverished and would have scant hope of chasing her wealth through the courts of England *and* France. This thought gave Jane a little sour satisfaction in the midst of the terrible bind in which she found herself.

The Queen had not yet given her permission, but neither had she forbidden the marriage. Jane felt the sovereign's shrewd eyes on her as she went about her duties in the privy chamber, but she knew that Elizabeth hated being dragged into other people's emotional tangles. To be sure, the Queen had enough on her plate these days with the prolonged and tortuous breakdown of the marriage of the Earl and Countess of Shrewsbury. Compared to the scandal engulfing two of the realm's most significant figures, a little trouble between a lady-in-waiting and an obscure French noble was not worth much thought.

Montfleury, or Clément, as he insisted his *chère Jeanne* call him, did not accost her again—not that she had expected another outburst of passion now that he had lost his audience. He made a great show of squiring her to court events, such as the one they were attending at present: Easter Day service at St. Paul's Cathedral. Jane sat next to him close to the pulpit, only half paying attention to the long sermon. Around her posed the flowers of the court, dressed in magnificent new clothes to celebrate the Savior's resurrection. She had chosen to wear black. Montfleury was decked in purple and rose-striped silk. She thought that said it all.

Jane's eyes traveled over the inattentive congregation and up to the rainbow patterns of the stained-glass windows. A bird had somehow gotten in and was flying across the nave, frantic to escape. It crashed into one clear glass pane, then fluttered to rest on the rood screen before trying a new escape. Jane found herself rooting for its success, but unless it left the heights and flew down to the open west doors there was little prospect it could find the way out alone. Tears pooled in Jane's eyes as it struck another window and fell, stunned, to the ground. It lay there in imminent danger of being trampled.

Jane couldn't let it die. She got up from her seat and pushed her way past the others in her row to escape to the side aisle. Montfleury raised an ineffectual protest, but she brushed his fingers off the back of her skirt. The priest faltered in his peroration but then continued, raising his voice a notch. Rushing to the bird before a careless boot put an end to its life, Jane scooped it up in her handkerchief. She could feel the heart beating incredibly fast, the poor bird terrified out of its wits. She had to get it outside. Pushing through a curious crowd, Jane forced passage to the west doors. Those who could not fit into the cathedral on this great festival thronged the steps—she couldn't leave the bird here in any safety. She headed to the north side of the cathedral and into the churchyard, empty today of the usual stalls selling books and pamphlets. Finding a likely tree, she went up on tiptoe to lay the bird in a forked branch and then stepped back to give it time to recover from its fright. The bird—a blackbird, she now saw—lay quiet for a moment, its round bead of an eye fixed on her, yellow beak stark against the inky plumage. Then it flapped to its feet, shaking off paralysis, and launched into the sky. Circling once, it landed on the top branch of the tree and broke into a paean of thanksgiving for its freedom. Jane felt a wild surge of joy that she had managed to save this one creature—a delight out of all proportion to the event. She looked around her to see who had witnessed the bird's resurrection. None of the fashionable crowd was in sight; she was alone, apart from an audience of beggars and cripples who usually haunted the churchyard. They probably thought her a mad-woman come to join their number.

Or a pocket to be picked.

With no wish to make herself a more likely target by standing still, Jane wrapped her black cloak tightly around her, glad that her sober outer garments would not attract attention for anything but their quality; then she started walking. She had never been on the streets on her own before. Neither her family nor her attendants had followed her out; she presumed they had lost sight of her in the Eas-ter crowds. A bubble of absurd pleasure welled up inside—she was free! What would they do if she just kept on going and lost herself in the city? All their stupid plots would fail—their alliance would be at an end. They had taken her compliance as a given, but they still needed her body present in the church to make the ridiculous farce of a marriage. What if she denied them that?

Laughing out loud, Jane hurried on, turning right onto Paternoster Row, then on to the broad expanse of Cheapside. Perhaps she was acting a little mad, but the escape was so enticing she did not care. They had pushed her to her limits and she had snapped free.

The streets were packed with citizens out to celebrate the Easter holiday, heading to and from the many Masses being said in all the churches. Bells rang peals, the sound shivering to pieces the icy detachment that Jane had been in for the past few weeks, reminding her that there was still love and life to be had in the world.

"Christ is risen, Alleluia!" called out one gap-toothed maid, heading the other way in a new straw hat.

"He is risen indeed, Alleluia!" Jane replied, giving the proper Eastertide response. She had to stop herself from grabbing the girl's hands and swinging her in an impromptu reel.

A young couple came out of one of the fine houses near the turning to Forster Lane, the wife cradling a babe in arms, another flaxen-haired infant hanging on her skirts. The father scooped up the little one and put her on his shoulders. Jane followed them northwards as they headed for Cripplegate and the fields beyond the city walls, an Easter family outing being risked despite the cloudy weather. She envied them their simple joys; she could not remember her father ever treating his family to an expedition, nor did she think the earl had ever swung her onto his shoulders.

As the family turned into Silver Street, Jane realized that she had unconsciously been heading towards Milly's. Her friend's shop was closed for the holiday, of course, and it was more than likely that

Milly would be out enjoying herself with friends. Still, Jane had no other commitments this day; she could at least leave a message and Easter greetings before she went on her way.

She rapped on the door.

No answer.

Jane stood with her back against the portal and closed her eyes to enjoy the shaft of sunlight bathing the step. She could wait. After all, there was nothing else worth doing.

Jane had missed Milly by an hour. Milly's father had arrived that morning, hotfoot from his duties on the continent, in high dudgeon to have received a letter from his former servant. Barely had they exchanged the usual greetings when he launched into the real reason he had won permission from his commander to return to London.

"What's all this, Milly? Have you taken leave of your senses? You can't seriously think you can marry that boy!"

Milly had forgotten how difficult her father was in person, finding it easier to love him at a distance. She tried to defer the subject, arguing that they must hurry or miss the service at St. Olave's across the street, but Silas was not to be deterred. He had had the length of a rough sea crossing to marshal his arguments and was determined to wheel out his battalions and beat his daughter's resistance into submission.

"I can't sit in church with this hanging over us." Silas flicked a dismissive hand to his cloak, which she tried to pass him.

"Father, it is not a subject that can be settled in five minutes—and that is all we have before the Mass begins. Do you want to pay the fine for missing the service?"

Silas grumped at that but followed her downstairs and into the little parish church. Milly had never thought she would be grateful for the Queen's laws that made missing Sunday worship a punishable offense, but this day she muttered a prayer of thanks for her stay of execution.

When the service finished, Milly suggested to her father that they walk in Moorfields beyond Cripplegate. If they were going to argue, she would prefer to do so without an avid audience of her apprentices and servants.

"Where did you stay last night?" she asked, trying for a neutral opening to their conversation.

"At the Swan with Two Necks, Wood Street," Silas replied, limping slightly as he escorted his daughter northwards and out of the city. "Arrived too late to disturb you."

"Thank you for your courtesy. You will of course stay with me for the rest of your leave?"

"If you'll have me." Silas glanced sideways at his girl, his gray-green eyes frowning at her from under his wiry salt-and-pepper brows. His hair and beard had gone the same color over the last few years, the result of his disgrace and subsequent incarceration in the Tower. He was still a stocky man, only five feet and some six inches, but no one would underestimate his fighting strength when they saw the breadth of his shoulders.

"You will always be welcome in my home, Father."

He sucked his cheeks in briefly, then let out a huff. "You're a good girl—done well for yourself, Milly. I know I've not been much of a father to you of late."

She pressed his arm. "I always knew you would have done more if you could. I was fortunate in my patron."

"Aye, the Lady Jane turned out to be a trump card. That surprised me—I always thought her consumed with vanity, and cold-hearted, even as a youngster."

"She's been a good friend. As has Diego."

Silas resisted his instinctive response to that remark, as they were in the midst of other holidaymakers out for a walk, instead confining himself to a grunt. He followed Milly's prompting and took the less-frequented sandy path between the laundresses' drying grounds until they reached a grove of trees. Someone had fashioned a bench of fallen logs beneath the bare canopy of the silver-barked beech.

"This is as good a spot as any for what I have to say." Silas handed his daughter to the seat, then stood in front of her with his arms clasped behind him. "You can't marry a blackamoor, Milly. It's just not done."

Milly squeezed her hands together. "Do you think Diego a good person, Father?"

"He's a loyal servant, I can say that for him."

"Is it only the color of his skin you object to?"

Silas scowled. "He's a servant."

"Take a look at me, Father. So am I these days—in service to my customers. There is little to separate us in rank."

Silas could not argue with that; it was his fall from grace that had brought about her own tumble from gentility. "He sent me word that he would *pay* me for you—some nonsense about buying the equivalent of many heads of cattle! As if I would sell my own daughter!"

Milly bit her lip. Oh, foolish Diego and his herd of cows! "He means to honor me—and you—as would be done in his country. There the groom pays for the bride."

Silas waved that away as if it were of no consequence. "And is he even a Christian, I ask you?"

"He respects our religion," Milly said carefully, knowing that Diego had a frighteningly all-encompassing view of faith—he did not deny the truths of Christianity, but neither did he renounce the gods of his upbringing. She was rather more orthodox in her views and had hopes she could influence him over time into a more correct path. "He's been baptized." Three times, in fact, by three different masters, he had confessed to her.

Silas stamped on a stick, snapping it in half. "And what of your children—they'd be neither one thing nor another—it isn't natural, I tell you."

Milly suppressed a shiver of excitement at the thought of bearing Diego a family. He was so protective of her; she guessed that he would make a wonderful if overanxious father. "They'd be loved and welcomed by both parents—what could be more natural than that?"

"But, Milly, just look at him. He's . . . he's not English!"

Milly knew this was the heart of the matter—a bone-deep prejudice against the foreigner, particularly one who announced his otherness in his skin. "I look at him, Father, and I see the boy who stayed faithful to me during our troubles, and a man who loves me now and will, I believe, carry on loving me in the future."

Silas kicked the broken pieces of wood into the undergrowth, disturbing a sparrow from her nest. "I suppose I gave up my right to order your life when I betrayed our country and you."

Milly touched her bracelet for comfort. "I will always listen to your advice."

"He might not come back from this expedition of Raleigh's."

"He'll return."

"You'll need my permission to marry, as you are underage."

"And I hope you will grant it. Otherwise we'll have to wait."

"You're set on this course? Do you really see all the difficulties your union will face—the hatred and plain spite of others?"

Milly took heart that he was ceding ground, talking as if the marriage was a real possibility. "I think I do. It will be much easier if I know I have your blessing."

He shook his head. "I'm not sure I can give you that, Milly. Not yet."

Outright opposition was what she feared; neutrality she could live with. "Wait until you see Diego again, Father. You'll understand why to me he is worth all the trouble."

Silas reached for her and tenderly cupped her jaw in his rough hand. "Stubborn wench."

Her eyes pricked with tears, knowing he had surrendered the power of decision to her. "Thank you, Father."

"I hope you have no cause to regret your choice. I know what it is like to live with the consequences of a calamitous decision."

She went up on tiptoe and kissed his cheek. "Come, let's break our fast at home. I have some fresh-baked manchet and honey."

He offered her his arm once more. "You know me well. An army marches best with a full stomach, and mine is as empty as a soldier's purse before payday."

Father and daughter arrived home to find the Silver Street household in confusion. Henny had returned from church only to discover a marchioness sitting on the doorstep. She had invited the lady into the shop but had then been at a loss what to do next. Old Uriah hadn't helped matters by saying loudly in the kitchen that the visitor had clearly run mad, as she had turned up in the middle of

London with no escort and no explanation for what she was doing there.

"My lady." Milly dipped a curtsy on finding Jane humming to herself in her shop.

"Milly!" Jane jumped to her feet. "Guess what? I escaped!" She put her fingers to her lips to suppress a giggle.

"Are you . . . are you quite well, my lady?" Milly glanced over her shoulder at her father, begging him with her gaze to go into the back kitchen. But she wasn't quick enough; Jane spotted him.

"Oh, Master Porter, you are here! Did you escape too?"

Silas bowed. "Aye, in a sense, my lady, but with my commander's permission. Good to see you again, lass, after all these years. Why don't you sit down? You are a little flushed from your walk."

He was right. Milly realized that Jane looked almost feverish.

"Oh no, it was a lovely walk—quite the best thing to happen to me all April. I caught this bird, you see." Jane frowned, ordering her thoughts. "No, not so much caught as saved—it was caught—in the cathedral. I let it out. Then I thought I'd leave them all behind. I told myself, why not?"

Milly was distressed to see that her friend was rubbing her arms under her sleeves, leaving red scratch marks.

"Whom did you leave, my lady?" Silas glanced out the window, expecting to see some sign of a search for her. A noblewoman did not go missing without someone setting out in pursuit.

Jane grimaced. "My loving family. They're trying to make me marry this Frenchman—not really a man, more a stuffed doublet. I told them no, but then they made it look as if I did want to and . . . and . . ." Her frantic humor was winding down, returning her to despondency. "And . . . oh, Milly, I'm in such a tangle! I have to marry him now. Even the Queen expects it. I thought I could walk away, but now that I think about it, where would I go?"

Milly took Jane's hands to stop her from doing any more damage to her poor skin. "You can stay here, of course."

Jane shook her head, tears spilling from her eyes. "No, no, they know about you. Henry said he'd tell the Patons and they'd break your tenancy—throw you out. That's how it all started—how they got me involved in this farce of a marriage."

Silas scowled. "Don't you worry about that, my lady. I'm here now. I'll talk to my lass's landlord."

Jane smiled through her tears. "I'm glad, sir, but they'll still come for me. I'm surprised they're not here already." The ramifications of what she had done were now occurring to her. "It'll suit my father to claim I took leave of my senses and went wandering: if he can't make me marry Montfleury, he'll be as happy to claim I am insane. Either outcome gives him control of me."

"Well, we can't have that, can we?" Milly announced brightly. "What can be more natural than a holiday visit to old friends? We met by chance when you left the sermon for a breath of air and I persuaded you to walk—most properly under the chaperonage of my father—in the fields."

"Is that what I did?" Jane reclaimed her hands and folded them across her chest, squeezing her elbows. She turned her blue eyes to the ceiling, trying to pretend they weren't swimming in tears. "Oh God, I have to go back, don't I?"

Milly wished she could make a different reply, but Jane was one of the Queen's ladies, not any old courtier free to come and go on a whim. "I'm afraid so, my dear."

Making a visible effort to pull herself together, Jane straightened her shoulders. Milly felt very proud of her; it was like watching a soldier willingly face a bombardment of enemy guns. "Then I wish you a happy Easter. If I could prevail upon your father to escort me back to the cathedral, I believe I will have people waiting for me there."

"It would be my honor, my lady." Silas clicked his heels together and bowed smartly.

Jane took his proffered arm. "Any advice, sir: one prisoner to another, I mean?"

Silas gave a sour laugh. "Take a good book to pass the time and don't trust the food."

CHAPTER 15

MILLY WATCHED THEM GO WITH TREPIDATION. She'd never seen her friend like that, so completely at the end of her tether, close to the breaking point. All that the Earl of Wetherby had done to Jane before to force her cooperation, she had resisted; now her family were about to crush her with their schemes. Milly suspected that James's rejection had softened her friend before the blow, making her all the more vulnerable.

"Oh, I could kill him." Milly stabbed a long pin into her heart-shaped cushion. "James Lacey has a lot to answer for."

Before she could think twice about it, she snatched a piece of paper from her writing desk and quickly scrawled a letter to Diego.

> *Silver Street*
> *19th April 1584*
> *My darling,*
>
> *You will laugh at my fickleness after I just sent you off to Plymouth, but I need both you and your master to return to London as soon as may be. Lady Jane is being forced into marriage and has urgent need of her friends. Please beg your master to put aside this voyage and*

come to her rescue. *I fear only someone of his standing will be able to help her escape. I know she loves him and I believe he cares for her too, else I would not presume to ask him to make this sacrifice. Whatever barrier he has put between their finding happiness together will surely crumble when he realizes that he is condemning her to be yoked forever in a miserable match.*

Hurry home.

Your own Milly

P.S. My father has arrived soon after receiving your letter. What were you thinking offering to buy me with cows! However, he is coming round to the idea of our getting married, but you need to be here to persuade him to take the final few steps.

There, that ought to do it. She quickly wrote a covering note to James Lacey, enclosing hers to Diego within. Her only problem was finding a messenger able to carry the letter to Plymouth—and she could think of only one man for the task.

Milly knocked on the door to Christopher Turner's room, his landlady at her elbow. "Master Turner! Kit! Wake up!"

Dame Prewet shook her head and folded her arms. "I told you, Mistress Porter, he is a right one, our Master Turner—never out of bed on a holiday unless you put a rocket under him."

"For God's sake, Kit, this is urgent!"

The landlady extracted a key from her girdle and jiggled it in the lock. "He always takes the key out on his side in case I have to get him up. Sleeps like the dead, he does." She pushed the door open.

"Lord, has he been burgled?" Milly exclaimed, seeing the state of the room. Clothes were strewn on every surface, a side table overturned, papers scattered like autumn leaves after a gale.

"Nay, dear, this is him. Man in his natural state." The landlady gave the recumbent form of her favorite tenant an indulgent look. He was lying on his back, covered to the waist in a sheet, one arm thrown above his head. "He pays extra to have his room cleaned."

"I hope the maid gets money for the risk she takes—who knows what she might find in here: a sleeping dragon or a nest of Catholic conspirators?"

"More likely linen that should've gone in the buck basket." Dame Prewet strode bravely across the chamber and dropped her bunch of cold keys on Christopher's bare chest. "Wake up, Kit. Someone to see you."

Christopher shot to his feet, a flash of bare flank briefly revealing that he did not bother with clothes when he went to bed. Milly quickly covered her eyes.

"Fie on thee, woman, you gave me a seizure!" Christopher grumbled, grabbing the sheet to his chest. "I'm naked!"

Dame Prewet chuckled. "You haven't got anything I've not seen before, lad. You don't raise six boys and not be familiar with all there is to know about a boy's this and that."

Chistopher clutched the sheet tighter, groping through the piles of clothes to find a clean shirt. "Well, my 'this and that' is not used to being put on display to the neighbors."

"It's only Mistress Porter. She has an urgent business with you."

"Out the door, you pair of Peeping Tom-esses. I'll let you know when I'm decent."

Obediently, Milly went and stood in the hallway, trying not to laugh. Who would have thought Christopher Turner, bold declaimer of outrageous verses, could be so shy about being caught in his Garden of Eden glory? She had to admit, if she hadn't already been betrothed, there would have been plenty for a girl to admire.

The door flew open.

"All right. What's this about? Why can I not spend the Lord's holiday in bed as I had planned?"

Milly smiled at Dame Prewet. "Thank you for rousing this charming bear from his cave; I think I can take it from here."

Dame Prewet headed back to her kitchen. "Leave the door open, mistress. I don't want no scandalous goings-on in my house— or even rumors of such."

"You can trust me," promised Milly.

"But not him. Mother of six boys, me. I know all about—"

"This and that. Yes, I remember." Milly grinned.

Christopher ducked his head out the door. "Has she gone?"

Milly followed him into the room. "Yes, you're quite safe."

"She has no shame, that woman." He began haphazardly piling up belongings into teetering piles, trying to excavate a chair for her.

"Don't put yourself to the trouble, Kit. I'll sit here." She perched by the window. "You've a lovely view."

"Aye, if you stand on the sill you can see when the flag's raised at the theater."

The dear silly dreamer was lost to the stage. So many hopefuls and yet so few achieved success. "I was talking of the orchard and the herb garden."

Christopher sat on the edge of his bed. "So, Milly, what's this about? Trouble with your blackamoor?"

"His name is Diego. And no, thank you for asking. It's about a friend of mine. Her family are forcing her into a marriage she doesn't want."

Christopher pulled his cuffs free of his jacket, evening out the white frill. "Sadly, she wouldn't be the first. Can't she find someone to intercede for her? The vicar—he's a pleasant enough fellow when you stand him a drink."

"This isn't a little local matter, Kit. My friend's one of the Queen's ladies and a marchioness."

Christopher whistled. "Not that dazzling lady I've seen going into your shop many times of late? My, my, you do keep exalted company, mistress."

"Jane and I knew each other as children."

"And now she's in trouble?"

Milly nodded.

Christopher shrugged. "I suppose 'love is love, in beggars and in kings.' What do you want me to do?"

Milly twisted her fingers in her apron. "She's got to get away from her family. She needs to marry the right man for her."

Christopher winked. "All right. I'll wed her, then. Whisk her away from her unloved swain—save her from her greedy kin."

Milly laughed. "No, you dolt. She needs her true love—and that's not you." She held out her letter. "I've written to him begging him to return."

Christopher plucked the missive from her fingers. "And the lucky man is where, exactly?" He scanned the direction. "Plymouth? You're writing to *James Lacey*? I can't believe this. How absolutely perfect!" He threw back his head and crowed with laughter.

"Please, Kit, don't jest about this. I'm serious."

"I should've guessed: lady in trouble and where are the Laceys? Not there. You're wasting your time, Milly; he won't come back for her."

"You don't even know him; how can you say that?"

"Oh, but I do. I met my wonderful half brother a month or so ago. I'm the last person you want as a messenger, trust me."

Milly dug in her pocket and pulled out some coins. "I do trust you, Kit. Please, you are the only one I can ask to do this. It's even better if you know him, as you will not mistake the man. And I've enclosed a fuller explanation to Diego—he'll help persuade his master. Can you not put aside your family differences to help my friend? Just this once?"

Christopher refused to take the money. "Find someone else."

"Who, pray tell? My father is on his parole to stay in London, then return directly to his post. Old Uriah would fall off his horse before he reached Southwark. You are my only hope."

He flopped back on the bed. "I'm not hearing this."

"Yes, you are. Please, I beg you."

"Milly, Milly, you don't know what you're asking me."

"Yes, I do. I'm asking you to save a lovely girl from a terrible marriage. I'll pay double your expenses. Please."

He sat back up and ruffled his mop of curls. "S'blood, it's not about money."

Milly paced the room in a simmering fury. "What, then? Pride? Running errands to your brother pains you so much?"

He grimaced.

"My God, that's it. The mighty Christopher Turner doesn't want to humble himself. Why, I'm not so proud." Milly dropped on her knees. "By all the saints, Kit, I beg you: do this for me."

"Don't."

"I'll talk to your master—make sure you won't get into trouble at the theater."

With a groan, Christopher pulled her to her feet. "I'm not needed next week."

"Then you'll go?"

"You're a bully, do you know that?"

Milly shrieked and clapped her hands. "You're going! Oh, thank you, thank you! But you've got to hurry: they're sailing any day to America." She thrust a coat into his arms and the coins into his hand.

"What!" Christopher juggled the items she kept piling on to him.

"You had better leave at once. My father's got a horse waiting for you at the Swan with Two Necks, and I've already packed you a bag of provisions."

Christopher found himself propelled out onto his own landing with a little red whirlwind behind him gathering up clothes for the journey.

"I'll be forever in your debt," Milly announced solemnly, handing him a leather satchel of clean linen.

Christopher rolled his eyes. "And why do I not find that thought reassuring?"

Plymouth Harbor

A little flotilla of boats accompanied the *Dorothy* and the *Bark Raleigh* out into the Channel. The day was set fair, a good south-easterly wind wafting them on the first stage of their voyage. James stood on the poop deck with Captain Barlowe, enjoying the sensation of the ship plowing a straight furrow through the jade-green waters, a flock of seagulls wheeling overhead.

"Aye, it's good to be on the way at last," murmured Barlowe, giving voice to James's own thoughts. "How's your man?"

"Not good, sir. I left him in his bunk with a bucket."

Barlowe snorted, the uncomprehending reaction of the strong-stomached. "I'll send someone to him, my lord."

"Thank you, but I'll see to his care. I'm sure your men have their own duties to attend to."

"True enough." Barlowe checked their progress against the Plymouth Hoe. "Time to fire our parting salvo." He nodded to the gunner waiting for the order down on the main deck.

The seagulls scattered in alarm as the gun boomed, the echo rebounding across the water from the land. The crews of the little boats cheered, then turned back to harbor, leaving the two ships to continue alone. James stood at the rail, looking not to land but out to the sea yet to be crossed. He took a deep breath, enjoying the clean cut of salt air in his lungs. Strange, but ever since Diego had turned up at his inn a fortnight since, James's spirits had begun to rally. His know-it-all brother and his servant had been right: he needed this adventure. The horrors of war had encased him in a kind of emotional ice; now, in the spring sunshine, he felt that carapace crack and slide from his shoulders. He was beginning to believe that life was not so bad after all; there were still things to live for, new horizons to explore.

James's mood took a bit of a dip when he returned to his cabin to face his sickly servant. Poor Diego looked washed-out and a little gray in the face. Ships were never sweet-smelling, but this little cabin could badly do with an infusion of fresh air. James pushed open the window, grateful that they had been given accommodation high above the waterline. Covering his mouth with a neckerchief, he dealt with the worst of the mess and sluiced out the bucket with fresh water.

"Turning servant, master?" croaked Diego.

"Glad you can find some humor in the situation; you look like death."

"Gets better . . . eventually." Diego closed his eyes and curled up on his little bunk under James's own.

At a loss what to do with himself on the long stretch of hours on board ship, James pulled up a stool to the writing ledge bolted to the wall under the window. He took a piece of paper from his portmanteau and cut himself a pen from the stock of quills. There was always a chance they would pass a homebound vessel on their outward journey, so he should have a letter ready to hand over. But to whom did he want to write? He dipped his nib in the inkpot and scrawled the date across the top of the page.

To my dear

He lifted the pen, hesitating over writing his brother's name in the space. It wasn't Will he wanted to write to.

Lady Jane,

Greetings from afloat Neptune's playground. We have set sail from Plymouth at last and already I feel the change has wrought much good. Thus far the divine powers have been kind to us, giving us fair weather for our departure.

James frowned at what he had written. The weather! In courtly language too. Couldn't he do better than that?

I thank you from the bottom of my heart for sending Diego to accompany me. I must have taken leave of my senses to embark on this adventure alone. You and the good seamstress are both wiser than I.

There—something heartfelt. An improvement.

As I sit by my little window looking out on the chilly waters of the Channel, I regret only one thing— and that is the way I parted from you. I fear I left you without telling you how deeply I admire and

He paused again, his pen wanting to write *love* but his mind telling him that was not fair on the lady. His aim was to cheer her up, not make promises he could not be certain of keeping. He scratched out *and*, inserting *your character.*

My departure had nothing to do with what passed between us in the garden, bitterly sweet though the memory is. I left London to flee myself. I hope I will return a better man, more worthy of your friendship. Until I have the good fortune of seeing you again, I pray you will welcome my letters when I have the chance to send them to England. I miss our conversations, and it is a pleasant pastime to imagine that you are with me, listening to these words as I write them. In that way, I can think you are partner with me in this voyage, seeing the sights as I see them and sharing the same thoughts.

Too intimate? The pen hovered over the passage, but James couldn't bring himself to score it through. He meant every word. The lady had a grip on his heart no matter how he pretended otherwise. It was unlikely that she would receive the letter for many months, and by then she would doubtless look upon his affection for her as an amusing episode and would have moved on to new scenes, new interests in the busy life at court. He let it stand unchanged, folded the paper and put it away to add to it later. Perhaps he would never send it, but at least this way Jane would be with him on the voyage.

Silver Street

The rain hammered the streets of London, turning the gutters into muddy streams, disguising the people as hayrick-shaped bundles of clothing as they huddled under cloaks and blankets hurrying through the wet. Christopher clattered into Milly's shop, throwing his rain-sodden cloak to one side. She rushed to take his hat—he looked like he'd found every puddle between London and Plymouth.

"Did you see James Lacey?" she asked anxiously after sending Old Uriah into the kitchen so they could talk privately.

"Oh yes, I saw him."

"But—"

"I saw him standing on the deck of his ship heading out of port. I was in time to hear the parting salute, but not in time to catch up with him. Can you believe my luck?" He collapsed onto the stool by the fire and rubbed his chilled hands together.

"And there was no chance of overtaking him?"

"How so, Milly? They had a good wind and a fast ship. Unless I sprouted wings at my heels like Mercury, what hope had I?"

She hung the hat on the rack over the fireplace. "I pray you pardon me; that was a stupid question."

Christopher grunted. "I know I let you down. But whatever you might think, I really did make all speed. It's this infernal damp weather—roads are like quagmires. Damn near lost my horse near Exeter."

Milly left him briefly to fetch a tankard of strong ale, which she tapped from the barrel in the back kitchen. "Here, drink this. I know it's not your fault."

"I left a message with the innkeeper just in case the ships are beaten back by the weather. Your James Lacey will receive it immediately on his return." He sipped the brew. "Ah, this is good. So, tell me what news here? Have I lost my position at the theater for being away so long?"

Milly shook her head. "Of course not. I told your master that you were engaged on important business for a gentleman at court—a potential patron."

Christopher closed his eyes and smiled. "Clever. Your father still here?"

"Gone back to the Low Countries, but promises to return in the autumn."

"I like him. When he saw me to my horse last week, he sang your praises with every step. For a traitor, he's an uncommonly pleasant fellow."

Milly swatted the top of his head. "Hush, we no longer speak of that. It is in the past."

"And your friend?"

Her expression turned grim. "Her wedding is set for September. I don't know what we are going to do now that your mission has failed."

Christopher gave a philosophical shrug. "You tried your best, love. It's up to your friend to refuse the suitor."

Milly shook her head. "There speaks a man with the freedom to choose. You don't know what it's like to be in her shoes. Jane is under pressure from her family, the court and now even the Queen, as she has been swayed by Lord Wetherby's arguments that the match is a necessary one."

Still the actor could not sympathize with the plight of one of the realm's most privileged ladies. He swirled the contents of his tankard. "If your friend is rich, she'll find a way."

"Sometimes, being rich is not enough. Sometimes, it's the problem."

"Look on the bright side, Milly."

"And what's that?"

He gave her a wink over the brim of his cup. "All those wedding clothes—some lucky seamstress is going to prosper."

CHAPTER 16

DESPITE THE DISAPPOINTMENT that Christopher's mission had failed to catch the ship in time, Milly was conscious that she owed him a huge debt for his efforts on behalf of people he did not know well or, in the case of James, even like. Remembering the actor's love of eye-catching clothes, she worked quickly to make him a new hatband of gold and silver thread, embroidered with his initials. Two days after his return, she went to deliver it in person as the first installment of her thanks.

She had just stopped briefly in Dame Prewet's warm kitchen for a neighborly chat before seeing Kit when the attention of both was caught by a commotion in the street outside. Milly rushed to the window in time to see a fine-looking nobleman, fair-headed and dressed in serviceable riding clothes of russet wool and black velvet compass cloak, as he dismounted from his mud-splattered horse in front of the house. He was accompanied by two outriders and a young gentleman in blue venetians and doublet on a sorry specimen of a hack.

The nobleman and his companion consulted with each other briefly before the elder signaled to one of his servants to knock on the dame's door.

"Dame Prewet, what kind of company have you been keeping?" exclaimed Milly.

The dame brushed her apron smooth, flustered by the visitors. "Not me, my dear. Must be acquaintances of one of my lodgers."

Milly now noted the green livery of the servants and the familiar features in the boy's face. "It has to be Kit's family." She hugged herself in a mixture of delight and trepidation as the dame opened the door to her callers. Finally, Christopher was going to get the attention he deserved from his half brothers. Fate had been kind allowing her to be here to witness this—if she had missed this opportunity by arriving a few minutes later she would have simply died of frustrated curiosity.

"Mistress Prewet?" rumbled a deep voice. "My master, the Earl of Dorset, inquires if Master Turner is at home."

The dame was practically falling over her own feet to usher them in. "Of course, sir, bid your master to step inside if he be so kind as to enter my humble home." She flapped at Milly with her apron. "Run upstairs, Mistress Porter, if you would, and tell Master Turner to hurry. We mustn't keep an earl waiting!"

Milly lifted the hem of her skirts to take the stairs two at a time and then thumped on Christopher's chamber door. "Kit, Kit, make haste! Your brothers are here."

Silence.

Was Christopher from home? Knowing his feelings on the subject of the Laceys, she realized he could well be halfway out the window.

Not waiting for an invitation, Milly threw the door open. She caught Christopher in the process of donning his shirt, head hidden in the folds of white linen. He yanked it down roughly, ripping the shoulder seam. Milly rushed forward to help him.

"Leave it," growled Christopher, picking up his doublet.

"Didn't you hear me, Kit? The earl and the youngest one—Tobias, isn't it?—are in the kitchen!"

"I heard you. What are they to me?"

Milly tugged his doublet straight at the back to fasten the points to his trunk hose. "Don't be so foolish. You have held your grudge against the Laceys for far too long. It was their father, not them, who failed you."

"Let me be the judge of that."

Milly was tempted to wallop him one: he was far too set in his ways, casting himself as the beleaguered hero with the world against him. When the world showed signs of coming over to his side, his instinct was to grumble and run.

"Well," she said tersely, fastening the last point, "they have journeyed all this way to see you; it is only polite for you to receive them this day."

"I'll see them, for what good it will do." Christopher picked up his hat, reminding Milly of her errand.

"Here." She pressed the new band into his cold fingers. "For you. With my thanks for going to Plymouth."

His ridged features softened somewhat when he saw his initials—*C. T.*—embroidered with a flourish. "That is perfect." He put it on his velvet cap, making sure the decoration was prominently displayed. "I am a Turner, not a Lacey."

Giving up on changing his attitude in the time available, Milly herded him from the room. She would be excited for him, even if he couldn't muster the necessary enthusiasm. "Hie thee below, Master Turner: an earl awaits you!"

Christopher checked himself on the threshold to the kitchen, betraying his nervousness despite his careless attitude. Milly wanted to give him a hug, but instinctively she knew he had retreated to a very lonely, private place, forged over years of rejection. She just wished he wouldn't keep pushing everyone away, his charm a kind of armor—superficially shiny but made of steel nonetheless. Gathering his courage, he strode into the kitchen.

"Good day, my masters." He bowed to the company, the sarcasm ringing. "To what do I owe this honor?"

The earl returned the bow with a nod. "Master Turner?"

"Aye, my lord."

"My brother James wrote to me concerning your situation. Would you care to step apart with me so we can discuss our business in greater privacy?"

Christopher looked as if this were the last thing on earth he wanted. "Nay, sir, I have never made a secret of being a bastard get of your late father—both ladies present know the truth."

Tobias Lacey coughed, amused by his older half brother's rudeness. "Tell it plain, why don't you?" he muttered.

The earl was still trying for diplomacy, though he clearly wished Milly and the dame banished. "In that case, I will continue. I regret most sincerely that you have been neglected since our father's death."

"He was noted for his absence before then as well," Christopher cut in.

"Indeed." The earl studied his new brother, trying to find the key to understanding him. He rubbed the golden hairs on his chin thoughtfully, his clever blue eyes intense. "As soon as I heard of your existence, I inquired about the circumstances of your birth and later dealings with the estate. My father handed over the responsibility for sending your stipend to his steward. Unfortunately, Turville took it upon himself to terminate the arrangement on my father's death. I admit the estate coffers were empty at the time, and he was acting from an overzealous desire to protect me, but, even so, he was wrong to do this. At the very least, he should have consulted me and I would have made other arrangements for you."

Christopher curled his lip. "Pray, what kind of arrangments? You would have sent me into the navy or dispatched me into the army? That's what many great families do with their unwanted sons, isn't it? I saw that you were quick enough·to send your brother abroad when you had an heir."

Expecting a difficult first meeting, the earl had clearly resolved beforehand not to lose his temper. "I think you mistake me, sir. James is desperately wanted by us all—he travels because we sincerely thought it for the best. A day does not pass without us praying for his safe return." The earl cleared his throat, emotion choking his voice. "As for you, sir, had you come to me, I would have desired to know you better and determined with you what profession you would like to follow. You are, first and foremost, our brother." He waited until the actor met his eyes. "You have a family if you want to claim it."

Christopher clenched his fists on his hips to hide his tremors. He had played many parts onstage, but this was one that he'd had no time to con. Milly's heart broke for him as he appeared lost for words.

Fortunately, Tobias decided it was time to lighten the atmosphere. "Still, I'd understand if you didn't want to acknowledge us. Will here can be a real killjoy—I'm always in trouble with him—

and Jamie is simply no fun at the moment. I'd appreciate an actor for an older brother—think of all those free seats to the plays I'll get! And those plays by Gascoigne, the soldier-poet, are real firecrackers, from what I've heard—quite the funniest things ever seen onstage. I can't wait to hear one."

"Tobias!" growled the earl.

The young gentleman ignored him. "But I must be frank"— Tobias pulled a wry face—"I only want you if you promise to take the attention off me by getting into deeper disgrace than I manage. I have hopes of you: the opportunities at the theater must abound."

Christopher smiled despite himself, quite disarmed by the lordling. Tobias had inherited a similar propensity to charm, but his was warmer, the product of a sunnier disposition.

"And what does your esteemed elder brother think of my profession?" Christopher asked Tobias. "Will he demand that I separate myself from such infamy as price of your favor, think you?"

"Lord, no!" Tobias turned to the earl. "Come on, Will—you wouldn't be a fusty old bore and take such a line, would you?"

Will smiled and shook his head. "Master Turner's choice of profession is his alone to make. I have no intention of forcing him to change for the sake of the family."

Tobias suddenly grinned. "Of course you wouldn't dare! Pot and kettle, that would be." He swung round to Christopher. "He married Ellie two years ago despite ruining a brilliant chance of rebuilding our fortune with an advantageous match. He told the rest of the family to go shake their ears—it was the most splendid thing he's ever done!"

"I did not tell you any such thing!" The earl gave his irrepressible brother a glare.

"Yes, you did—according to Jamie."

Giving up on that tack, the earl made an attempt to bring the conversation back on course. "You are drifting from the point, Tobias—and disclosing far too much information that should remain private."

But the youngster, much to Milly's delight, was not to be quelled. "Don't mistake me, Kit—that's if I may call you Kit?"

Bemused, Christopher gave a nod—what else could he do in the face of such candid eagerness?

"Good. Kit, then. Ellie—I mean the countess—is really the best thing to happen to Will and to Lacey Hall. You'll like her when you meet her—she giggles most easily and is excellent fun. Little Wilkins is a bit of a bore at the moment—cries and spits up the whole time—but he'll get better in a year or so."

Tobias had obviously taken it as already agreed that Christopher would be welcomed into the Lacey fold. Milly knew her friend was not yet prepared to throw his lot in with them so soon. What would he do? He wouldn't scorn them now, would he, and spoil the chance for reconciliation?

"Wilkins?" Christopher asked faintly.

"My son. Your nephew." The earl's face transformed with a broad smile. "He's four months old. The countess would have come with us otherwise."

"Nothing would have stopped her," agreed Tobias.

The two Lacey brothers paused and looked to Christopher for his response to their olive branch.

Pick it up, Milly urged him silently.

Christopher ran his fingers through his hair, crumpling his hat in his other hand. "I admit, sirs, that your approach has taken me by surprise. I have not been used to attention from the Lacey family. I find it somewhat"—he paused, searching for a word that was not outright offensive—"hard to trust."

The earl nodded as if he quite understood. "Then let us prove ourselves with our constancy. You are welcome any time at any of my homes, but you will find me most often in residence at Lacey Hall. I would offer to restore your stipend, but I anticipate that you may refuse?"

"Aye, my lord." Christopher's tone was now genuinely respectful. "I do quite well as I am."

"Even so, all of us need a helping hand from time to time. You have family now, Kit. Please remember that. And your sisters would like to meet you too—Lady Catherine and Lady Sarah." Sensing that he had achieved all that could be hoped from this one meeting, the earl turned to the dame and thanked her for her hospitality. "Come along, Tobias. We've business at court yet this day."

Court! Milly realized that she had an opportunity to plead for help on Jane's behalf. Then she recalled that there was no love lost between the earl and the girl who had jilted him. He might even think Jane's marriage problems only her due—Jane had warned her that they had parted before an explanation could be made and, unless James had had time to tell his brother the truth, the earl was still thinking the worst of her. Taking a second too long to consider the advisability of making an appeal, Milly lost her chance as the Lacey party were taking their leave and walking out the door. Still, it was good to have the Laceys to go to if all else failed. She would have to give the matter more thought.

"Well now, Master Turner, that's a fine thing: an earl for a brother!" exclaimed Dame Prewet, watching through the window as the party departed in the direction of the river. "I'll have to double your rent."

Christopher took his landlady's teasing in good part. "You should halve it, madam—think of the honor I do your house, lodging my seminoble carcass here."

"You'll visit them?" Milly asked, her mind still wondering if she had just missed a golden opportunity.

Christopher rubbed his forearms thoughtfully. "Mayhap. But not yet. I need time to adjust to their change of heart. Mine is not so mercurial."

"No, you're plain stubborn." Milly sighed. "Give over your resistance, Kit. They are splendid people: take the gift that is being offered you."

"I'll still be only a bastard."

Milly shrugged. "Of course—and so is half of London. The earl wasn't offering to make you one of his heirs—he was volunteering to be your brother. Poor man: he doesn't know what he is letting himself in for—I've seen your bedchamber, remember?"

Christopher gave her the first carefree smile she'd seen on his face that day. "Oh, he knows. He's got Tobias for a younger brother, hasn't he?"

Chapter 17

Greenwich Palace

CLÉMENT MONTFLEURY HAD COME for his daily courting visit as approved by the Queen. Jane had to force herself to remain seated in the sunny corner by the window as he strolled around her father's fine chamber. She would have preferred to run screaming from the room.

"And when we get home to France, *ma petite fleur,* we will have such a grand celebration. The whole countryside around the estate of *mon père* will rejoice that I have brought home such a beautiful English bride." Montfleury flicked at a clock on the mantelpiece, disturbing the finely balanced mechanism so that it struck prematurely.

Jane got up. "Oh, is that the time? I really must go."

He seized her hand, bending her arm forcefully so she took her place again. "*Non, non,* it is not the hour, *ma belle Jeanne.* This clock, it goes off too early." He kissed her aching fingers in a gesture that could be mistaken for affection. "Remember, everyone watches, everyone sees at court. We must be the perfect lovers."

Why? Jane wanted to shout. What was the point of this elaborate farce? The "everyone" he was so worried about knew full well that he did not care for her as a man should for the woman he is to marry. He was only pleasing himself by making her put up with his ridiculous attentions.

"How go the preparations for your wedding clothes, my dear?" Montfleury asked loudly, spotting the Earl of Wetherby standing by the door in the inner room of his suite.

Jane studied her hands, bathing them in the sunlight as if that could bleach away his touch. "They are progressing." She had in fact given no orders for new clothes—had not been able to stomach the idea.

"Excellent. I want you to look magnificent on the day we wed. You must be a credit to the house of Montfleury."

She felt too dispirited to bother with a response. What did it matter? She could come dressed in a sack and they would still insist she marry. Her father had made it all too clear that if she refused to go through with the wedding, he would lodge a plea with the Queen that Jane was not mentally capable of managing her own affairs and should be placed under his control—in effect, imprisoned at his pleasure. Jane had not needed much persuading that even marriage to Montfleury would be better than that.

The Frenchman did another promenade of the room, a frown burrowing two creases at the top of his pronounced nose. "I am concerned, *ma chère,* that you do not seem interested to hear what arrangements I have made for after our wedding, where we will live and so forth."

"I assumed, sir, that we would live in France." Jane pleated and unpleated her skirt with restless fingers, crushing the expensive silk. Milly would be cross with her for treating it like this. She brushed the cloth smooth.

"Not necessarily. I have looked through your holdings. You have a dower interest in a pretty property in Kent, very convenient for my business in the southern ports. I thought you would lodge there."

Jane remembered the place—it may be pretty but it was little more than a drafty manor house, deadly cold in winter. "Indeed, sir? And do you plan to live there with me?"

He flicked at a speck on his sleeve. "From time to time. I will be very occupied with my interests. I have to travel much."

Jane did not know whether to laugh or cry at this announcement. She had imagined an exile in France with his family, but it appeared that after their wedding visit, he intended to abandon her in England and go on his merry way. She would be living a half-life in retirement, but perhaps that was better than living unloved among strangers. However, she could foresee one problem.

"I understand, sir. You do know that my late husband's stepsons dispute my claim to the dower rights?"

He sniffed. "They are, how you say, *vulgar* men. I have met with them and asserted your claim. I have sworn that you are not a virgin, that your marriage was complete."

Jane blushed. "You told them that!"

He shrugged, entirely unembarrassed by the subject. "But of course. I said we had anticipated the marriage bed and I found all was in order—you had been a wife in truth as well as name." He examined her flushed cheeks. "I hope, *ma chère*, that I do not perjure myself? You have rid yourself of your innocence? It would be very inconvenient if you had not, as your stepsons are demanding that you be examined by a doctor and for some reason they cast doubt on my having bedded you."

Jane had never felt so humiliated in her life. "I would not wish to inconvenience you, sir. The matter has been seen to."

"*Bon.*" He bowed. "Then I bid you good day, my lady. Until the same time on the morrow."

Jane watched him go. He paused to exchange a few words with her father, both men at ease with each other; soon laughter rumbled in the next room. Montfleury had a skill for making male friends. His outward effeminate appearance disguised a mind like a trap, quick to snap up any and every advantage. But did he really care so little about her honor? A strange husband to hope his future wife was not chaste. Maybe he thought sending her to the lonely manor in Kent would be defense enough from further indiscretions.

The irony was that for the first time in her life she had reason to be grateful for her stupid interlude with Raleigh. Without that, she did not doubt that Montfleury would be pushing her to take a lover to secure her dower rights; or worse, he would have forced himself to volunteer for the role. That did not bear thinking about.

> *13th July 1584*
> *Outer Banks, somewhere in North America*
> *My dear Jane,*
>
> *God has blessed our little expedition beyond our expectations. Fine weather has wafted us with all speed across the Atlantic, and miraculously we have arrived without loss of life or serious incident. We made*

landfall in the Caribbean and were fortunate to find
sweet water on our first island and no hostile Spanish
to greet us. We then turned north and made our way
along the coast of the land called Florida until we met
with a chain of islands our captain calls the Outer
Banks.

James lifted his pen from the paper and gazed out at the new land he could see through the window. They were sheltered in a lagoon, a perfect harbor once past the dangerous shoals. The coastline flourished with vines and tall cedars—it truly looked to be a land of milk and honey, such as had been promised to the Israelites in the Old Testament. Many among the crew were expressing the same thought; some believed they had found a new Eden, innocent of mankind's devious ways. Only Diego was unimpressed. He had been the first to note the natives in their little boats spying on the strange ships, and had pointed out to Barlowe that the land was clearly inhabited. It would be foolish to think it a safe terrain or somewhere that could be counted as their discovery.

"Ah, son, but it's not a Christian prince that owns this land, so it's ours to claim," Barlowe had replied affably, as if the presence of other people was no more problematic than reports of a herd of deer.

Diego had been furious with the captain, but wisely waited to make his thoughts known to James in private. A charge of mutiny would not make for an easy voyage. While James could see the logic of Diego's position, he himself was less worried in the rights of the locals; the land looked big enough to support both American natives and European settlers with much room to spare.

James returned to his paper.

> *Diego has recovered from his seasickness now that we are in the shelter of a lagoon, and I am busy trying to fatten him up for the homeward journey. I have never seen someone so o'erset by the sea. Tell Mistress Porter that he should remain on dry land for the rest of his life.*

Diego entered the cabin. "The captain's putting ashore. He asks you to join the landing party."

James grinned and stretched. "Excellent."

Diego plucked the quill from James's fingers before he dribbled ink on his sleeve and rested it carefully on the writing desk. "Writing to her again?"

James pulled on his doublet over his shirt. "Of course."

Diego held out James's hat. "You are in love with the lady, sir. You might as well admit it. And she loves you."

Clapping the round brimmed hat on top of his salt-matted hair, James laughed. "I know. I had to take myself away in order to come to my senses. Somehow it all seems much clearer out here." He glimpsed his reflection in the cracked shaving glass he'd tacked to the wall. "Not that any woman in their right mind would want me now—I look like a heathen."

Diego shook his head. "No, sir. Heathens are much cleaner than you—trust me, I know."

The pair joined the ship's company waiting by the boats. First, Barlowe led them in a prayer, thanking God for their safe arrival. He then divided his men up between the craft. James and Diego found seats in the second vessel, arriving on the beach only a few yards behind the captain. Barlowe did not wait for the seamen to pull the boat out of the surf; he was over the side, wading through the shallows with the enthusiasm of a child on the first snowy morning of winter.

"Gentlemen, have you ever seen a land like it?" The captain waved his arms to the smooth sand, pale yellow with a sprinkle of black grains. Sandpipers flocked to the water margin, sticking long beaks into the tidal flats. A flotilla of pelicans bobbed on the sea a stone's throw from the landing party, oblivious to the strange new creatures invading their fishing grounds. James marveled at their capacious beaks, wondering how they could manage to fly with so much weight up front.

Now on dry ground, Barlowe took his musket off his back and primed the chamber. He stamped his foot on the sand. "Witness, my lords and gentlemen, I claim this land in the name of Her Majesty, Queen Elizabeth."

Fortunately, only James caught Diego rolling his eyes in exasperation. He nudged him in the ribs, warning him to behave.

Tucking his powder horn away, Barlowe wiped his brow and gestured inland. "Come, let's see what fresh meat we can find."

After loading his gun with powder and shot, James followed. Diego had a hunting bow, which he held at the ready; he appeared far less overawed by this experience than the Europeans. They trailed the captain up the dunes, treading in his footsteps in the virgin sand, and entered the forest, awed by the huge red cedars that flourished so close to the stormy Atlantic.

As they penetrated deeper inland, James regretted his woolen doublet—the humidity was punishing. He unhooked it to let it gape open, but still the sweat trickled down his back. Envious of Diego, who had sensibly dressed only in a light shirt and linen Venetians, he vowed to take more notice of his servant's preparations in future. Diego looked almost at home.

It was no good. James wasn't going to be able to hit a thing with perspiration dripping in his eyes. He pulled off his doublet and hat, then his leg hose.

"Here, man." He passed them to the nearest seaman. "Put these back in one of the boats for me and there'll be a groat waiting for you when we get back to the *Bark Raleigh*."

The sailor grinned at the prospect of making easy money. "Aye, aye, my lord."

James wafted his shirt free of his sticky back.

"Better?" asked Diego wryly.

"Much."

Diego passed him a bunch of berries he'd just plucked from an obliging vine. "They're good—I've tried them already."

"Food taster now? Is there no end to your talents?"

"Probably not."

A musket exploded ahead.

"A hit!" shouted Barlowe.

He was hidden from their view by the sudden exodus of a flock of white cranes rising from the brush all around them. James laughed: they were like the spirits of the blessed on Judgment Day rushing to greet their Lord. Their long legs dangled as they flapped into the air; then they wheeled away, making a deafening clamor like the shouts of the heavenly host in the book of Revelation.

"Glorious!" he exclaimed.

"Not good eating," remarked Diego more prosaically, putting his arrow back in the quiver.

They caught up with Barlowe, who had just dispatched the deer he had brought down with his shot.

"How like you this land, my lord?" the captain asked James, tucking his knife back in his belt and nodding to a crewman to drag the beast back to the beach for butchering. "I have never before seen such abundance of game. There's nothing to match it in Europe."

"You are right, sir." Movement above caught his eye. James shouldered his musket, aimed and fired, bringing down a duck on the wing.

"Good shot!" Barlowe applauded. "We feast tonight—on the beach. You, lad." He turned to his cabin boy. "Tell the cooks to build fires to roast the meat on the strand."

Their hunt continued to prosper, game absurdly easy to kill as it wandered into their path, too innocent of European men to flee the report of the firearms. After months of salt pork, the mood was near euphoric as the catch continued to mount. Leaving the crew to their slaughter, Diego filled a couple of baskets with berries to add to the bill of fare, and then joined James sitting on a sunny rock by the fire pits.

"This is a slice of heaven," remarked James, spitting a pip into the sea.

Diego winced as another salvo echoed in the trees. "Until we arrived."

· ❈ ·

The natives made contact with the English crew a few days after they had landed on the island. The Indians approached with caution, but without fear, first showing themselves on the next promontory along from the ships' mooring, then paddling right on to the beach. James was intrigued by their appearance: their skin was the hue of burnished copper, their clothes minimal, their body ornaments a mixture of paint, metal rings, beads and feathers. He had never seen anything like them before, even in the books in Raleigh's library.

James stood back as Barlowe led the initial exchange of greetings and presents on the sand. "Extraordinary," he murmured to Diego. "They wear only a scrap of cloth to hide their manhood. They truly do live in a state of innocence here."

Diego folded his arms. "Look about you, master: it's hot, you are all sweating in your shirts, hose and doublets, yet you think them strange for being appropriately attired. Who is the most extraordinary in the eyes of God?"

"But the Bible teaches modesty."

Diego gave a wry smile. "I do not think they've had the chance to read that chapter, but the book of nature teaches us to adapt to our climate. Doubtless in winter those fellows will be swathed in furs enough to satisfy the most prudish observer."

James scratched his head, his brain trying to catch up with the new concepts his man was teaching him. Diego had for many years been an outsider to the world in which he lived; he was used to seeing the difference between what was essential and what was merely temporal, scorning the flimsy rules dreamt up by men to make sense of their ways of doing things. Diego was right that it was instructive to imagine oneself in the shoes—no, not the shoes, as they weren't wearing any—in the place of these friendly natives. Two big ships had landed on their shore and they had reacted with no sign of hostility, biding their time to take the measure of their guests and approach without a show of force. James doubted the people of England would have reacted so calmly to such an invasion.

"The world is much bigger than I thought it," James admitted.

"With respect, sir, you've only scratched the surface by your voyage here. Go east and the marvels multiply like rabbits in spring."

James looked anew at his servant. "How exactly do you know all these things, Diego?"

He shrugged. "I worked for a Venetian trader for a short time. Those merchants have connections to places you would not believe."

The exchange on the beach led to a visit to the ships by the little party of Indians. They seemed impressed but somewhat puzzled by the two craft, touching everything and chattering away to each other in their own language. One repeatedly plucked at Barlowe's sleeve, saying "Wingandacoa."

Amadas, who thus far had managed to keep his temper under control, much to everyone's relief, seized on this word. He clapped his hands, making the poor visitors jump. "So this is the name of this place, is it, sir? Wingandacoa?"

The crew all repeated the name eagerly, trying to get their tongues round the outlandish sounds. The natives smiled and nodded eagerly.

Diego leant across to James. "I do not think that was what he meant at all. I think he was merely complimenting Barlowe on his shirt—I doubt they have seen linen before."

James bit down on his laugh. "We can't tell them that now. Captain Amadas is so pleased to have finally made progress communicating."

Diego gave another shrug. "I do not suppose it matters in any case. You'll give the place your own name that you don't have trouble pronouncing."

The following day the natives returned in larger numbers, led by their leader, a fellow dubbed Granganimeo. He was a striking individual with yellow-daubed skin and a cockscomb tuft of hair atop his shaved head. Seated between the two captains for an impromptu picnic on the beach, he appeared in very high spirits and at one point suddenly began hitting himself and the two Englishmen, laughing loudly. Amadas looked fit to spit at this uncalled-for attack, but Barlowe restrained him, choosing instead to thump himself on the chest and join in the laughter. The Indians seated with James and Diego began copying their leader. James grinned through the onslaught—some of the blows were bruising.

"What's this supposed to mean?" he asked Diego through gritted teeth.

Diego hit one lively fellow back with equal force. "I think they are enjoying themselves." The Indian he had just thumped held out both his hands and joined them together, smiling broadly at them both. "Something about all being one happy family, I would guess."

"They are going to love this at court." James ducked one particularly enthusiastic wallop to the head. "I can just see the Queen and this Granganimeo fellow getting on like a house on fire."

After a few more days of such pleasantries, the Indians invited their guests to visit their home island of Roanoke. James was numbered among the party, instructed to survey whether the site would prove a good choice for the planned colony. Barlowe and Amadas reasoned that the natives were so friendly that it would be of huge benefit to the novice settlers to have them on hand to help live off this land.

"But what if they do not want a crowd of foreigners taking over their hunting grounds and fields?" Diego asked James in private.

James had been wondering the same thing himself. He doubted that the natives had any idea at all about what was planned for them. Still, he was a loyal Englishman; he had a duty to perform. "But look around us—there is so much uncultivated land. A small party of farmers is hardly going to encroach on them. And the natives stand to benefit—they'll hear the gospel, have a chance to improve their lives through trade."

"I expect that is what Caesar said about the Ancient Britons when he first landed—they will learn to treat him as a god and have the honor of being traded as slaves."

"But we did benefit. The Romans brought us their civilization."

"And thanks to them every schoolboy has to learn Latin."

James chuckled. "Well, I suppose there were drawbacks."

Roanoke surpassed even the Englishmen's fondest hopes. Granganimeo's settlement was small—a mere nine houses fortified by a wooden palisade, the people not too numerous to frighten a group of colonists. The sailors were greeted warmly when they disembarked, seeing for the first time their hosts' families, the women and children, who until now had remained hidden. James could not help noticing that the ladies were as lightly clad as their spouses; even Diego appreciated this detail after being unimpressed by much else.

"Excellent country this!" Diego remarked as one particularly pretty girl presented him with a slice of melon.

"Keep your eyes to yourself: remember you are a betrothed man," chided James without too much force.

"I am trying not to think what my Milly would make of all this. If American customs were to catch on in London, her business would be ruined."

James laughed and shook his head. "As much as we may applaud the idea of seeing our ladies Indian-style, I think I could not bear others to be a witness."

The chief's wife, dressed in a long leather cloak marking her high status, emerged from her house and brought order to the chaotic scenes on the beach. She ordered the native men to carry the foreign guests into her home—a gesture that James prayed was one of respect rather than preparations for dinner. Rumors that these natives indulged in cannibalism had done the rounds of the ships on the journey over. He had tried not to pay too much attention to such fanciful tales, but the prejudice remained. Once the visitors were installed by her hearth, the chief's wife began tugging at their clothes. The other women joined in, pulling off hose and jackets, laughing as they did so.

James looked at Diego, wondering if he should panic.

Diego surrendered his shirt without a murmur. "We stink," he said simply.

Sure enough, the clothes were whisked away to be washed by one party of women while a second detachment brought warm water to the guests. They insisted on bathing the sailors' feet and hands before the meal was served.

"What excellent creatures!" enthused Barlowe, his skin looking very pink in contrast to his weather-beaten face and hands. "They are like the hosts in the Bible—like Our Lord himself on Maundy Thursday washing his disciples' feet!"

"Either that, or we had quite put them off their food," whispered James to Diego. He looked around the circle of buck-naked Englishmen. "Problem is, now I've lost my appetite."

CHAPTER 18

Lacey Hall, Berkshire

TIME WAS RUNNING OUT FOR JANE, but Milly had a plan: she would act on her idea of appealing to James's family. It had to work, because she was at the end of her wits as to how else to save her friend. Taking advantage of the lull in business when the nobility departed from London for the summer months, she left her shop in the hands of her most capable apprentice and set out for Berkshire to make a personal appeal to the only other friend she knew Jane trusted entirely: Lady Ellie, the Countess of Dorset. If she could persuade the lady, she hoped the earl would swiftly be set straight on what had happened two years ago. They owed Jane their happiness; it was time to repay that debt.

The journey was about thirty miles and would take at least a day or two on the old hack she had hired. Christopher Turner had refused point-blank to accompany her. It was too soon, he claimed.

"How much time do you need, Kit, to come to terms with the fact that they are kind people?" she asked in exasperation.

He ducked giving her a straight answer, mumbling something about plans to tour with his acting company over the summer.

Pressing him further, Milly discovered that he was embarrassed to meet with the earl's mother—the lady who had been neglected while the old earl dabbled with his mistress.

"The earl didn't mention her, did he?" he challenged Milly. "That must mean I'm not really wanted there while she is still in residence."

Milly didn't think it meant anything of the sort, but he was hardly rational on the subject.

"I tell you what, why don't you report back what she is like. Consider this full payment for my trip to Plymouth."

Milly was surprised that Christopher, who had always acted the victim of his birth, felt he bore some of his mother's guilt for her choice to become an earl's leman. Yet if he felt his reconciliation with his family had to take place with tiny crab steps sideways to the main aim, then that was his affair.

"I'll do as you bid, Kit. But don't keep spurning the Laceys—it will get more embarrassing the longer you leave it."

"Thank you, Milly-o." Christopher threw his arm round her shoulders and squeezed. "You are still my queen of the embroidery bower even though you've foolishly fallen in love with that roving jackanapes."

"Go to, you knave." Milly pushed gently away, remembering suddenly how she had promised Diego to keep Kit at arm's length— she wasn't doing very well with that pledge. "And, yes, I'll let you know if the coast is clear for you to venture on to Lacey land."

With no Christopher to protect her, Milly decided to take Old Uriah on the journey to Lacey Hall. A less convivial companion she could not imagine. He moaned about the horses, the inns, the roads.

The only thing that made him smile was seeing a nobleman's heavy coach stuck in a muddy puddle.

As evening fell at the end of the long day's travel, Milly was relieved to see the roofs of the great house appearing at the end of the road. She shifted in her uncomfortable pillion seat, her clothes still damp from the earlier rainstorm.

"See there, Uriah: that's our destination."

He grunted. "About time too, mistress. I was worried we'd end up sleeping under a hedge, preyed on by wild creatures and vagabonds."

Out of sight, Milly grinned at his back. This was Berkshire: hardly the wilds of America. "If they don't offer us a bed here, there's a village just a mile on, according to Diego." She wondered if she was getting the first glimpse of her future home. One of the places she might settle with Diego would be this household, if London did not welcome their marriage. Admiring the sweeping parkland in the late burst of sunshine, she had to admit there were worse fates than living here.

Uriah steered their mount to the domestic offices at the rear of the building. As they rounded the honeyed sandstone edifice, it glowed in the sunset like a castle from some folktale housing the fairy king and queen, windows twinkling like diamonds. Even the servants' areas of the estate were well tended, a flourishing walled kitchen garden visible through an open gate. Delicate pale-orange globes decked the apricot trees trained to a warm southern facade, some blushing to ripeness. Milly was beginning to think the inhabitants might not be quite human and that she had stepped into a poet's story.

The illusion was shattered by the sound of a loud argument in progress in the servants' courtyard.

"Get your lazy carcass down here at once, Afabel Turville!" shrieked a young fair-haired woman with a toddler on her hip. "That wretch of a miller has delivered a sack short again. I won't pay him for cheating us."

Milly got her first glimpse of the man who had cut off Christopher without a shilling when Turville, a much older servant, red of face and hair, shoved his head out a window on the first floor. "Hold your peace, woman! Do you want the family to hear your caterwauling?"

"You took delivery without counting again, didn't you?" continued the goodwife, not lowering her voice a jot. "Just because you share a barrel of ale with the man on a Saturday does not mean you should let him swindle you on a Tuesday!"

The clop of the horse's hooves finally reached the woman's ears. She spun round, revealing a pretty face beneath her modest coif. Her little daughter, a charming blond imp with a heart-stopping smile, shared her good looks.

"How may I help you?" the goodwife asked, for all the world as if the argument had not been going hammer and tongs but a moment before.

Milly gave her a friendly smile. "Mistress, I have a gift for your lady from my Lady Rievaulx."

The young woman's eye lit with avaricious interest. "Then you'd better come in. Not often we get gifts from London."

A groom ran out of the stable to take the hack's bridle. Milly and Uriah dismounted at the block, both staggering slightly with the effects of being in the saddle for too long.

The goodwife beckoned them to follow. "Come into the kitchen. I'll see if the countess can receive you. What name should I give?"

"Millicent Porter of Silver Street," Milly replied.

The woman swung round. "*You're* Milly Porter! Oh yes, we've heard all about you."

Milly was dumbfounded. "You know about me?"

"Of course. I was in service to Lady Jane Perceval before I married Turville." The woman pursed her lips, then hitched the child higher on her hip as if to remind herself of the benefits of the match. "Who would guess she'd end up as one of the Queen's ladies?"

Milly realized she knew exactly who the goodwife was: Nell Rivers, now Mistress Turville, one of Jane's less pleasant lady's maids, who had left her service to marry the earl's steward. She was no doubt kicking herself for missing the opportunity to attend her lady at court. "Indeed, who would've thought it?"

"Rest here awhile. I'll see if my lady is receiving." Handing the infant over to Milly to tend, Nell made to leave. "Oh, her name's Janet—after her godmother, the marchioness."

Interesting—Jane had not mentioned standing godmother to her maid's offspring. Milly smiled down at the little girl's face. There was something of a resemblance to her friend in the imp's blue eyes. She thought it best not to ask how that had come about, though her quick mind leapt to the fact that Jane's brother had been at court when Mistress Turville had been in service there. Milly had never thought much of Sir Henry and his goings-on—he was notorious for his amours. She had always given him a wide berth.

The child tugged at the embroidered collar of Milly's coat and giggled, her eye caught by the robins Milly had painstakingly sewn onto the cloth.

"Like birds, do you, sweeting?" Milly tickled her cheek.

The giggle became a glorious chuckle, which prompted Milly's laughter. Then her heart gave a funny little lurch. She tried to ignore Diego's absence most of the time, but she was missing him terribly. Determinedly optimistic, she had schooled herself to believe that he would be safe; the infant reminded her of what they could have together, but only if he returned from the voyage. She closed her eyes briefly, murmuring a prayer. He had to be safe. Had to.

Nell came back within five minutes and brusquely transferred Janet to Uriah's lap as he sat by the fire. "Keep an eye on her," she told him sternly.

Uriah was so astounded to find himself roped in as nurse so soon after arriving that he did not think to protest. Around them, the kitchen servants were busy preparing the evening meal—there were surprisingly few of them considering the size of the household; Milly surmised that, in this far-from-wealthy family, it was usual practice to expect everyone to lend a hand.

"Come, the mistress is eager to see you." Nell bustled through the short service corridor and into the grander parts of the house. Milly emerged into the entrance hall just in time to note the departure of a pack of dogs following at the heels of a young man leaving the front door.

"That's Master Tobias," Nell said shortly. "The youngest Lacey boy."

Milly remembered him fondly from the encounter in Dame Prewet's kitchen but doubted he would recall her, as she had kept in the background. "How many of the family live at home? I believe there are more brothers and sisters, are there not? And the dowager countess?"

"There are plenty of them here at the moment, that's the truth." Nell frowned, as if the insult of family daring to occupy their own home was more than she deserved. "Only Master James is abroad."

Nell opened the door to one of the fine chambers off the hallway. The plasterwork musical motifs intertwined with fruit on the coffered ceiling hinted at its purpose, though for the moment there was no one playing the collection of family instruments. Instead, on either side of the fire sat the Earl and Countess of Dorset, both watching the newcomer approach with keen expressions.

Taken aback to be brought into the earl's presence as well as that of the countess, Milly halted on the threshold. She hadn't planned to make her case in front of the man Jane had jilted; he could hardly be expected to be a friend to her cause.

"Mistress Porter, please do come in." The earl gestured to a third seat by the fire. "Now I see you, did we not meet briefly in London? Do you bring word from our brother?"

Milly remembered herself sufficiently to dip into a curtsy. "My lord, my lady. And, no, I do not come on behalf of Christopher—though he sends his regards." Well, he would have done if she had thought to prompt him, so it was not an absolute lie. "I come on behalf of the marchioness, Lady Jane."

The young countess, a petite dark-haired beauty of Milly's age, smiled at her husband. "Will, I've just worked out who this is! She is the one who has conquered Diego's heart—the one James wrote about in his letter announcing Christopher's presence in Silver Street. I can quite see how she won him—she's lovely."

Milly blushed, knowing that she fell far short of that measure. "Thank you, my lady."

"Don't embarrass her, love." The earl stood and gallantly handed

Milly to the chair. "We can tease her about her suitor later—once she knows us better. Have you been offered refreshment?"

"Not yet, sir. I've only just arrived."

The earl turned to Nell. "Mistress Turville, pray order the kitchen to send up wine for our guest."

Nell bobbed a curtsy and reluctantly left the room. She had been hoping to eavesdrop on this conversation, but evidently the earl knew her habit well and had moved to prevent it.

"So, Mistress Porter," began the countess, "you have a gift for me from Jane. How is she?"

Milly darted a look at the earl. He was smiling indulgently at his wife, not at all the picture of the rejected suitor.

The countess caught the direction of her gaze. "Oh, don't mind him. He's long since got over Jane giving him the boot."

The earl cast his eyes heavenwards at his wife's blunt language.

"I always told him there was more to that than he thought, but it wasn't until James wrote to us from Plymouth that we understood quite what she had done for us," the countess continued.

That was a relief—James had already cut most of the briars from her path. "My lady . . ."

The countess placed her hand on Milly's knee. "Please, we are all Jane's friends here. Call me Ellie, as she does."

"Lady Ellie—"

The countess laughed. "I suppose that will have to do. I forget what an important person I am these days."

"Lady Ellie, I am afraid I lied. I did not bring a gift from Jane. I haven't been able to see her for some weeks, as her family are keeping her close."

The earl frowned. "How so? I thought she was a Queen's lady

now, under the authority of the sovereign. James said her marriage to Rievaulx had brought her independence."

Milly rubbed her hands together, afraid that he would not believe her. "True. But her father and brother have made a match for her with a Frenchman and have ensured she cannot refuse him. They've even gained the Queen's approval by arranging for Jane to be caught in what looked like a compromising situation with the man."

"Oh, this is terrible!" exclaimed Lady Ellie, her big brown eyes wide with distress.

"And this is all against her will?" The earl was more suspicious of Jane's motives than his wife.

"I promise you that it is." Milly cast around for something to bring the earl in on Jane's side but could only come up with the truth. "She wants nothing to do with this Frenchman. She loves your brother, my lord. She would've married him if Master James would have had her. He hurt her deeply by running off as he did. But he left, and now she's in this awful trap. Her father and Sir Henry have threatened to have her declared unfit to govern herself if she resists them."

"They want her money." The earl went to the heart of the matter.

"That is so."

Lady Ellie jumped to her feet and paced to the window. "It's that horrid brother of hers, isn't it? I can believe anything of Sir Henry Perceval."

"Her father is as bad, my lady. The apple didn't fall far from the tree when it came to Henry."

"Oh, Will, we have to help her. But what can we do?"

The earl ran his hand over his golden beard, thinking. "I'm partly to blame. It was my idea to send James off to America. I beg the lady's pardon for causing her yet more pain."

The countess turned back to Milly. "When is the wedding?"

"It's almost upon us. This Thursday."

"Two days." Lady Ellie returned to her seat and sat down with a sigh. "That does not give us long to come up with a solution."

"And we can't do anything from here. We'll have to go to court," concluded the earl.

Milly felt a knot in the tangle of her concerns for Jane loosen. This pair had a much better chance of influencing the Earl of Wetherby than she ever did. "Thank you. I am more grateful than I can say. I'm only a seamstress—my influence does not count at court. I cannot even get into Whitehall to see Jane at present."

Lady Ellie shook her head. "You may not count at court, but you certainly matter to Diego. He is part of our family, so that makes you one of us too. You have our support in this."

"Wiiill!" A girl tumbled into the room from the far door, her red-gold hair flying behind her.

The earl rose and, with what looked like years of practice, caught her before she tripped over in her dash to him. "Lady Sarah, we have a guest."

The girl cast a quick glance over Milly and decided she couldn't possibly outweigh the importance of her own complaint. "But Tobias ruined my bower. He let the dogs run right through it!"

"Your bower?"

"You said she could build one by the new maze, remember?" whispered the countess. "In the hazel grove."

"It was my fairy bower!" wailed Sarah. "I'd spent ages and ages weaving the garlands and preparing a feast for Robin Goodfellow and the elves—I was going to invite my friends on the full moon tomorrow night so we could watch out for them—but Tobias trampled it all!"

"And so has spoiled your midnight revels?" The earl was quickly catching up with the gravity of the sin. "But did Tobias know you were building it there? And why did the dogs run through it?"

Sarah frowned, twisting an end of one curl with her finger. "I may have borrowed a little cold meat from the kitchen to offer the fairy folk."

The earl raised an eyebrow.

"All right, I took a side of honey-glazed ham from the pantry. But . . . but the dogs have eaten it—they fought over it like . . . like . . ."

"Like a pack of dogs?" suggested the earl, gamely keeping his face straight.

"Yes, and now it's all spoiled and none of the fairy people would be seen dead in my bower—it's a mess and smelly and horrid and I hate Tobias!"

"I see." The earl stood, momentarily at a loss how to remedy the situation, when his youngest brother sauntered into the room, doubtless fully aware that his sins had been confessed prior to his arrival.

"What ho, brother and sisters mine," Tobias said cheerily. He then spotted Milly. "Ah, and who's this?" He bowed and smiled broadly at her, bathing her in the full rays of his charm, dark eyes twinkling somewhat like the mischievous elf Robin Goodfellow that Sarah had been trying to tempt. "What fair damsel has come to Castle Lacey to bait the dragon earl in his den?"

Milly could not help but be reminded of the overblown gallantry of Christopher Turner. A few years younger, Tobias was obviously treading down the same paths with the female sex.

"Hold thy peace, Tobias," warned the earl good-humoredly. "She's Diego's. We met her at Dame Prewet's, if you recall."

Tobias knelt at her feet and kissed her fingertips. "She has tamed the African lion—she is a miracle. I am honored to meet you, fair damsel."

His flattery was interrupted by the renewed eruption of his volcano of a little sister. "To-bi-as!" She launched herself at him, batting him about the head. "What are you going to do about my den?"

He held her off at arm's length. "Will, what are *you* going to do about this little harpy?"

"I hate you!" Sarah's face was flushed with rage.

"I hate you too, smelly." Tobias's insult was delivered with such a happy grin at her fury that Milly seriously doubted he was in earnest.

"Right, that is enough!" bellowed the earl. "You, Sarah, sit down like a lady next to Ellie. You, Tobias, stand by my chair and try to be a gentleman for five minutes."

Sarah appeared cowed by her brother's shouted order and shuffled quickly into place. By contrast, Tobias merely glanced at the clock on the sideboard, as if marking the minutes exactly before he felt free to behave as he normally would. Milly looked inquiringly at Lady Ellie, wondering if she should leave the family to it, but the countess gave her a small smile and shook her head slightly. Good. Milly rather wanted to see how all this would turn out.

"I see two problems before us," the earl announced like a judge at the assizes. "One: that Tobias did ruin Sarah's hard work; and two, that Sarah did take food from the kitchen without permission." The earl held up his hand to forestall their protests. "The remedy is as follows. Tobias, you will report to your sister's bower and repair the damage. Weave flower garlands and so forth until it is back to how she left it."

"Will!" groaned Tobias.

The earl ignored him. "Sarah, you will confess your borrowings to the cook, apologize and give her the worth of the ham in coin— from your own pin money. No wheedling of Ellie or our mother to make it up for you later. Agreed?"

"Yes, Will." Sarah's reply was subdued, but she felt she had to justify herself. "I didn't think of it as stealing, you know. My tutor's been prosing on about Roger Bacon and the need for experimental proof for the existence of things we cannot see, so I wanted to conduct an inquiry as to whether the elves truly exist. You must agree that I needed good bait."

Milly was vastly impressed by the advanced education the girl was receiving when most ladies had to be content with sermons on manners and morals.

The earl scratched his chin to hide his smile. "How very intelligent of you, sweetheart. Do let me know the result of your investigations, but next time ask first before you take something from the house, and do not forget to think through all the dangers of your experiment, such as the reaction of other creatures, before laying out bait."

Sarah nodded solemnly.

"Now, do we have an accord?"

Tobias checked the clock. His time was almost up. "I hear and obey, my lord."

The earl was also aware that the interlude of his brother's good behavior was almost over. "Then, Sarah, go back to your maid and dress for supper. And, Tobias"—he examined his brother and gave him up as a dead loss—"just try to do something about the fact that you look like you've not seen a comb for three months."

With a perky salute, Tobias left the room. Wisely, Ellie held Sarah back for a moment then released her when the coast was clear.

"Well," said Milly, thoroughly entertained but aware she had to find lodging before it got dark, "I had better be leaving."

"Nonsense! You'll stay here the night, of course." Lady Ellie rang a bell to summon her own maid. "You're one of the family—by association."

The earl put his arm round his wife's shoulders. "I wouldn't press that fact at this moment, love. After seeing that display, she might want a separation from the Laceys."

Milly laughed. "Oh no, I think you are all just the right kind of family."

CHAPTER 19

Approach to the English Channel

SHUT IN HIS CABIN, James finished his sketch of Roanoke Island for the draftsman to interpret in a more presentable fashion for the sponsors Raleigh hoped to attract to fund his colony. He bit his tongue in concentration as his nib scratched out the settlement, the woods and the proposed site for the new houses for the colonists—he wasn't a natural artist, but he had a soldier's eye for what he wanted to convey. The visit had been an amazing success. The crew had spent some five weeks among the villagers. Remarkably, the locals had continued to be obliging and seemingly welcoming of the idea that the foreigners might return (that was, if they understood what Barlowe and Amadas said, which James sometimes doubted). The crowning achievement was to have persuaded two young Indian men to accompany them on the voyage home. One of them, Manteo, charmed the crew with his delight in all the novelties they had to show him; the other, Wanchese, an inhabitant of Roanoke itself, was more suspicious but made an imposing presence. The captains had calculated that their appearance at court would do more for attracting public attention to the enterprise than any number of learned treatises on the subject. James just hoped someone remembered to tell the Indians to keep a bridle on that body-thumping business.

A groan came from Diego's bunk. With the ease of frequent practice, James handed him the bowl in time. "Remind me never to allow you to set foot on a ship again."

"I'll hold you to that, master."

James passed him next a tankard of watered-down spirits to rinse his mouth. "Your lady is not going to recognize you: you are thin as a rake and almost as pale as me."

At the thought that he was almost home, Diego smiled and closed his eyes, hands laced across his chest.

James studied his servant with great affection. The voyage had lifted their relationship beyond that of master and man: they had become friends. They both knew it would be difficult to maintain their informality in the more rigid society of England, but James hoped it would last. For one, it made life so much more interesting. He would have to give thought to how he could even out their unequal positions, find some way of advancing Diego's career. It would be a challenge, particularly for a person of Diego's unusual parentage, but on the other hand, that made the blackamoor unique, and perhaps rules would be easier to bend for the exception? James hoped this would prove the case.

James rolled up his finished map. "I don't think I've thanked you for choosing to come with me."

"Aye, I'm a hero—I know it." Keeping his eyes shut, Diego smirked at the ceiling. "But has it worked?"

James pushed back his sleeves and linked his hands behind his head, rocking back on his stool. "I think it has. The memories of the winter campaign are less painful. I feel better about myself, having been of real use in this expedition."

"That is good. You have lost your haunt."

"My what?" James spluttered, touching the cross on his prayer book. "I'll have you know we mariners are a superstitious lot—you can't talk of such things."

Diego nodded. "Aye, one should not name them. But it is true—you are free of it. The voyage by water confused it, as I thought it would."

James rolled his eyes, recognizing that it was a hopeless task to correct his friend's idiosyncratic view of the world.

"Your brother would say your humors are once more in balance," Diego continued sagely. He knew full well what these blinkered Englishmen thought of his knowledge of the spiritual realm and enjoyed tweaking their tails.

"That is a relief, or he might have set the doctors on me, forcing some foul-tasting tonic down my throat in the name of cheering me up."

"But this voyage was your medicine."

"That it was." James absentmindedly tapped the pile of letters, all unsent, that he had written to Jane over the weeks he had been away.

Diego peeked at him through half-closed lids. "Are you going to give them to her?"

James shrugged, trying to disguise the hope he had been nourishing that she had not yet given up on him. "I've no right to disturb her peace. I left her. She doubtless has moved on to new scenes, new loves. Someone with her looks and her attractions will not remain unnoticed by the gentlemen at court. How can I hope to compete?"

Diego gave a world-weary sigh. "Well, if you do not put yourself in the field, then of course you will not win her heart."

"You think I should?"

"Master Lacey, you would deserve the title of idiot of the year if you do not."

James laughed. "Diego, about this plain-speaking habit of yours."

"Yes, sir?"

"Do not stop. It is all the tonic I need."

The Red Lion, Plymouth

James and Diego disembarked from their ship and staggered to the inn to secure lodgings for the night, their legs refusing to cooperate now they were back on dry land.

"I feel drunk," admitted James, leaning heavily against Diego as he steered clear of one disapproving merchant's wife, into whose path he had stumbled. "She's blaming me and for once I am entirely innocent."

Their arrival went almost unnoticed. The good people of Plymouth, from Sir Francis Drake, the mayor, to the humblest pot boy, had all turned out to gawk at the outlandish strangers the captains had brought back from America. Wanchese stalked down the quayside as if he had a bad smell under his nose—and to be fair, the docks did smell very pungent; Manteo gamboled along at his side, smiling and waving at his audience.

"That man could have a marvelous career onstage when his ambassadorial duties are over," commented James.

The landlord assigned them their old chamber for the one night.

They had no wish to linger in Plymouth on this visit, eager to bring news of their triumph back to London. Their host was just leaving them to their supper when he remembered the message that had been entrusted to him by Christopher Turner all those months before.

"My lord, I have a letter for you. Missed you by a whisker when you set out, and I promised faithfully to deliver it immediately when you returned."

James's euphoric mood sobered. Urgent letters rarely brought good news. "Let me have it at once, man."

"Aye, my lord."

The landlord returned with the missive, a little battered from having spent the summer on a shelf waiting to be handed over.

James snapped the seal and found enclosed another letter, as well as a scrawled note from Christopher Turner.

"That's Milly's hand!" exclaimed Diego, barely restraining himself from tugging the enclosure from James's fingers.

James glanced at the direction and passed it to Diego. "For you."

Diego quickly read the letter. "This is not good. Not good at all." He handed it back. "You should see this."

Reading the dire news about Jane's forced marriage, James sank back in his chair, letting the paper dangle from his fingers. "We're too late. This was written months ago." He brandished the letter. "Jane will have been wed by now."

Diego took the paper back and folded it carefully to tuck away in his pocket. "We do not know that was the outcome, sir. It is possible other friends came to her aid, or her family changed their mind."

James shoved his fist through his hair and tugged. "Possible but unlikely. God's blood, I'm being punished for being so weak. I should never have gone."

Alarmed that all the good work of the voyage was about to be undone in a trice, Diego was quick to deny this. "Say not so, sir. You did not engineer this plot against the lady—you are not to blame for taking the steps to mend your spirits."

James was in no mood to listen to such comforting words. "We'll set out at once. I may be too late, but until I know for sure, I cannot stay here."

Diego gazed longingly at the pallet bed he had been planning on occupying until late the next morning. "I will order the horses to be made ready."

"We'll leave the rest of our baggage to be sent by carrier's cart. Make arrangements with the landlord, will you?"

"Aye, sir." Diego turned to the night sky visible through the window. "We have a full moon in our favor."

"Then let us waste no more time. I want to be in London as soon as possible."

Whitehall Palace

The court had returned to Whitehall after the summer's progress. Jane knew she had entered her last few days of freedom before the marriage was solemnized in Westminster Abbey, but still she could not think of a way of escaping her fate, not without bringing a worse outcome down on her head. At times in the small hours of the night, so desperate was she that she had contemplated taking her own life, but she rejected the thought, as that would bring eternal damnation. No man, and certainly not a Frenchman, was worth her soul.

Blanche Parry, the senior lady, was the only one in Elizabeth's circle who recognized that Jane was suffering. Mistress Parry stopped her in the hallway outside the Queen's apartments the day before the wedding.

"You've lost weight over the summer, my lady. It does not suit you," the dame declared in her forthright manner. "I would speak with my mistress, but I know your father has done so already. He says you are ailing because you are anxious to be wed. Is this the truth?"

Jane felt like a shipwrecked mariner suddenly finding flotsam to cling to in his sea of troubles. At last, someone who cared about her, and not the benefits she could bring them. "No, mistress, I would wish never to be married again. Please, I need help."

The old lady frowned. "Hmmm, I will see what I can do."

Jane sighed, struggling to keep her head above the waters that surrounded her. "What can you do? What can anyone do?"

"You may be surprised. Fifty years of service is not to be discounted lightly, even by princes of the realm, such as Her Majesty." Blanche patted her arm and hobbled off to the Queen's chamber.

As Jane prepared herself for bed in her bare room, she clung to the possibility that Mistress Parry would earn her a last-minute reprieve. Her wedding finery lay spread out on a chest—she had chosen her amber satin doublet with black edging, a mourning garment, which reflected her mood entirely. She still hoped she would not have to wear it.

Someone knocked softly on the door. Jane had already sent her maid away, wanting this last night on her own so that no one would witness her pacing.

"Who is it?"

The knock came again.

Reasoning that no villain should have been able to get inside the closely guarded palace, Jane opened the door a crack. "Who's there?" Maybe Mistress Parry had succeeded in her errand and had come to break the good news?

A foot insinuated itself into the gap. "It is I, my lady. Come to wish you well on the eve of your wedding day."

Richard Paton, Marquess of Rievaulx. Jane was tempted to squeeze his foot in the door but her better nature prevailed. She stepped back. "Richard, you call unseasonably late."

Her stepson entered with his usual arrogance, not waiting for an invitation. "It was unavoidable, my lady. My horse cast a shoe near St. Albans and I arrived much later than anticipated." Jane found his apologetic expression hard to believe. "I could not, of course, let you leave our family for that of your new husband without wishing you well."

Jane pulled her robe more firmly over her nightgown and belted it closed. "I thank you for your attention. You may report that you have done your duty by me." She moved back towards the door, signaling that the interview was at an end.

"Please, my dear lady, do not be in such haste to be rid of me. This is the last chance for us to make peace before we take our separate paths." Richard stepped farther into the room, revealing a servant standing behind him. The man carried a tray loaded with a jug and two glasses. "I know that we have not always dealt well together, and I regret my part in that."

"Really?" Jane doubted that very much. For some reason, Richard had decided to change his tactics towards her. Perhaps he hoped to bring her over to his side when dealing with her husband on her dower rights? If so, he must think her more malleable than a warm wax seal. She had not so easily forgotten their recent altercations.

The servant placed the tray on a little table and retired, leaving the door ajar for propriety's sake. Richard poured two glasses and sipped his appreciatively. "Ah, a good vintage." He held the other out to Jane. "Come, let us drink to the morrow and the start of your new life as Lady Montfleury. It has a pleasant ring to it, does it not? You must be very pleased with yourself."

Jane touched Jonas's wedding band, still on her finger; she persisted in wearing it despite the protests of her intended, who did not like seeing another man's mark upon her. She had vowed not to remove it until she was standing in the church porch, and even then she planned to place it on her right hand. Montfleury could take offense if he wished, but she would not surrender that part of her life to him.

"Where will you live after your marriage?" Richard asked affably, offering her the glass again. "Your good health."

Jane took it but did not drink, merely raised it to her mouth in pretense of joining him in the toast. "In Kent."

"The Grafton property?"

"Yes, I believe that is what Montfleury intends."

Richard sniffed. "It is a small estate, but the fishing rights are lucrative. You should do well there." He raised his glass in a second toast.

Jane was amazed by his lack of complaint on the subject. "Thank you, Richard. I confess I am much relieved that you no longer protest my interest in the property." She raised her own glass and sipped.

He watched her wet her lips with hawkish interest. "I decided that there was no point in wasting my money on pursuing the case through the courts—I'd lose the fortune that I intend to regain to lawyers."

Her throat began to tingle. Jane looked down at her wineglass, then back up at her stepson's face, now wreathed in a vindictive smile. He took the drink from her and poured the remainder out on the floor. "Let me help you to the bed, my dear."

"What have you done?" Jane gripped her throat. Her ribs felt as though heavy stones pressed against them; she strained to breathe.

"Taken back what is mine. It will be too late if you marry, so, sadly"—he pulled a grotesque face—"death is the only answer. How tragic that such a young lady should have such a weak heart."

Poison. How could she have been so foolish as to trust him? Jane wanted to scream—scratch at his eyes—but her head swam, her body wracked with chills. Cramps in her stomach bent her double. Her heart pounded, struggling to beat. Close to losing consciousness, she felt his arm twine round her waist, pulling her over to the bed.

"Lie down, sweeting. I prefer to think you did not suffer unnecessarily." He arranged her on her side, gently folding her arms across her breast like an effigy on a tomb. As a final gesture, he slid the ring from her finger. "Sleep well, dear stepmother." He pressed a kiss to her damp brow and silently slid from the room.

It was so quiet in this part of the palace. Pain raged inside Jane's body but she could not make a sound. She thrashed out at the jug on the table. It shattered on the ground but still no one came. She could hear distant laughter in the courtyard below, but everyone was leaving the bride to her last night's lonely vigil.

"Help!" Jane whispered, tears trickling down her face. "Help me! James!"

Milly was delighted to discover that entry to the Queen's palace was a simple business when you were in the entourage of an earl. Will Lacey cut through the flunkeys like a hot knife through butter.

"But Her Majesty is abed!" spluttered one manservant, bobbing at the earl's heels as he strode down the cloistered passageway from the stableyard. Milly and the countess followed a few paces behind.

"Then I will leave news of my arrival with her chamberlain and pay my respects on the morrow," the earl declared with admirable hauteur.

"But, my lord . . . !"

Will swung around to face the hapless servant. "Yes?"

"Everyone has retired. It's past midnight!"

"Then I suggest you rouse whoever is in charge of lodging guests. We can hardly be the first visitors to court to arrive late."

The poor man disappeared with the thankless task of waking his master.

Lady Ellie frowned. "Do you think we should go to Jane at so late an hour? If only the roads had not been so muddy, we would have been here hours ago!"

Will pulled his gloves off, finger by finger. "No use lamenting something we cannot change, love. And if Jane is so opposed to this marriage, there is no point us waiting until the very day to see what use we can be to her. She'll need her friends around her this night." He turned to Milly. "Do you know where she lodges?"

257

"Yes, my lord—that is, if she has the same room as before."

"Then lead on."

Leaving one of the Lacey servants to inform the chamberlain where they had gone, the three set off for Jane's quarters. A light still burned in the room, suggesting that the occupant was having a sleepless night.

Milly rapped on the door, but there was no answer.

Will shook his head. "She must have fallen asleep with the candles still lit. Does she want to burn the palace down?"

Something was wrong—very wrong. Milly lifted the latch. "My lady? Jane?"

The room was a mess—wine spilt on the floor, Jane herself curled up on the bed.

"Drunk?" wondered Will aloud. "She can hardly be blamed for drowning her sorrows, but still—" He broke off as he spotted her hand lying limp over the edge of the mattress.

Milly and Ellie rushed across the room.

"Quick, Will: summon help!" ordered the countess.

The earl strode out into the corridor, bellowing for assistance. Milly felt for a pulse: it was there, but erratic.

Ellie slapped Jane's cheeks lightly. "Jane? Jane? Can you hear me?"

Jane's eyelids flickered but she did not open them.

"What do you think is wrong with her?" Milly asked frantically.

Ellie surveyed the evidence in the room. Spilt wine with no attempt to clear it away; a smashed jug. "I'd say it must be something she drank—the onset was very sudden."

"You mean poison?"

Ellie nodded and snagged a quill from the inkstand. "Open her mouth—we must make her sick."

Jane retched as the feather scratched the back of her throat. Her skin was still clammy and horribly pale.

Ellie held her until she had emptied the contents of her stomach into the chamber pot. Then Ellie bent over and kissed the top of her head. "My poor Jane, what have they done to you?"

Or what had she done to herself? Milly could not help but wonder if her friend had been so desperate as to try to commit suicide. "Will she be all right?"

She took comfort in the fact that the countess was well known for her learning; her father had been a noted alchemist. If anyone understood the properties of strange substances, it would be her.

Ellie rubbed Jane's hands vigorously to warm them. "I cannot say with any certainty. Some poisons are not cured by inducing the patient to vomit; indeed, they have no antidote. All depends on how much Jane took."

As she spoke, the Queen's own physician hurried into the room, followed by what appeared to be half the household. A grave-looking elderly man with a gray beard, the doctor quickly surmised what treatment had been administered so far and nodded approvingly at the countess. "Excellent—you've already given the emetic."

"No emetic—a feather in the throat," Ellie corrected him.

"No matter: it has the same result. Do we know what poison she imbibed?" He knelt at Jane's bedside in a flurry of black robes.

"No, doctor, but her heart rate is uneven and she is having difficulty breathing."

"Hmm, possibly wolfsbane. I do not know anything that can

counter its effects; we have to wait it out. Has she got any worse since you found her?"

"No, sir."

He allowed himself a flicker of a smile as he pressed Jane's limp hand. "That is a good sign. Her own body is battling the poison; we must pray she wins that war."

Emerging from behind the scandalized courtiers and servants blocking the door, Clément Montfleury pushed his way to the front of the crowd. "*Mon Dieu!* What is happening? Why is my bride like this?"

Jane gave a low moan, audible only to Milly, Ellie and the doctor.

"Will, Jane does not need an audience," the countess appealed to her husband. "Please, will you ask everyone to clear the room?"

The earl stepped between the bed and the spectators. "Good sirs, the lady is in the best possible hands. She must have peace."

Montfleury bristled like a diminutive cockerel facing down the sheepdog. "But she is to be my wife!"

"Then you must have her best interests at heart, *monsieur*. I pray you, everyone, clear the room and let the physician do his work."

"We are supposed to marry in but a few hours from now!"

"Sir, is her health of no concern to you?"

Montfleury snapped his fingers at the earl. "Your innuendo is not welcome, sir. The welfare of my *chère Jeanne* is my chief occupation." With a sniff, the Frenchman departed along with the others. Milly would have thought better of him if he had insisted on staying, but evidently the unpleasant realities of nursing a patient through her illness did not appeal to his fastidious tastes.

The earl also withdrew, promising to guard the door against any more unwelcome visitors. Once he had gone, Milly set about cleaning the chamber while Ellie and the doctor monitored Jane's condition. It looked as though they were in for a long night.

The watch was crying two o'clock by the time Jane began to revive.

"Water!" she whispered hoarsely.

With the physician's permission, Ellie raised a cup of watered-down wine to Jane's parched lips. They had taken the precaution of ordering it up from the Queen's own stores to ensure it had no taint.

Jane's eyes fluttered open and came to rest on Ellie's face. She raised her hand feebly to touch her friend but gave up the effort. "Ellie. What are you doing here?"

The countess smiled at her through her tears. "Come to save you, it would appear."

"I feel terrible." Jane put her hand to her throat.

"You look terrible, my dear."

"What time is it?"

Ellie raised an eyebrow. "What does it matter?"

"I'm supposed to be getting married on the morrow." Jane closed her eyes again.

"I don't think that will go ahead now. You've been poisoned."

Blue eyes snapped open. "Richard! Oh God, I remember now—Richard Paton—he gave me the wine." Frantically she groped the fingers of her left hand. "He took my ring. Ellie, he took Jonas's ring!"

"Hush now. We'll see to all that. You must sleep—recover your strength. No one is going to harm you again. We won't let them."

Jane turned her face to the pillow, her grief for the loss of her wedding band outweighing all else at that moment.

The doctor rose from his knees. "Lady Dorset, I would say the marchioness is mercifully out of danger. The most worrying symptoms are subsiding, but I would expect her to feel weak and have some lingering pain in her stomach. That should fade after a day or so." He frowned at the red stain on the rush mat. "I will report her allegations against her stepson to Her Majesty, but it is most difficult to prove poisoning—it is such an insidious art, nigh on impossible to detect unless you catch the perpetrator in the act. The person responsible was careful to leave no sample for us to test." He left, promising to return in the morning to check on the lady's progress.

"What does that mean?" Milly whispered to Ellie.

Ellie smoothed the hair from Jane's brow. "I think he is hinting that it will be hard to pursue a case against someone as important as the present Marquess of Rievaulx, particularly when it is well known they bear ill will each to the other. Her allegation could be construed as a malicious attempt to blacken his name."

"But he can't be allowed to get off scot-free!"

"But taking it to a court of law may not be the best avenue to keep her safe from that wicked man."

"So what can we do for her?"

Ellie shook her head sadly. "That is the question, isn't it?"

"She needs a champion—someone to stand up for her with her family and that awful Montfleury person."

The two girls exchanged a glance, both reaching the same conclusion.

"I hope James comes back soon," said Ellie.

Chapter 20

Jane woke to find Ellie and Milly sitting either side of her bed like two lionesses guarding a cub. Wisps of copper hair drifting free of her cap to tickle her neck, Milly concentrated on embroidering a hatband while the countess read aloud from a manuscript of poems, dark eyes twinkling at the more absurd passages. Jane lay still, allowing herself to enjoy the scene before she had to face the reality of what had happened to her and what was still to take place, unless some miracle intervened.

"What day is it?" she asked at length.

"Thursday." Ellie reached out and squeezed her hand. "I'm pleased you are back with us."

"I should be getting married at noon."

Milly squinted at the sun shining through the window. "I think you'll miss that particular appointment."

Jane lay silently for a few moments, taking stock of her condition. Her stomach ached, her limbs felt weak and heavy, but otherwise she was unharmed, which, considering the close brush with death of the night before, seemed a marvel. "I survived. I thought I was dead."

Ellie smiled at her through her tears. "Nay, Jane, it will take more than a few sips of poison to do away with the Dowager Marchioness of Rievaulx."

Her words jogged Jane's memory. "My ring."

"I know, my dear. Will is doing what he can to regain it for you."

"Has my stepson been arrested?"

Milly stabbed her cloth with a huff. Ellie gave her a stern look, reminding her not to upset the patient. "Not yet."

"Why not?" Jane tried to sit up against the pillows but Ellie pushed her back.

"Stay still. You are ordered to complete bed rest by the Queen on the advice of her physician."

"Tell me."

Milly scowled. "I'll tell you why, Jane. The thieving knave claims you suffer from a weak heart, denies poison had any part in your so-called fainting episode yester eve. He admits calling on you, says you gave him the ring as a sign of the peace made between you both, and calls his servant to witness that he left you in good health at around eleven."

"He lies."

"Of course he does, but he's a marquess, therefore he must be right." Milly snapped her thread in her fury. "Oh, he's full of sympathy for your poor health, is our mendacious marquess, but says that a poor female couldn't possibly understand such things and would be quick to cry poison when learned minds know better."

"That's not true."

"He even uses your survival as proof that you are mistaken, says you panicked, suspecting poison, and induced your own symptoms.

He's even persuaded the Queen's physician that this is a possible explanation."

Jane lay on her back, hands fisted at her sides, glaring at the faded bed curtains. "When I get out of here, I'm going to corner Richard and stick his codpiece full of pins—while he is still wearing it. And that is just as the prelude to my revenge."

"Good for you, Jane. I'll hold his arms. I have some very long pins in my workroom—let me know how many you need."

Ellie shook her head. "My, my, what a bloodthirsty crew I have fallen among. I was content to leave his punishment to Will, but perhaps your idea has merit."

"Gelding is too good for that man—he should be executed for his crimes!" Milly continued.

Jane flinched—giving vent to her anger was one thing, contemplating the marquess's death quite another. "He is Jonas's son, for all that."

Milly was less than impressed. "Humph. Perhaps his mother wasn't honest: he shows none of the kindness you met in your husband. I struggle to believe they are kin."

Their conversation was interrupted by a disturbance just beyond the chamber.

"You cannot go in there, sir!" bellowed Will. Feet scuffled—something heavy fell to the floor.

"I'm taking her to church!" thundered the Earl of Wetherby. "I do not care if she is at death's door: she's marrying Montfleury this very day."

Will said something in return, but as he was speaking more softly now, his words were lost.

Wetherby knew no such moderation. "She brought this on herself. I don't believe for one instant that the marquess would do this to her. She's been trying to wriggle out of this match ever since the papers were signed. I won't stand for it!"

Ellie's normally kind face grew incandescent with outrage; Milly jumped to her feet, placing herself between the bed and the door.

"If he dares lay a hand on her, I'll box his ears!" she vowed.

Jane closed her eyes, embarrassed that her friends should hear how little love her own family bore her.

"Daughter!" The earl had apparently forced his way into the room, as his voice came from much closer. "Stop this play-acting and get up. We've a wedding to celebrate."

"The Queen has ordered her to rest." Will sounded as angry as her father. She could sense both of them at her bedside, but she took the coward's way out and kept her eyes closed in the feeble hope that if her father was convinced she was too ill to get up he would leave her alone.

A meaty hand gripped her shoulder and shook. "Stop this, you disobedient she-devil! I know you're well enough. You will obey me. Ouch! Good God, wench, that hurt!" The fingers quickly released their hold.

"Oh, I pray your pardon, your lordship. My needle must've slipped." That was Milly. Where on earth had she pricked Jane's father? That didn't bear thinking about.

Jane gave up on the attempt to ignore the incursion into her chamber. She opened her eyes and saw that her father had brought Henry with him; her brother was keeping Will back as her father attempted to get her to rise.

"I told you she was playing us false!" crowed her father.

"This is ridiculous!" interjected Ellie. "Your daughter was poisoned but a few hours since and you are intent on dragging her to church! Have you taken complete leave of your senses? I appeal not to your heart, as I know you do not have one, but surely common decency should tell you to let her rest."

"Poisoned, i'faith? Nay, she merely tried to renege on our agreement with Montfleury by staging her collapse."

The little countess went head to head with the man, despite the fact he outweighed her by a good five stone. "And if she did, what would that tell you? How can you push your own child into a marriage when it is clearly so repulsive to her?"

"So you admit it was a plot to escape the wedding?"

Ellie could have screamed with frustration. "No, sir, I said no such thing. I am trying to make you see reason."

Clutching the sheets more tightly, Jane sensed that her father was girding himself up to drag her from her sick bed, Queen's orders or no. He was so desperate for this marriage to proceed—greed had gone to his head. He was prepared to haul her from the sheets as a goodwife tugs the carded fleece to spin into profitable yarn. For all her friends' arguments on her behalf, the basic fact remained: she was still going to have to marry the Frenchman.

Jane was preparing herself for the unseemly tussle when there was a further commotion at the door. Two more people forced their way into the chamber.

"Diego!" squeaked Milly, abandoning her post at Jane's side to throw herself into her lover's arms.

"James!" Will laughed in relief, taking Henry's arm. "In the nick of time. Come give me a hand here. The Earl of Wetherby and his son were just leaving."

"It would be my pleasure." James took Henry's other arm as they hauled him out into the corridor.

The tide had turned, as Laceys now outnumbered Percevals. "My lord, I'm sure the Queen will not be impressed when she hears that her express orders that her lady remain abed have been challenged," Ellie said pertly.

Seeing the game go against him, Jane's father ignored the countess and glared down at his daughter. "I'll expect you to proceed with this wedding as soon as the Queen gives you permission to rise."

Jane was tempted to say in that case that she thought she had discovered a calling to a life in bed, but decided not to risk it. "I thank you for your kind wishes for my recovery." She gave him a flinty smile that sparked off another barrage of insults as her father reluctantly retreated.

The room finally cleared of Wetherby and son, Jane could turn her full attention to the wonderful fact that James was back—here, in this very room. Her emotions were in turmoil. He looked well—sunburnt and shabby but in very good health. She feasted her eyes on him as he greeted his brother and sister-in-law. Then he reached her side and kissed her hand.

"So, Lady Jane, what trouble have you been brewing while I've been gone? And whom do you want me to do away with to put it right?"

That was the moment when finally, after all the shocks of the last few hours, Jane burst into tears.

· ❀ ·

The others left Jane and James alone, taking discreet positions at the far end of the chamber so that Diego could tell them about the voyage. As she went, Milly tugged free the ties securing the bed hangings to give them added privacy. Deciding this was no moment for respectful caution, James slid onto the bed beside Jane and gathered her into his arms so she could sob against his chest. Her tears dampened his shirt, her cheek hot against his heart. He ran his hand over her long hair in a soothing gesture, letting the crying run its course. Aware how fortunate he was that she still appeared to care for him and by some miracle had remained single, he silently prayed that he would find the right words to comfort her, the right actions to help her.

"Ah, love, what have they done to you?" he asked as her sobs subsided.

Her shoulders shuddered as she took a deep breath, trying to regain control.

"I'm not sure what we walked in upon, but I know about the marriage. Milly wrote to Diego, but the letter missed us. I understand that you have no wish to wed Montfleury?"

"Not him," she whispered, fingers tracing the loosened lacing at his throat.

James allowed himself a small smile, bent and kissed the top of her head. "Then you won't have to."

"It's not that simple, Jamie."

He put that aside for now. If he had to take her out of the country, he would; there was no way she was going to be forced into marrying the French coxcomb. When he had left for his voyage, he had imagined she would have crushed the pretender to her hand under her boot heel long before now. As she had not, he was more than happy to do the deed for her. "What else has been going on? Have you been ill?"

"Poisoned."

He jerked in shock, almost dislodging her before he pulled her back against him. "What?"

"Rievaulx did it—wants my dower rights and probably my dowry too." She turned her face to look up at James, her blue eyes pools of sorrow. "He took the ring, Jamie."

James forced himself not to leap from the bed and go hunt down the marquess right that moment. "He's a dead man."

She reached up and brushed his jaw with her fingers. "No, he's not worth it. I don't want you to get into trouble for me."

Another matter to leave for later discussion, James decided. He was not letting Rievaulx get away with hurting her. "I'll get your ring back—I promise."

She snuggled against him. "It is enough to have you back. Tell me of your voyage."

James let her rest, her head against his heart, as he related the adventures in Roanoke, shaping them to amuse her. He could sense her silent attention to every detail as she caressed the fabric of his shirt, reassuring herself that he really was there. Seeing her so battered by those who should have looked after her, he could not but feel fiercely protective. Her welfare had become his first priority. The most important thing right now was to help her rest from her ordeal, so he sought a way to make her sleep. Deliberately, he shifted from the more entertaining anecdotes to give her details of his surveys, reeling off long lists of facts he had noted for his map. Sure enough, it worked like a sleeping draft and her breathing evened out, her hand went limp. She slept.

Easing out from under her, he arranged her on her feather pillow and tucked the sheets around her. Her fingers twitched as if still reaching out for him. He brushed his thumb across the back of her hand in reassurance, then walked softly to the other side of the room.

"All well?" asked Will.

"She's resting." James slumped next to his brother on the bench.

Will threw his arm round James's shoulders. "What a homecoming."

"Aye. It's a tangle."

From her perch on Diego's knee, Milly wrinkled her nose. "But from the mess of raw silk, we can draw the thread. There has to be a way."

"You know, when I left her, I was convinced she was as happy as she could be, as safe as the Queen's jewels serving as one of her ladies. What happened?"

"Her family happened." Milly stroked Diego's hands, folded under hers.

"Tell me the details. Jane gave me the outline but I lack the shading."

Milly, being closest to the action over the past months, briefly explained the machinations of the Percevals, Montfleury and the Patons. James could feel his anger rising but he had to see beyond emotion if he was going to be of any use to Jane.

Will crossed his feet at the ankles. "Do we understand you consider the lady yours now, James?"

He nodded. "If she'll have me."

"About time too," muttered Ellie before giving James a beautiful smile. "She wants you; she always has."

"Then, brother, I think you should lead this campaign," said Will, ceding command.

James stood up and strode to the window, then back to his little circle of recruits in Jane's army. "As I see it we have three problems: making her family back away, turning Montfleury in another direction than marriage and getting justice for Jane with that bastard, Rievaulx. What is the Queen's attitude to all this?"

Will glanced over at the curtained bed, afraid that they were disturbing Jane with their discussion, but there was no sign she was awake. "Thus far Her Majesty has been persuaded to take Wetherby's side. Appearances made that inevitable."

"We need more allies then: those who are closer to the Queen."

"The Queen's ladies should be on Jane's side," suggested Ellie.

James shook his head. "No, someone even closer to the Queen than that."

Will groaned. "Are you thinking what I am thinking you are thinking?"

James gave a gruff laugh. "Lord, Will, you sound like my old philosophy tutor, full of obscure sentences. I don't know. You tell me."

"I don't want to mention the name unless I absolutely have to."

James grinned. "You can't deny he owes me. I did a good job for him in America; he should be feeling grateful. And we have to move Jane somewhere her family cannot reach her, else they'll marry her off when our backs are turned. Indeed, that should be the first thing we do. Diego, would you go see if Master Raleigh is at court?"

With a kiss on the tip of her nose, Diego shifted Milly from his lap. "Aye, sir."

"Will, if you'll stand guard here. I'm going in search of a marquess."

Will stood up. "Jamie—"

"Save it, Will. This is a reckoning that has to be paid, one way or another."

CHAPTER 21

JAMES FOUND RICHARD PATON CLOSETED with his brothers in their lodgings close to the palace. Far from the finest rooms available, it proclaimed better than a glimpse into the account books that the Rievaulx estate was not doing well under the new marquess. If Paton was struggling to keep up appearances at court, then his fortunes were sunk very low, explaining but not excusing his desperation to do away with his stepmother to claw back some much needed income. As the surly manservant showed him upstairs, James wondered if the marquess would remember him from the altercation outside the abbey all those months ago; from the suspicious expression on Paton's face when James entered, he guessed that he did.

"Master Lacey, how may I help you?" the marquess asked coldly, not bothering to rise for his visitor. "I am rather pressed for time this day, as I have been called away on business."

Fleeing the scene of his crime, thought James bitterly; Paton hoped that out of sight would be out of the Queen's mind.

"I would beg only a moment of your valuable time, sir." James almost lost his composure when he saw the Rievaulx ring on the man's little finger. He linked his hands behind his back to rein in the urge to rip it off. "I would ask you to accompany me to the fencing hall."

Paton snorted. "I have no time for play, sir."

"Not play." James let his smile glint with wolfish hunger. He wanted nothing more than to sink his dagger into the villain's heart, if he could find it, but he had to keep this civilized. And legal. He would do Jane no good if he was in the Tower for murder.

Paton surveyed the younger man with contempt. "Then what is it? A challenge?"

James shrugged. "If you like, but a challenge would suggest I consider you worthy of one when in truth I think you worse than a dunghill rat."

"What!"

All three brothers leapt to their feet. Excellent.

"You insult me, sirrah!" spluttered the marquess.

"No, I insult rats mentioning them in the same breath as you." James drew his sword to stop their advance on him. "What I propose is a wager. You attempted to poison my lady, and compounded that sin by stealing a ring from her when she was powerless to defend herself."

The marquess unsheathed his blade. "There is no proof, only her word against mine. The courts will not believe a jade like her."

"Ah, and there's your mistake, sir, for I am not a court of law. I intend to make you pay and care not how we go about it. I could kill you and be on the continent before the sun sets—it matters little to me as long as my lady has justice."

"Justice? Pah!" spat Otho, the most hot-blooded of the brothers.

He stabbed his dagger into the tabletop. "She deserves to be kicked into the gutter."

Paton gestured him to be silent, evidently realizing that there was nothing more dangerous than a man who believes he has nothing to lose. "Your wager? What is it?"

"We take this to the fencing hall and settle the dispute before witnesses. If I win, you give me the ring and your solemn vow that you will not come within sight of my lady, or harass her through your agents, for the rest of your miserable life, that's if I see fit to grant you that."

"If you lose?"

"Your choice of penalty, as befits a gentleman."

The cunning brother, Lucres, laughed. "Tell him to cut his own throat—that should do it."

The marquess drummed his fingers on the table, the ring glinting in the firelight. "You leave the country—if I let you live."

James nodded. "So be it."

It was a short step from the lodgings to the fencing hall. James made sure he kept behind the Paton brothers, not foolish enough to risk exposing his back to them. When they arrived, James found Diego waiting for him in the portico, accompanied by none other than Walter Raleigh.

"Sir." James bowed, thinking quickly what this meant for his wager with the marquess. Would Raleigh feel obliged to step in to prevent it?

"I am most gratified to see you back safe and sound from the voyage." Raleigh returned the bow. "You must tell me all about it, but it appears you have other business at the moment."

"Indeed." James cut a glance at the three Patons, wondering if they were about to appeal to Raleigh to avoid the combat. "The marquess and I had a philosophical argument and agreed to settle our differences in a test of our swordsmanship."

Raleigh gave the Patons a contemptuous look. "A scholarly quarrel? I heard the bastard poisoned the Lady Jane." The marquess was quick to hide his consternation, but it was there, under the cool demeanor. "Have at him with my blessing." He gestured for them to proceed into the hall.

"The Queen sent you?" James asked when the Patons were out of earshot.

Raleigh gave a wicked smile. "Not as such. Your servant anticipated your argument would bring you here and Mistress Parry and I agreed that it would be in the lady's best interests for me to attend. I volunteered to stand witness so that fair play is observed. But the Patons don't have to know that, do they?"

James had to admit that Diego's plan was better than his. With the Queen's favorite on his side, implying Her Majesty's support even if the reality was far less certain, any repercussions from the encounter would be minimized.

"Thank you, sir."

Raleigh clapped him on the back. "Can't say I like your brother, but it seems there's one Lacey I've learnt to stomach. And the lady too has earned my respect—I am no friend to those who seek to harm her."

"Thank you." James would prefer Raleigh to have no feelings at all towards Jane.

Raleigh grinned as if party to his thoughts. "Besides, I wouldn't want to lose the opportunity to hear your report if you fell unjustly to the marquess's blade."

James grimaced. "You're all heart, sir."

"Aren't I?"

The marquess did not look at all happy that Raleigh had elected to watch their bout but had to acquiesce. A number of other gentlemen already exercising their skills in the fencing hall looked up on their entrance; Raleigh's arrival anywhere was guaranteed to attract notice. The hostile atmosphere surrounding James and the Patons alerted all but the most thick-headed to the fact that something extraordinary was afoot, and many of them drifted over to join the audience.

James limbered up in his corner, focusing on the task at hand, not on the excited chatter around him.

"How far do you intend to take this?" Diego asked, checking James's rapier.

He gave Diego a wry smile. "Not to the death, unfortunately. I'll settle for humiliation and the return of the ring. As long as the court knows he's guilty, that is enough for now."

Diego wiped the blade with a soft cloth. "And if he beats you?"

"Not an outcome I will allow."

"I have just spoken to the fencing master. Paton's good. Practices most days."

"Then I'll have to be better."

"My lords, gentlemen." Raleigh held up his hand for silence. "Lord Rievaulx and Master Lacey have come here to settle their differences. I stand here for the Queen to ensure fair play is observed. The gentlemen have both pledged their word to abide by their agreed penalty if defeated. You fight until what? To first blood? Disarmament? Or points?"

"Disarmament, by whatever means," James said quickly. He did not want this to turn into a polite competition for points; neither did he desire to end it before he'd bloodied Paton more than once; he was in the mood for something much more satisfying.

"My lord, you agree?"

Paton scowled. "This is ridiculous—I haven't time for this."

Raleigh raised a mocking brow. "Yes, yes, I agree. I'll give the young pup a scar to teach him respect for his superiors."

The older men in the audience, unaware of the cause behind the contest, applauded, naturally lending their support to their peer against the youngster.

"Positions, then, gentlemen."

James took his stance an arm's length from the marquess, attempting to gauge what kind of fighter he was. Stocky in build, Paton probably relied on body strength rather than reach and speed, James's own advantages. Fortunately, James had trained against Diego, who, while much slighter, had a similar height to Paton's. He had taught his master to expect the unexpected from the shorter opponent.

"Begin!"

The fighters engaged, each testing the other's skills in a series of opening moves. The rapiers were thin and deadly sharp. You could use them like a whip, bringing the flat down on your opponent's wrist, forcing him to drop his blade; or, if you were going for blood, the most vulnerable area was the eyes, but that was considered poor sportsmanship and James wanted to make this a clean victory. That was if he could get through Paton's defenses. Damn, the man was more skilled than he'd expected.

The audience applauded an elegant exchange of strike, block and parry that had the two men dancing around like courtiers doing the coranto.

"Bravo!" shouted one old lord.

So pleased to amuse you, thought James sourly.

Forty-eight hours without sleep were catching up with James; fighting as he was in bare feet for grip, his instep caught the edge of an uneven flagstone and he lost balance for a second. Paton thrust his blade through the gap so the tip caught James's chin, then his shirt, snagging in the material but not reaching flesh. The audience clapped.

The combatants parted to return to their positions. Diego passed James a towel so he could wipe off the perspiration and blood.

"I've seen you fight better."

"So have I. I should have slept before attempting this, but there's my foolish pride for you."

"And he would have slipped away from London, escaped your retribution."

"True."

"Still, you had better raise your game."

James threw back the towel. "As if I didn't know that."

Paton's confidence had been boosted by James's stumble. He went into the second bout with an arrogant swagger.

"Chosen your country of exile, Lacey?" he sneered. "How about Russia? That should be far enough."

James did not rise to the bait and lose his temper. He merely raised his blade and narrowed his focus to his opponent's torso, watching for the telltale signs of which way Paton was going to move. The point against him had been the call to alarm that he needed; he did not intend to give away another one.

Blades clashed, steel scraping on steel like the carvers sharpening their knives for a feast. James dug deep and found his old rhythm, pressing from defense to attack, making the older man sweat to be in time to parry the blows. Some cuts came perilously close to finding home in flesh, but the marquess managed to deflect at the last second. The younger spectators cheered, seeing their champion return to form. When James considered he had let it drag out long enough for Paton, he swiped across the man's collarbone, leaving a shallow cut on his upper chest. The marquess staggered back, clutching the injury.

James lowered his blade. "That was for my lady, for the distress you gave her. Hurts like hellfire, doesn't it? Now you feel something of what she felt yester eve when you left her to die."

The audience fell quiet, realizing that something more serious than a contest of skills was at stake.

"You mention that whore to me?" rasped the marquess. "She's a blight on the family name."

"You are mistaken." James's tone was clipped, still in control. It was going to be very difficult to resist the temptation to ram his blade through the bastard's heart. "You are a disgrace to your father, Paton. He asked you to protect his wife and you break your word by trying to murder her."

"Enough of this nonsense," spat out the marquess. "Are we going to fight or are you going to stand there and preach?"

James flourished his blade. "Definitely fight. *En garde!*"

The next bout was vicious, the rules out the window as Paton went for eyes, kidneys, any area that would disable the younger man. James's blood was up—he took pleasure in unpicking each attack, making the marquess look clumsy and vastly outskilled. Several times Raleigh looked on the point of intervening, but that was impossible while the battle heat was on both men. First blood had long since been drawn, but neither contestant was ready to concede. Satisfied that the marquess's shirt was stained red, blood dripping from a slice down his cheek, James had finally had enough of tormenting Paton. He let the marquess make one wild swipe, then came back swiftly to lay the flat of his blade in a stinging blow across the back of his opponent's right hand. The marquess's blade clattered to the ground as he nursed his paralyzed fingers.

Stepping forward, James seized the injured hand and pulled off the ring before Paton had time to recover. "My lady's, I believe."

Raleigh swiftly took position between James and the other Paton brothers, who looked ready to take up where their elder had left off. "I declare Master Lacey the victor. On the honor of both your houses, you must now abide by your agreements and leave this place with no further violence."

"I'll get you for this, Lacey," growled the marquess.

"I think you misheard, my lord," Raleigh said coldly. "If you pursue your revenge outside these walls, you will be dishonored and no longer received at court. Indeed, I believe you have quite outstayed your welcome on this occasion and should return to your northern estates until the Queen summons you back."

If Paton's eyes had been thunderbolts, Raleigh would have been struck down where he stood, leaving nothing but a smoking pair of shoes. The marquess nodded curtly. "I wish him joy of his whore, then."

His move to leave was stopped by a blade poked in his chest. The sword's owner was Raleigh.

"Careful, my lord. You slander one of the Queen's ladies without cause, and that I cannot allow, as it strikes too close to Her Majesty's person. You may not depart this place until you withdraw your comment."

The marquess looked close to apoplexy. Raleigh was as good as saying that to insult Jane was a treasonous act. Many of his peers had been sent to Tower Hill for less. "I retract my words. I mean no offense to Her Majesty." He sounded like he was spitting pebbles.

Raleigh dropped the point of his sword. "Good. I am glad you have seen the error of your ways."

Paton summoned his brothers with a jerk of his head. "You may rule here for now, Raleigh, but how long will that last?" He stamped out, pushing a path through the crowd when people did not move out of his way quickly enough for his taste.

Raleigh shook his head. "Well, that told me, did it not, gentlemen?"

The audience laughed, as he had intended, and dispersed to spread the gossip about the marquess's humiliation in the corridors and anterooms of the palace.

"Is it enough for you?" Raleigh asked James shrewdly.

James sheathed his sword. "Not nearly. But it will have to do. I'd hurt her more if I took this any further."

Raleigh tossed him his doublet. "Come, I understand I need to offer sanctuary at Durham House to a marchioness."

Jane woke to find James sitting by her bedside, feet propped on the covers, chin dropped to his chest as he slept. She smiled to herself. He really was here. The distance that had opened between them before he left for America had been closed by last night's disaster and he was hers once more.

But for how long? As soon as she got out of this bed, she would have to deal with the awful mess she had gotten herself into with

Montfleury. If there were a prize for the worst person at handling their love affairs since old King Henry, then she would be the winner. She clenched her fists, forcing back the onset of panic. No, she would not give in to hysteria; there had to be a way. At least now she had friends about her. And James.

Just then his foot slipped from the covers, jolting him awake. He opened his eyes to find Jane gazing at him, amused at the momentary confusion in his sleep-befuddled face. He lifted his chin and she saw that he had a shallow scratch along his jaw, a bloody line almost hidden by his beard.

"Did you cut yourself trimming your beard?"

James rubbed his hand over his short whiskers. "Aye, beard trimming—but it was a marquess I was shaving." He twisted something off his little finger and flourished it.

"My ring!" Jane reached out for it.

Smiling, he took her hand and slid it on her finger. "There, love, back where it should be. But not for too long, I hope. I pray you will agree to wear my ring very soon."

Jane tried to pull her hand away but his hold was firm. "Jamie, what about my family and Montfleury? I'm in such a muddle."

"And I am an excellent solver of muddles—let that be my wedding present to you, as I have precious little else to offer."

"But, Jamie . . ."

He shook his head. "Hush, love. Just trust me. I got you back your ring, didn't I?"

Jane had been slow to work out how that might have come to pass, but now she realized Richard would not willingly have surrendered it. "Did you . . . did you kill him?"

James caressed her chilled fingers. "I was tempted, but no. I fought him for the ring and sent him packing. Raleigh stood up for me—that helped."

"Raleigh?" Jane choked in surprise. That gentleman was not one to whom she would look for favors.

"Strangely, he has taken a liking to me, and you have his respect—his term, by the way."

"Well." Jane was lost for words.

"He's doing more. He has gained permission from his mistress for you to remove to Durham House for your convalescence. We need to have you somewhere your father will find it hard to gain entry. The palace is too open to him, and I fear he will make some surprise move if we do not keep you safe."

Humiliation rippled through Jane at the thought of being under Raleigh's roof. "But I can't go to Durham House!"

"I know your brother is his friend, but on this matter Raleigh is siding with you. He has promised to keep Henry away."

James wouldn't understand what he was suggesting unless she explained. Jane closed her eyes, not wanting to look at his face as she confessed. "No, James, it is not that. It is just that Raleigh and I, well, we have a history." She swallowed, her heart racing again as if she'd drunk more poison.

James was ominously silent.

"It . . . it was two years ago." Jane could feel tears pricking her eyelids. Was this when she would lose him? Was her stupid mistake going to blight the rest of her life? "I thought I loved him and that he loved me. Foolish, idiot girl!"

James cleared his throat. "I see. I see."

"I think my brother knows, Milly too. And my maid at the

time." This was torture. "I told Jonas, of course, before we married, but he forgave me. He was like that—never saw another's sins but only his own. No one else is aware of what passed between Raleigh and me, though the rumors have followed me, as you know. I . . . I pray your pardon for not being what you thought I was." Silence.

Oh God. "Do you . . . do you want to leave?"

She felt her fingers taken once more in his warm palm. "Jane, love, look at me."

"I can't. I'm too scared."

"Look at me."

Reluctantly, she opened her eyes. He had leant forward so his face was only a few inches from hers.

"Do I look like virgin territory myself?"

She shook her head, smiling despite herself at the thought.

"Do you want me to apologize for the beds I have been in before yours?"

"You haven't been in my bed," she whispered. It was going to be all right, completely all right.

"And that is a great shame and an oversight I intend to correct with the first priest I can persuade to marry us."

She caressed his jaw with the tip of her finger. "Thank you. I can't tell you how much I've been dreading this."

"Nay, do not thank me. Like you, I have my regrets, but I don't want to bring them into our marriage. It is enough to know that from here on there is just you for me and, I hope, me for you."

"Oh, yes. No one else."

He gave a sudden grin. "Which is why you are not marrying that cockless Frenchman and are wedding me instead. We will then go on to make a new start, forging good, lusty memories to drive out all others."

Jane allowed herself an anticipatory smile. "I told Raleigh he was a disappointment as a lover."

"You did what?" James roared with laughter. "The poor man. He's a saint for offering you sanctuary when you gave him that particular kick in the crown jewels."

"I thought it only fair."

James abandoned the chair to recline beside her, head propped on one hand. "Quite so. He was a blackguard for seducing you—but I can understand the temptation." He kissed her lightly. "I haven't made a habit of bedding virgins in my past, but I cannot swear that I've not hurt a few hearts in my passing. We'll pay Raleigh back by being outrageously happy and smirking when he sees us in an amorous embrace—and I'm planning plenty of those just to make him choke with jealousy."

"A sweet revenge." She returned the kiss.

"Aye, that it is."

She let the silence stretch for a moment, wondering if she could trust this new country of love that he had led her into. It was hard to believe in this landscape of green hills of contentment and sunny prospects stretching to the horizon when she was far more used to dark confinements and storms coming out of nowhere. "Are you sure, Jamie, that you want me? Really sure?"

He caressed her hair, fingertips playing with the delicate skin behind her ear. "Very sure."

"But you didn't want me earlier in the year."

He sighed. "I wanted you, but I didn't want you to have me as I was then. I felt empty—worthless. I soon realized how I felt about you when I sailed. There's something about being at sea that sets all in perspective—I was able to slough off the skin of the old guilt and become something shiny and new again. America does that to a man."

Was he just telling her what he thought she needed to hear for her recovery? "You needn't pretend with me, Jamie. I won't be offended if you admit you . . . that you . . ." She couldn't bring herself to say it—that he despised her as she despised herself for her weakness, her faults.

James hugged her closer. "I can see you do not yet trust me, madam, and require proof. Fortunately, I have it."

"Proof?"

"Of my feelings for you. This lovesick swain penned you many letters while on his voyage of discovery." He tugged a pouch from his belt and placed it in her hands. "Here's proof that the clouds of despondency cleared my mind very soon after leaving these shores—and you were the sun that rose to smile down on me."

Jane hid her face against his chest, almost afraid to test whether this was true. "I will look forward to reading them, sir. I would not take you for a lovesick swain—seasick, perhaps."

"Ah, but that role was already taken. Rest now, my love, or Ellie will beat me around the ears for overtiring you. Read the letters when I'm gone or I'll blush to see your eyes on my pitiful outpourings."

"You, blush? Never!"

"It has been known to happen." He kissed the top of her head. "You have more power over me than you can guess, my lady."

CHAPTER 22

BEFORE SECRETLY MOVING JANE to Durham House, James acted on Milly's advice and dismissed Jane's maid; the woman had betrayed too many of her mistress's secrets to Henry and could not be trusted. All went smoothly: Jane transferred quietly by river with no Perceval interference and was soon lodged in a chamber with Milly to keep her company.

Alone for the first time since talking with Jane, James chose to walk back to Whitehall. He wanted time and space to make private peace with Jane's confession of her brief affair with Raleigh. He had known as soon as she started on her story that this was one of the moments in his life that he would regret eternally if he got it wrong. He was quite sincere in not blaming her for a lapse when his own balance sheet looked far worse. Still, he did not like the idea that Raleigh had known her first. She was his—his territory. The thought that another colonizer had got there before him turned his stomach.

And, of course, he admitted, that was entirely unreasonable of him. It had all happened before she even knew him and she had led a blameless life since. As Diego had pointed out about America, territory could not be claimed so easily. Being first was something of a fiction. What mattered was who lived there now. He should start making new memories with Jane to further his claim, not fret about the old.

As he turned towards the palace gate, a rough-looking middle-aged gentleman stepped into his path, his doublet showing the scuffs and stains of a traveler. Fearing that the Patons had come back for revenge, James put his hand to his sword, then realized he did not recognize the person as belonging to the Rievaulx entourage.

"May I help you, sir?" he asked, deciding to try politeness first.

"Master Lacey?"

"Aye."

"My name is Silas Porter. I am Milly's father."

James let his hand drop from his sword hilt and gave the stocky soldier a military-style nod of the head. "Sir. I am pleased to make your acquaintance."

Silas returned the gesture. "May I walk with you? I am afraid I cannot enter the palace—I lost my welcome there some years back."

It was not hard to guess what Silas wanted to talk about; James anticipated that they would need privacy for the discussion. "Let us walk on the riverside."

He led the way beyond the sprawling royal complex to the road leading to the village of Chelsea. Here the country reasserted itself—more trees than houses, a fine view of the bend in the river taking the Thames into the heart of England, a whitewashed mill, a waterwheel turning slowly in a mill race fed by the Thames. Three boats rowed downstream, brightly dressed courtiers their cargo, bees returning to the court hive and its queen.

"Your man wants to marry my girl," Silas said with no more ado.

James sighed. Was this going to be another approach like that of Christopher Turner? "So I understand."

"What think you of the match? I know my lass has her heart set on it, but I fear for them both."

Silas's point was fair. Their union would attract much harmful attention. "Diego is a fine man and a good friend. They both deserve their happiness."

Frustrated by the position in which he found himself, Silas ground his fist into his open hand. "But how can we make sure they are safe? I have done a poor job thus far, but I must make a stand if I think she is condemning herself to a lifetime of misery."

"In this case, misery, if it comes, will come from the outside, for they are well suited and, I sincerely believe, can make each other more than content. That is more than can be hoped from many marriages."

Thinking about that for a moment, Silas kicked a twig from his path. "I know that, but men can be cruel. Sometimes two people are not enough."

James wondered what arguments he could employ to sway the father. Then he saw the answer. "But, Master Porter, you are mistaken: they are not only two."

"What! She's with child!" spluttered Silas, leaping to quite the wrong conclusion. "I'll geld your man if that is so!"

James gulped back a laugh. "Goddamn my foolish tongue, no! I am not gifted at this kind of talk, sir, pray pardon me. I'm a soldier, not a poet, but even a rough man such as I can tell you your daughter is virtuous."

"Humph, just as well. Forgive me: I am apt to rush my fences."

Silas smiled with rueful self-knowledge. "I'll hold my peace. Let's see what two fumbling warriors can make of this."

Without needing to speak, they paused by mutual consent at a little landing place and sat down on an upturned boat. Strangely, despite the difference in age, James felt in harmony with the other man, sensing they shared many characteristics in common—a rash temper being one of them.

"Pray pardon me for causing you a moment's alarm. What I mean, sir, is that your daughter has friends to protect her—as does my man. I've already told Diego that if London proves too hot to hold them, then they will always have a home at Lacey Hall. And, if I do not anticipate too much, they would also be very welcome in my household when I marry my lady."

Silas perked up with interest. "Oh? What lady is this who would welcome a marriage like my daughter's?"

"Lady Jane, the Dowager Marchioness of Rievaulx."

Silas guffawed and slapped his knee. "Excellent, i'faith! So you have stepped forward to claim the lady—cut her free from the toils in which she was caught. I wish you joy—that lass is another pearl."

James warmed to his heartfelt praise. "And I'm the lucky swine who intends to have her."

The breeze picked up, whipping the water against the posts of the landing stage, reminding James that he still had much to do that day, but he couldn't find it in his heart to hurry Milly's father.

Silas scratched his chin for a moment, thinking through the options. "Where will you settle?"

James shook his head. "That is as yet unclear. My lady serves the Queen and may wish to continue to do so. I have to make my way, and court does offer the most chances for a man in my position."

Silas grunted. "Aye, second son—I know what that feels like. But a court life is good. My Milly is a damned fine woman of business. I don't like to think that her dream might be dismantled just because Londoners are too prejudiced to use her services. If she has your protection, and that of the lady, I think the commoners will not snub her."

James hadn't given the matter the thought it deserved, but he realized Silas was right. There was little point in Milly and Diego's retiring to Lacey Hall when their skills were ones that were valued by the nobility and gentry. If he was going to raise his manservant's fortunes, court would be the place to do it.

"So you do not object to the match on principle?"

"What father likes to see his little girl go off to another man?" Silas shook his head at his own selfishness. "But, no, I've always liked Diego, even if I never thought him to be a prospective son-in-law. I'm a traveled man and not narrow in my views. My last remaining reservation is that he is not quite orthodox in his beliefs. A few years back that could've ended at the stake."

James privately thought Diego was completely over the line as far as doctrine was concerned, but seeing he had his own doubts, that did not shock him unduly. He rather hoped that they both would benefit from the influence of their more orthodox wives. "Fortunately, under this queen, we live in happier times. Diego's beliefs are those of his homeland, overlaid with what he has learnt among us—nothing as incendiary as being a Catholic."

James had meant that as a jest, but Silas winced. His own treason had been rooted in his adherence to the faith of his upbringing; he'd since learnt, as many others had, to keep quiet and seek the common peace. "If you give him your support in this as well as in the rest, then I am content."

Pleased that he had been of use to his faithful companion in so vital a matter, James held out his hand and shook on the agreement. "Very good. You have my word. Now, will you come back with me after I've run my errand and break the news to the bride and groom? They are both at Durham House with Lady Jane."

"Aye, gladly. But what errand is that?"

"I have to persuade a Frenchman that he has no desire to wed my lady."

"'Swounds, I'd like to see this. Need a second?"

"Verily. I could do with a reasoning voice if I lose my temper."

Silas chuckled. "You've got the wrong man, then, son, but I promise to hold your cloak if you want to thump him."

Inquiring about Whitehall, James quickly discovered that Montfleury lodged at Master Mann's in Red Cross Street, one of the many fine houses of owners who supplied the needs of the overflow from the court. With Silas still in tow, he arrived outside the substantial three-story building in the heart of the city at the supper hour, hoping this would mean the Frenchman was at home. The landlord confirmed that Montfleury was within, but appeared reluctant to admit them.

"He's with guests, your worships," Mann prevaricated. "Don't like to be disturbed when he has company."

James fished out a coin from his purse. "I assure you, sir, he'll be delighted to see us."

The money disappeared with admirable swiftness into Mann's apron pocket. "In that case, sirs, you follow me. Shall I announce you?"

Silas grabbed the back of the landlord's jerkin. "Nay, in these cases, 'tis best we surprise them."

The host quickly surveyed the two men, both capable and with the unmistakable air of soldiers. "You're not going to shed blood under my roof, are you? I've no love for the Frog, but I keep a decent house, I do."

James pushed past Mann before he changed his mind and barricaded the stairs to them. "Have no fear: we come in peace."

"Just don't leave him in pieces!" quipped the landlord, before making himself scarce.

James paused outside Montfleury's room. Within he could hear several masculine voices, all talking in quick-fire French, punctuated by frequent bursts of laughter.

Silas nudged him. "What are you waiting for?"

True, this scene was not going to get any easier, with or without witnesses. James put his hand to the latch and entered.

As anticipated, they had interrupted supper, but the scandalous company they had not foreseen. Montfleury lay like some debauched god on a pile of red and purple cushions, dressed only in a shirt and hose; his male companion was similarly attired; the third man at the low table had the added garnish of a lightly clad girl on his lap. They looked up in surprise to find intruders at their feast.

James focused his scorn on Montfleury. "So this is how the bridegroom prepares for his wedding while his betrothed lies in her sickbed. I am touched to see how deep runs your concern for her well-being."

Recovering from his momentary surprise, the Frenchman shrugged and raised his glass to the newcomers. "I can be of no use to the lady, so I enjoy myself. It is not a sin." He smirked at his handsome companion.

James wasn't so sure about that. "*No use* is correct. As a husband, you would be nothing but a burden to the lady—and she to you—so I have come to rid you of that particular bridle on your freedom. I'm here to tell you that I'll be marrying Lady Jane. Your choice is to withdraw your suit quietly or fight me for her."

Montfleury snorted with disdain. "Gods, you Englishmen are so amusing, coming like a little bulldog to bark at my gate. I do not need to fight you—I have the family's permission, the Queen's approval, what more do I require?"

James smiled with studied nonchalance and helped himself to a fistful of grapes from a basket on the sideboard. "The lady. You forget the essential ingredient. That is the entire problem with this match—you have no use for a woman and she has no use for you. It makes no sense for you to persist when you will only end up standing at an altar, a notorious geck and gull. No honor for your house in that."

Silas slapped Montfleury's companion out of the way as he took over the young man's cushion. "Do up your laces, lad," he said briskly. "So much lilywhite flesh at the supper table turns my stomach."

Confused by the rough manners of the old soldier, the boy

scuttled back to the bed like a crab hiding under a stone. The drab giggled and offered Silas a plate of pastries.

Montfleury sat up straight, shying away from Silas, who made a point of crowding him as he filled his plate from the delicacies displayed on the low table. "You are naive, sir. This wedding is not about the lady."

"A marriage? And not about the lady? That's a fine pickle," commented Silas, winking at the girl.

"*Pas du tout,* marriage for the nobility is commerce. It is business." Montfleury scowled at Silas.

James insinuated himself into the gap on Montfleury's other side. "So if the terms of that business could be changed so that you benefit as much, if not more, from giving up the match, then you would be persuadable?"

"*Bien sûr,* but how can that be? These things are always done with a marriage alliance; how else will we trust the word of an Englishman?"

James grinned, seeing his way at long last. "First, you must understand that icicles will form in hell before I allow Jane to go to you. She's mine." Montfleury looked as if he would argue that point but James forged on. "If you regard my marriage to Jane favorably, then I will do all in my power to further your business interests in England. In addition to my wife's estates, my brother, the Earl of Dorset, has wool to trade and would be a key partner for you in the import of French wines to southern England, close to court, rather more lucrative than the northern realm your Wetherby controls. My brother is a particular friend of Lord Burghley and his son, so through him you have a connection to the Queen."

James was encouraged to see that Montfleury was giving his

words serious thought, his man-of-pleasure air being replaced by that of a businessman.

"Not to boast too much of my own influence," continued James, driving a further wedge into the gap his arguments had created, "I am on good terms with Raleigh and have just returned from a trip to America, where some exciting opportunities for investors are about to open up. With Lady Jane and I as your friends, you would have a much better reach to the most powerful people in the land than if you settled for the partnership only with the Earl of Wetherby."

Not yet convinced, Montfleury toyed with the pips on the edge of his plate, moving them around with his fingertip like counters.

James poured himself a glass of wine. "You do realize that Jane is quite independent of her father as to what she does with her fortune? Her last husband saw to that. Now that I have returned, and her opposition to the betrothal has firmed with my support, she will not bend to your browbeating any longer. We will even defy the Queen if we must and leave the country, but that would be a shame for all parties, as we take her fortune with us. Face it, Montfleury, you are going to lose her in any case. Why not salvage what you can? If you follow my advice, you can carry on with your preferred manner of living, without the encumbrance of a wife; you'll prosper in your business and return home in triumph."

Montfleury brushed the crumbs of his meal from his sleeve. "All right."

"All right what?"

"You have convinced me." His gaze lingered provocatively on James's face. "I do not want the girl and you do—that is very clear.

We will break the betrothal agreement together so neither party can be sued for breach of promise."

"A good point. I had not thought of that."

Montfleury smiled with condescension at the younger man, letting his admiration for James's courage and attraction to his charms show in his expression. "You can be assured of my friendship, Monsieur Lacey."

His fishing trip was spoiled by a dig in the ribs from Silas. "Enough of that, man; he's about to be married and doesn't share your particular tastes."

Montfleury gave a philosophical shrug. "It was worth a try. There are always those that do, even if they keep it hidden." He now turned his assessment on to Silas, making the normally indomitable man blush.

"Gads, man! And neither do I!" Silas leapt to his feet, tugging at his collar.

The Frenchman raised his glass to them both. "I had guessed— you are both so very straitlaced and proper, but you must allow me to tease. *Eh bien,* I will summon my lawyer and see to the documents."

James glanced out at the darkening streets. "I should return to Jane. We can wait until the morrow."

"No need. It will not take long, for he is here."

The third man in the chamber, who had up till now remained silent, brushed the girl from his lap and got up to make a clumsy bow to the visitors, at a disadvantage without his trunk hose. Only now did they perceive he was sitting on the black-satin-edged robes of a clerk.

Silas and James exchanged a look, then gave in to their laughter. Montfleury joined them; more reluctantly, so did the man of law.

"Allow me to introduce Master Wriothesley. Come, let us settle this matter. Landlord, more wine for my guests!" bellowed Montfleury, banging a pewter tankard on the table. "We have a broken betrothal to celebrate."

CHAPTER 23

Durham House

MILLY COULD NOT BELIEVE her good fortune. Her father had arrived at Durham House with James, his mind already made up to bless her union with Diego. She had anticipated many more months of arguments and pleading; instead, he had kissed her kindly, shaken Diego's hand and asked them what they were waiting for. It left her speechless—not a common state for her.

"How much do you ask for your daughter, sir?" Diego inquired seriously as Jane and James retired to the other end of the chamber to give them privacy for their negotiations.

Silas groaned. "Not that again, lad! You've got it all wrong—I am supposed to give you a dowry to go with her."

"But I would honor her by presenting you with coin for very many cattle."

"And I refuse. I intend to settle two hundred pounds on her."

Milly put her hands on her hips and glared at both her menfolk. "I am here, you know."

"She's regained her voice," observed Silas to Diego.

"Aye, I did not expect that miracle to last long."

"You"—she poked her father in the chest—"cannot afford to give up your savings, but if you wish to invest them in my business, then you are welcome. And you"—Diego's breast was the next to receive the dig from her index finger—"will need your coin to set up your fencing school, not to mention buy yourself a decent horse so you can lay believable claim to being a riding master."

Silas turned to Diego with renewed interest. "Thinking of teaching the skills of the sword and saddle to the gentlemen at court?"

"It is one plan," Diego admitted. "My master supports the idea."

Silas grinned. "Then I think I know where I want to invest Milly's dowry. I'm more suited to take an interest in your enterprise than in her fancy furbelows." He held out a hand. "Need a partner, lad?"

Diego shook his palm and grinned. "Aye, sir."

"When I get booted out of the army, I think my skills might be of use to you. You'll want some old-fashioned sword work as well as your fancy Italian rapier-and-dagger flummery."

"Indeed I will."

Silas scratched his cheek. "There's a place over in Southwark that might work—near enough to the Queen's palaces but outside the city boundaries."

On her feet, Milly batted both men again to get their attention. "Before you two start hiring fencing halls, can we settle the little matter of *my wedding*?"

Diego pulled her down onto his knee and kissed her.

"Enough of that, lad," said Silas, shading his eyes. "You're not married yet."

"Then let us have a handfasting this night and marry after the banns can be read," suggested Diego. "In my village we would not wait once the father had agreed on the price."

Milly's cheeks flushed. "This night? So soon?"

"Aye, why wait?"

Silas nodded and pushed back from the table. "My lady, Master Lacey, our turtledoves here want to exchange their promises. Will you stand witness, Lady Jane? And Master Lacey, will you preside?"

James brought Jane forward, her arm linked in his. "It will be our pleasure."

Diego took Milly's hand and raised her to her feet. They stood facing each other in front of the fireplace, James between them, Jane and Silas standing behind Milly to give her their support.

James took the right hand of each. "I know not the words for such a ceremony, certainly no fine ones, so I will keep this plain and simple. Diego, do you swear you will love this woman all your life, protect and cherish her, be faithful to her?"

"I will."

Milly's eyes filled with tears as he gazed lovingly down at her.

"Millicent Porter, do you swear you will love this undeserving knave, Diego, for the rest of your life, keep him from harm as much as you are able, and be faithful unto him?"

"Yes, oh, yes!"

James smiled broadly at her enthusiasm and joined their hands, wrapping both of his round to press them tightly together. "Then, God bless you both. Congratulations, Diego, and good luck, Mistress Milly."

Diego swooped on his handfasted bride and kissed her. When they broke apart, Milly frowned.

"What is the matter, sweetheart?" Diego asked.

"You have no surname. What am I to be called?"

He laughed and kissed her wrinkled brow. "What foolish things worry you English."

Silas stepped forward and clapped his hand on Diego's shoulder. "Here, I'll adopt you, lad. Milly, you stay a Porter; we'll just bring him into our family."

"Very neat," agreed Jane. "And you won't even have to change the initials on your handkerchiefs."

James enfolded Jane in his arms and bent her back a little so he could look in her face. "But you, love, will you be happy to alter the stitching on yours to J. L.?"

Jane nodded her head shyly. "If the Queen allows."

They all knew the Queen was unpredictable in her moods and took a strong dislike to any of her ladies marrying, so that was by no means a certainty.

"And if she refuses? What think you of turning colonizer and going to Roanoke with Raleigh's settlers?"

Milly thought Jane would be about as useful in a new colony as an ermine cloak in the tropics—an estimate of her abilities with which Jane evidently agreed, because she did not look thrilled by the prospect James offered her.

"I want to be with you whatever the cost," Jane admitted, a frown wrinkling her brow, "but I pray it does not come to that."

James kissed her hands. "So do I."

Diego nudged him from behind. "Admit it, sir: you are not so very opposed to the idea. You would rather enjoy seeing your lady adopt local customs, style of dress and so forth."

Now it was James's turn to look uncomfortable. "Diego, hold your peace."

And though later that night Milly tried to winkle out of Diego what exactly he had meant by that remark, he remained stubbornly silent about which local customs he had in mind and distracted her instead with a kiss.

Whitehall Palace

After a week's recovery, which had given her plenty of time for reflection as she read and reread James's letters, finding each one a balm soothing the sore places in her heart, Jane decided it was time she took matters into her own hands. She had the assurance of his love in written form to give her strength; with that behind her, surely nothing could defeat her? Thanks to James, she had Montfleury's agreement to end the betrothal with no blame on either side; Jonas had made sure she was financially independent of her father, so she needed not fear her father and brother as long as she married quickly before they had time to move against her. Men had helped her to this point but England was in the power of a woman, and Jane's future was going to be decided within this feminine sphere: only with the Queen's approval would her path be clear. James, bless him, in his renewed vigor to be her champion, did not understand this; he was still discussing at length with his elder brother how to gain agreement to the match, talking dynastic considerations and other such masculine perspectives. But Ellie and Milly knew: they agreed with Jane that a female touch was now needed; the Queen should be approached as a woman as well as a monarch—a tricky assignment. Without alerting the Lacey brothers to their risky move, Jane had conferred with her friends to prepare for her gamble, leading up to this morning's visit to the royal apartments.

Knowing how Her Majesty hated her ladies' taking advantage of their position, Jane had never as yet used her appointment so close to the sovereign's own person to further her personal ambitions. Today she was going to make an exception.

Mistress Parry emerged from the bedchamber to select the Queen's jewels for her first engagement. Twisting the Rievaulx ring for luck, Jane dipped into the bedchamber and curtsied by the door. Elizabeth, seated by the window with two attendants putting the final touches to her elaborate headdress, looked up. Her pale skin was almost translucent in the bright light—a ghost inhabiting the regalia of the queen.

"Lady Rievaulx, I am pleased to see you have recovered. Approach."

Jane took five more paces across the room, curtsied again as was customary, then closed the distance until she knelt at Elizabeth's feet.

"You are well?"

"Yes, thank you, Your Majesty."

The air smelt of a heavy flower scent. The sovereign prized cleanliness, bathing regularly and using the finest perfumes. On a table at her right hand lay the cosmetics the Queen used to deaden her skin to the specter-white she favored. The pallor made a striking contrast to her wig of red curls threaded with gold and silver locks. From a distance, Elizabeth remained an imposing figure; close to, it was hard not to notice the spiderweb of lines on her skin and the signs of age around her increasingly scrawny neck. No longer beautiful, she was still Gloriana. Jane admired her mistress's determination to maintain her image; all the ladies understood that on it depended the strength of Elizabeth's hold over the fickle men of her court, and by extension over the country. It was the ladies' secret and their privilege to ensure she was never seen in less than resplendent form.

"You missed your wedding day." The Queen's lips crooked into a smile. "I see you are devastated."

"It proved to be a fortunate delay, Your Majesty, as it gave my Lord Montfleury and me a period for reflection." Jane's heart thumped as if she had just run up seven flights of stairs, and she struggled to control the nervous trembling of her hands.

Elizabeth waved a finger, inviting her to explain.

Jane cleared her throat. "After the impetuous haste with which we rushed into the betrothal, we realized we would not suit. We have parted on good terms."

The Queen motioned Mistress Parry to approach with her burden of rings and necklaces. "This is the second time you have been party to a broken betrothal, Lady Rievaulx. I do not like my ladies to blacken their names with such bedroom sports. The marriage should proceed."

"There was no bedroom sport, madam; a mere misunderstanding on the part of an overly anxious father."

Elizabeth held a diamond up to the light. "But appearances are everything for a woman."

"I agree with your opinion on the matter, Your Majesty. Which is why I do not think it wise for me to remain single for long. I would like to put myself above reproach."

Elizabeth cast the diamond back into the casket. "Lady Rievaulx, I am not a fool. You have something to ask."

Jane feared she might faint with the fearful risk she was about to take. The Queen might request plain speaking, but she rarely liked it when someone dared to comply. "My first desire is to serve Your Majesty," Jane began.

Elizabeth inclined her head, accepting the obedience as her due.

"But I also wish to marry James Lacey, brother to the Earl of Dorset."

The Queen frowned, attempting to recall the face of one of the many gentlemen who thronged her palace corridors.

"He is recently returned from America," prompted Jane.

"Ah yes, Raleigh spoke of him favorably. This would be a brilliant match for him, would it not? Your fortune is substantial."

"But he deserves greatness. I believe you would find him a faithful servant to Your Majesty. My fortune could not be better spent than by raising a worthy man in your service."

The Queen stroked a string of pearls famous for having belonged to her rival, the imprisoned Mary Queen of Scots. In this kingdom, most things eventually became Elizabeth's, except love and marriage—sweet fruits she dared not taste. But would she allow such happiness to befall another? "You were once betrothed to his brother."

"The Earl and Countess of Dorset are my very good friends, Your Majesty, and fully support this match."

"I do not doubt it, or you would not dare speak of it but would go marry hugger-mugger and then pray for pardon, as others have done. I detest such subterfuge."

Jane knew it well. The Tower had many guests who had offended the Queen in this manner. "I have no wish to go behind Your Majesty's back in that way. I speak to you as your faithful servant, begging that you will grant me this wish so I can serve you even more loyally in the future."

"You do not intend to ask leave to withdraw from court?" She chose a ruby hairpin from the jewelry box and handed it to Mistress Parry. "I do so hate disturbances in my household."

Humbly, Jane shook her head. "No, madam. My marriage would allow me to stay. Montfleury had intended to take me away, so I dare to hope that you will think this arrangement far preferable."

The Queen's silence was painful: Jane's future lay in the balance as Elizabeth ran her fingers over the perfectly matched pearls of the necklace.

"Your father?"

"I hope to persuade him that this connection is to our advantage once he has reconciled himself to the loss of Montfleury as son-in-law. I comfort myself with the thought that he once sought an alliance with the Laceys."

The Queen smiled. "Well argued, Marchioness Rievaulx. I never did favor your father—too dismissive of our sex for my taste. And as for the Frenchman, he was not a convincing lover, was he?"

The tension in Jane slowly shifted to relief as she sensed the Queen swinging her way. "No, madam, I do not think it would have been congenial for either party."

The Queen snapped her fingers. "The diamond-and-pearl brooch, Blanche. I am seeing the Venetian ambassador and it was his present to me at New Year."

Jane remained kneeling, waiting for the verdict she knew was coming.

"We have many demands on our time this day. Ladies, you will be required to attend me in the council chamber." The Queen stood, accepting a mantle of fine gold cloth. "Lady Rievaulx, why are you still there?"

"Your Majesty?"

"I would have thought you of all my ladies have no time to dawdle. Not only do I require your presence at the Privy Council meeting—wear the ivory satin, it is very becoming—but you also have a wedding to arrange, do you not?" Elizabeth swept out, followed by her train-bearer.

Blanche Parry paused to kiss Jane on the top of the head. "Well done, my dear. Now I think you can be spared an hour to go tell your young man the good news."

Durham House

Jane found James closeted in his rooms with Will, Silas Porter and Diego in attendance. More surprisingly, Christopher Turner was also present. She had heard rumors of a reconciliation, but had not yet seen him with his legitimate brothers. She stood at the door for a moment, eavesdropping. The men were gathered round a table planning how to approach the Queen; the player was being consulted on the possibility of using a specially staged play or sonnet sequence to soften the Queen's heart.

My, my, they were really running out of strategies if James was turning to poetry, thought Jane. She was delighted, however, to see that the half brother was slowly being brought into the family circle. There was nothing like a crisis to draw kin together.

The countess and the seamstress were leaving the men to it, enjoying a cozy gossip by the fire. Stepping over the threshold, Jane had no need to tell Ellie and Milly the news, as her expression said it all. The two young women laid aside their sewing and gathered up their menfolk.

"Come, dear, I have some purchases I wish to make," the countess informed her husband.

Will looked mightily alarmed. "Ellie, my sweet," he pleaded, like a man spying the gallows in his near future, "can you not persuade Jane to go with you? You know I am hopeless at telling you if something suits."

Ellie pulled firmly on his elbow. "It won't be so bad—we're going to spend all our money at Milly's. Diego can give you moral support through your trial. Master Porter, Master Turner, I think we have all just become *de trop*, or should I say unnecessary to James's happiness for the present."

Turner was the swiftest to pick up the hint. He glanced at Jane, then kissed the countess's knuckles with practiced flattery, making Will's hackles rise. The earl moved to relieve him of her hand.

"Some would say that I am always *de trop*, Your Grace," said Turner. "But my will as well as your Will are yours to command this day."

Ellie gave her husband a laughing look, quite understanding of Turner's teasing of his older brother. "Come along, gentlemen. Let us take ourselves elsewhere."

James looked somewhat nonplussed to find his conspirators

summarily removed from him. "Will, Kit, Diego, Master Porter, we have something rather more important than clothes to discuss!" he protested.

"No, you don't," replied Milly pertly, bundling her father and Diego out of the room. "Ask Jane." She snapped the door closed.

"What was that all about?" James turned to where Jane waited by the fireplace. "What did she mean?"

Hugging her knowledge to herself for a moment, Jane enjoyed his bewilderment. "We need to discuss your clothes."

He scratched his head. "Why? I am not much interested in them so long as they do their task of keeping me dry and warm."

"Your wedding clothes," Jane continued. "I think you would look very fine in blue."

James thought he now understood. Smiling, he shook his head. "Ah, love, I'd like nothing better than to don my finery for you, but we must not put the cart before the horse."

Jane stepped to him and took both his hands in hers. "Ah, love," she echoed, "the horse is now in the traces and ready to proceed."

"But . . . how . . . ?" His befuddled expression was comical.

"I spoke to my mistress this morning, telling her there was a poor vagabond gentleman around court who needed marrying off—to me. She saw that it would be doing the realm a favor, so she agreed."

"What? The Queen agreed?"

"Yes, as long as she does not lose my services, which I swore she would not, so I am afraid I cannot go to America."

Radiant with happiness, James slipped his hands free to frame her face for a sound kiss. "Lady Jane, you are a miracle."

She tugged his patched black doublet. "So?"

"So, what?" He looked puzzled.

"Are you going to change this for blue?"

Chuckling, he pressed her to his chest. "Oh yes. But at the church in Stoke-by-Lacey, if you have no objection. I'd like to wed you among family."

Jane brushed her lips over his heart. "Excellent. You see, I know a very good seamstress with a quite remarkable shop who would appreciate the custom."

James laughed. "You mercenary fiend—you are just protecting your investment. Later. We'll go there later. For now, I want to spend as long as possible admiring my wife-to-be. Come, wench, and kiss me."

"Wench!" Jane pretended to huff at his term. "I'm the Queen's lady."

"Maybe. But first and foremost you are my lady, and I claim you as mine own."

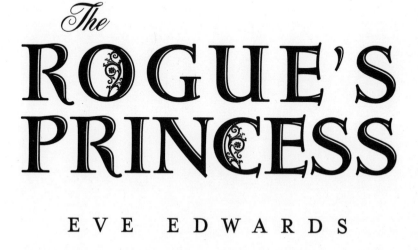

The
ROGUE'S
PRINCESS

EVE EDWARDS

If you loved *The Queen's Lady,*
you'll want to see how Kit Turner falls for
the modest and beguiling Mercy Hart.
The Rogue's Princess is their story.

COMING IN JANUARY 2013!

Turn the page for a sneak preview.

1586

"Master Turner, have you been with Master Burbage long?" asked Mistress Belknap, signaling for her servants to begin pouring the welcome cup of mulled wine.

Kit seized one from the tray, remembering just in time to take prudent sips, rather than downing it in one. "Indeed, ma'am; since I was a boy. He taught me everything I know about the business."

"And a better teacher you could not hope for."

"You echo my thoughts exactly." Kit almost yawned. The strain of keeping back his usual flowery style of address was as tiring as holding the reins on a team of spirited horses. And he still hadn't caught a clear look at the shortest of the girls, his quarry for the evening. It was time for him to cut her from the herd. "Mistress Hart, tell me, do you enjoy hearing a play?"

The sea of rainbow skirts parted as the Belknap girls turned to their guest, granting him his first clear sight of her. Kit felt he had just been thrown from the saddle. He had not been expecting to encounter such a creature in an alderman's parlor. She was stunning: more curves packed into her five feet two inches than on many a ship's figurehead, a sweet heart-shaped face and the most earnest pair of green eyes he had ever seen. As he watched, a faint blush rose over her strawberries-and-cream skin, making him even hungrier, though this time not for food. He couldn't help letting his gaze drop to her chest, where small fingers played nervously with the laces on her modest peach-colored bodice.

Peaches—that was absolutely the last image he needed right now, when he was trying his utmost to behave.

"I've never heard a play, sir," the girl said shyly.

So she didn't attend the theater. For the moment that did not matter to Kit; he was willing to be anything she wanted as long as he could get her talking.

"What about music? Do you like Byrd's madrigals or do you prefer Tallis?"

The girl shuttered her eyes with a sweep of her long dark lashes. "You must think me very ignorant, sir, but I am not familiar with the latest music. My father does not approve of anything but psalms sung at home."

The Belknap daughter in orange was watching the interchange with amusement, her squirrel-bright eyes leaping between them. Kit guessed that meant she knew that he was not quite as he appeared this night, an easy deduction if she had last seen him skewering Saracens onstage.

"Mercy has a lovely voice, Master Turner," the Belknap chit said. "Perhaps later you could teach her one of Lyly's songs?" She turned to her friend. "They are very good, Mercy; nothing unsuitable about them, you'll see. Even the Queen asks for them to be played—Lyly's her favored poet, and he trains the boys of St. Paul's to be excellent performers."

The girl appeared to be struggling against a desire to prod her friend in the ribs for making the suggestion. "What's right at court is not necessarily welcomed under my father's roof, as you well know, Ann."

So that was Ann. Kit sensed an ally in the orange-garbed maiden. "And you, Mistress Ann, how like you the fashion for madrigals? I see they have even begun to print the sheet music so that each one has his stave facing the right way when a quartet of singers gather around a table—a welcome innovation."

"Marry, sir, that is very convenient in a house that has a tuneful family, but ours is sadly lacking in that respect." Ann's eyes twinkled with merriment. "My sisters and I are most politely asked not to sing the responses at church for fear of throwing the others off key."

"But do you play?"

"The lute, but badly. Mercy here is far more accomplished than I, even though she pretends not to excel at anything so worldly." Ann staggered but continued smiling as if nothing had happened. If Kit was not mistaken, the little daughter of the cloth merchant had just kicked her friend in the shins—which were well padded by layers of skirts from any true injury. This parading of Mercy's skills was proving a very entertaining subject, confirming his suspicion that she was eminently easy to tease. He always appreciated that in a girl, not having a very serious approach to life himself.

He placed his hand on his breast and bowed. "Then, Mistress Hart, I would be desolate to leave this night without hearing your voice or enjoying a few melodies from your accomplished fingers."

'Swounds, he wished he hadn't created that image, as his mind was now full of entirely inappropriate images of her wandering hands and his all-too-willing flesh. She was a decent girl, far too modest for such sport, and he shamed her by even entertaining such ideas in private. *Behave, Kit, behave.*

"I'm sure she will be more than happy to oblige," Ann replied, prudently moving out of kicking distance. "Oh, Mother? Do you know where we put the lute after Mercy's last visit?"

Mistress Belknap beamed her approval. "Oh, Mercy, are you going to play for us? You know how I love to hear it after years of being tortured by music lessons for my own daughters." She leaned confidentially towards Kit. "Sadly, sir, they all make the lute sound like the strings are still attached to the gut of some unfortunate creature."

"To sound so awful must be a skill of sorts," suggested Kit gallantly.

"One of use to bird-scarers, perhaps," muttered Mercy, thinking only Ann would hear her little commentary.

Happily, Kit caught her words and laughed out loud. His damsel had a sharp sense of humor. Until today, he had never believed in that nonsense about falling in love on first meeting, but he was reacting to this girl as he had to no other. The fact that she was completely oblivious to her effect on men was all part of her charm, and he felt quite drunk in her presence. He was wracking his brains to think how he could get her on her own for a few minutes to further their acquaintance.

Mistress Belknap took Mercy's hand. "Will you play for us, love?"

"Have mercy on us, Mercy!" chorused the three daughters—then fell into giggles, telling Kit this was all part of a familiar joke that played on her name.

Mercy buckled under the combined pressure, as Kit anticipated she would. Already he was certain that his maiden had not a selfish bone in her very comely body. "To please you, ma'am, I will." She took a worried glance around the room. "But only if all the company are happy to hear me. I would not want to put myself forward and seem a proud sort of girl wanting all the attention for herself."

"I know, Mother!" exclaimed Ann, acting as if the idea had only just struck when doubtless the lovely little Machiavelli had been busy plotting. "Why not persuade Master Turner to join her? All of London knows he's a fine performer. Your guests would be *desolate* not to hear him before they leave." She smiled broadly at Kit as she parroted his words back at him.

He bowed to kiss Ann's hand. "It would be an honor."

"Oh, Master Turner, is it not very rude of us to ask you to sing for your supper?" cried Mistress Belknap, looking thoroughly delighted by the idea. Her feast was about to become a famous success if they could get London's brightest star to shine for them in private.

"Ma'am, I have been singing for my supper since I was a little lad, so I have no qualms about adding another to the count." Kit decided there and then that he was also falling in love with the Belknap family, since they were allowing his plan to be apart with the maiden to tumble so perfectly into place.

"Then it is agreed. After supper you must have a place to rehearse. The closet off the parlor should suit. I will ask the servants to set candles and music in it ready for you. Ann will help you select the songs." *And act as guard on my young guest's virtue,* Mistress Belknap's eyes warned Kit.

Kit thought Ann would make a wonderful third to their party. "I can hardly wait to get started. There are several love songs that I am sure Mistress Hart will enjoy learning, and I am a most willing tutor."

Mercy could barely eat a thing. How had this happened? She had come in all innocence to a family supper and ended up agreeing to entertain the entire company of aldermen and their wives with secular songs, accompanying the handsomest man in London. There was no way in Christendom that word of this would not get back to her father, and she hated to anticipate his reaction. He wouldn't shout at her or scold her much, but she knew he would be so disappointed. The heaviness of that would weigh round her neck like a milkmaid's yoke for weeks, if not months. Faith would give her that sad look, the one she reserved for serious breaches of decorum. Edwin would splutter something about the wild company she kept and the well-known liberality of the goldsmiths. All three of them liked Ann, but none entirely approved of Jerome Belknap because, among God-fearing folk, he was known to be very free-thinking. To hear that Mercy had taken part in such a frivolous gathering would be the proof they had been waiting for that all was not as it should be under Belknap's roof. There would be a sermon in it at least.

"More marchpane, Mistress Hart?" Master Turner offered her a plate of her favorite sweetmeats, but the sight of them turned her stomach. She was too nervous to eat.

"No thank you, sir."

Mistress Belknap had placed the pair of them side by side at the board in order for them to "discuss music." Mercy had decided the lady was as bad as her daughter when it came to encouraging flirtations. For the Belknap ladies, it was all a piece of harmless fun, not meant to go beyond the bounds of decent behavior, but for her, it was a torment. It would have been bearable if every smile on the young man's face had not made her heart flutter. She was feeling by turns hot and cold in her borrowed clothes, wishing that Ann's peach camlet bodice was not so tight round the bust and the ruff not so frothy. She had no clue how to behave under the man's unguarded looks of admiration. He had not been offensive—far from it, he had been nothing but polite. She reassured herself that he appeared a sober-enough fellow in his black doublet, a wealthy senior apprentice perhaps to the Master Burbage Ann's father so liked. Mercy wondered what line of business they were in to make his voice so famous. Were they makers of musical instruments? That would explain his expectation that she had frequented places of entertainment; doubtless he had to risk going to them himself for the sake of his craft. The Hart family stood apart from the current fashion for the stage. Though Ann had never said as much to her, Mercy suspected the Belknaps even went to the Theatre—that was how liberal the father was. Some churchmen said it was the very nest of the devil's brood, but Mercy had a sinful hankering to see what it would be like.

"Why do I get the impression, Mistress, that I make you very nervous?" her dining companion asked in a low voice. "Or it is the prospect of our performance?"

"Yes," whispered Mercy, chasing a piece of piecrust around her plate with her spoon to avoid looking at him.

"Yes to what? Yes, I make you nervous, or yes, you are worried about playing with me later?"

Mercy flicked her eyes to his face, wondering if the double meaning had been intentional, but he was studying her expression without so much as a glint of a naughty smile. He had to be honest or a very good actor. She decided the lascivious thoughts had been entirely of her own creation and begged God's pardon for them.

"Yes to both. I am . . . um . . . not accustomed to dining in such company. I live a very quiet life at home."

"I had guessed as much. And earlier you said you had never heard a play: why is that? I thought almost all of London went."

Mercy glanced around her, checking that they were not overheard. "I have been told the stage is given over to very dangerous spectacles, plays that teach immoral behavior and drive the watchers to"—she lowered her voice—"acts of lewdness."

He brushed a hand across his mouth, hiding his expression momentarily. "But you have not attended a performance to judge for yourself?" His disapproval was plain in his voice; this was clearly a sore point with him.

"I doubt it would be allowed." Even as she spoke, Mercy wondered if that was the truth. Her father had never banned her from going, merely made his own thoughts on the subject clear to his children. She knew Aunt Rose had slipped away to see the occasional play without making a great announcement of it to the family. These absences had been handled by everyone's ignoring the subject on the principle that if they weren't acknowledged, no one would have to take offense.

"That is a shame, for how else can you make up your own mind? I would argue that the play is the very place to teach morality, on occasion far more successfully than from the pulpit." As he gestured vigorously to emphasize his argument, a lock of his wavy black hair fell forward, teasing the solid line of his jaw. Mercy squeezed her fingers round her knife and spoon to stop herself from reaching out to brush it back. "By seeing vice punished and virtue rewarded, would you not be improved by the experience? It is a perverse mind that takes away evil lessons from the plays put on the London stage, all of which are first approved by the Queen's own servant, the Lord Chamberlain."

"You make many good points, sir," Mercy said soberly, not wanting to anger the young man. "I have much to learn, it seems."

"And I would be more than happy to teach you." His dark eyes held hers for a thrilling few moments before he blinked and turned away, breaking the spell. "Come now, Mistress Hart, you must eat something. One of these custards, perhaps?"

Mercy nodded dumbly, wondering where her wits had fled to when she most needed them about her. He broke off a corner of the creamy tart on his plate and placed it on her spoon, then watched as she nibbled it, his eyes fixed on her lips. To her mortification, Mercy felt her cheeks blush. She had been right in her first suspicions: he was attracted to her, and, Lord help her, she was horribly drawn to him too. But then again, was it so bad if he liked her? She was of marriageable age. As a respectable apprentice invited to dine with aldermen, would he not be a suitable husband for her? Ann would say so. She was forever reeling off the selling points of the potential spouses among the young men of Cheapside as if they were so many bullocks going under the hammer at Smithfield. Was it not Mercy's duty now that she was grown up to turn her thoughts to a future beyond her family if she was not to be an unmarried burden on her brother?

Suddenly the prospect of leaving her home did not seem as terrifying when she had a young man looking at her with such devotion. And he seemed so kind and concerned about her feelings. So quiet and respectful.

She swallowed her mouthful and gave him a blinding smile. "Thank you, sir. That was delicious."

"Hmmm." He seemed quite lost in the contemplation of her mouth. She licked her lips self-consciously. He shifted uneasily in his seat, rearranging his long legs under the board.

She looked behind them at the roaring hearth. "Are you uncomfortable, sir? Is the fire too hot?"

"Not the fire." He cleared his throat. "Mistress Hart, I believe our hosts have finished. What say you that we retire to practice our songs together?"

Trying to ignore the fact that she had rashly convinced herself on little evidence that this flirtation could be the prelude to true love, Mercy got swiftly to her feet, eager now to be apart with the young man. She caught Ann's eye, signaling that they were ready to go. "Yes, let's do that. I am ready to learn a new song if you will teach me."

About the Author

Eve Edwards (eve-edwards.com) has a doctorate from Oxford University. She has visited Tudor houses, attended jousts, and eaten Elizabethan banquets to get the sights, sounds, and tastes right for this novel. And, yes, she can testify that it is possible to eat neatly Tudor-style, without a fork. She lives in Oxford and is married with three children. The Lacey Chronicles begin with *The Other Countess*.